SPACE BATTLE LUNCHTIME

VOLUME TWO:
A RECIPE FOR DISASTER

ONI PRESS

AN ONI PRESS PUBLICATION

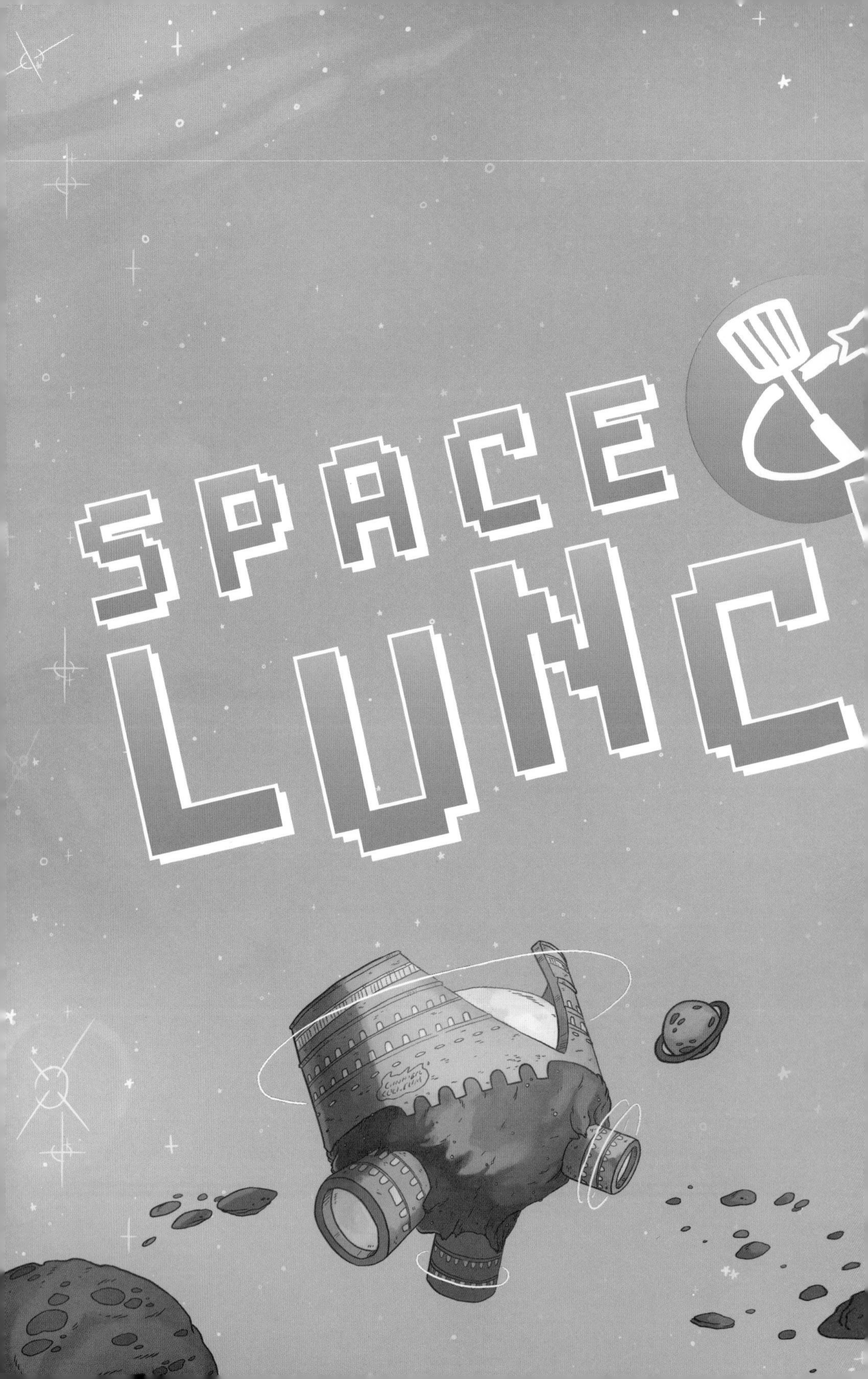
SPACE
LUNC

BATTLE
HTIME

VOLUME TWO:
A RECIPE FOR DISASTER

BY NATALIE RIESS

EDITED BY ROBIN HERRERA

DESIGNED BY HILARY THOMPSON

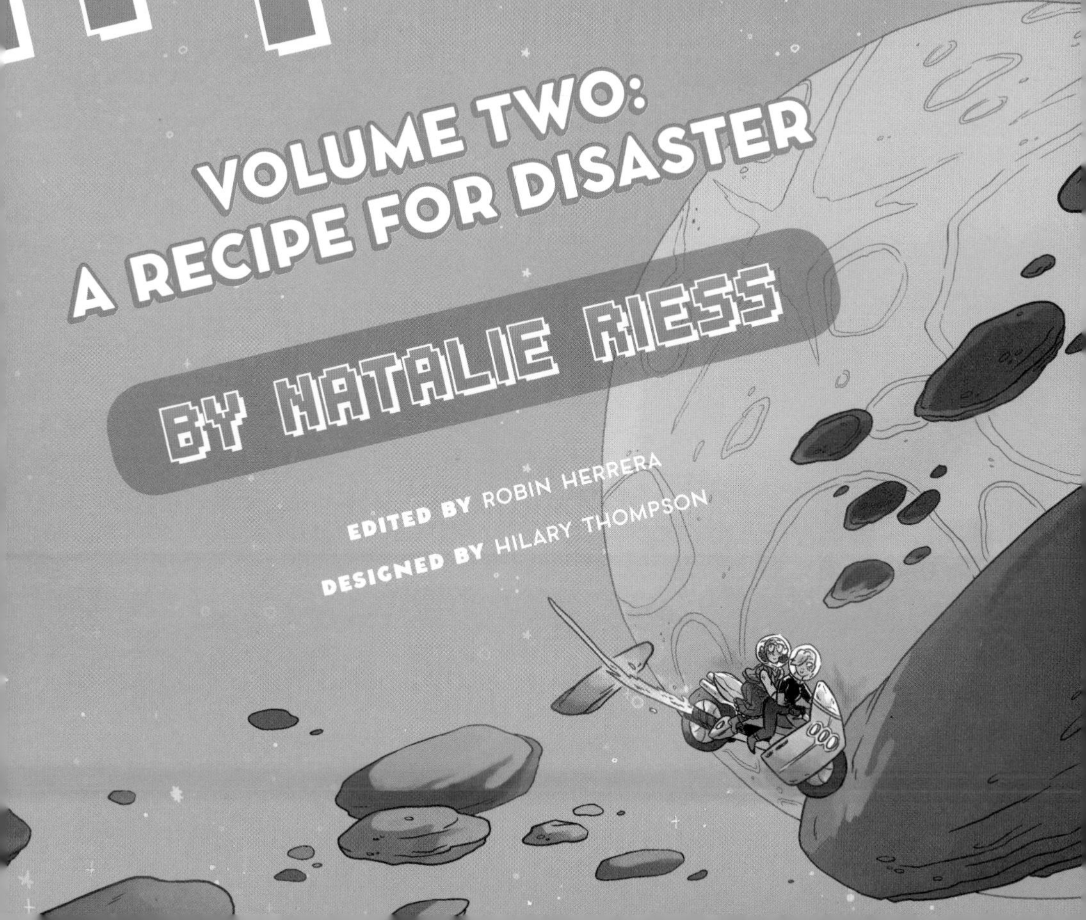

PUBLISHED BY ONI PRESS, INC.

PUBLISHER JOE NOZEMACK

EDITOR IN CHIEF JAMES LUCAS JONES

V.P. OF MARETING & SALES ANDREW MCINTIRE

SALES MANAGER DAVID DISSANAYAKE

PUBLICITY COORDINATOR RACHEL REED

DIRECTOR OF DESIGN & PRODUCTION TROY LOOK

GRAPHIC DESIGNER HILARY THOMPSON

DIGITAL PREPRESS TECHNICIAN ANGIE DOBSON

MANAGING EDITOR ARI YARWOOD

SENIOR EDITOR CHARLIE CHU

EDITOR ROBIN HERRERA

ADMINISTRATIVE ASSISTANT ALISSA SALLAH

DIRECTOR OF LOGISTICS BRAD ROOKS

LOGISTICS ASSOCIATE JUNG LEE

ONIPRESS.COM
FACEBOOK.COM/ONIPRESS
TWITTER.COM/ONIPRESS
ONIPRESS.TUMBLR.COM
INSTAGRAM.COM/ONIPRESS

ORIGINALLY PUBLISHED AS ISSUES 5-8 OF THE ONI PRESS
COMIC SERIES *SPACE BATTLE LUNCHTIME*.

FIRST EDITION: JUNE 2017
ISBN 978-1-62010-404-0
EISBN 978-1-62010-405-7

1 3 5 7 9 10 8 6 4 2

LIBRARY OF CONGRESS CONTROL NUMBER: 2016937918
PRINTED IN SINGAPORE.

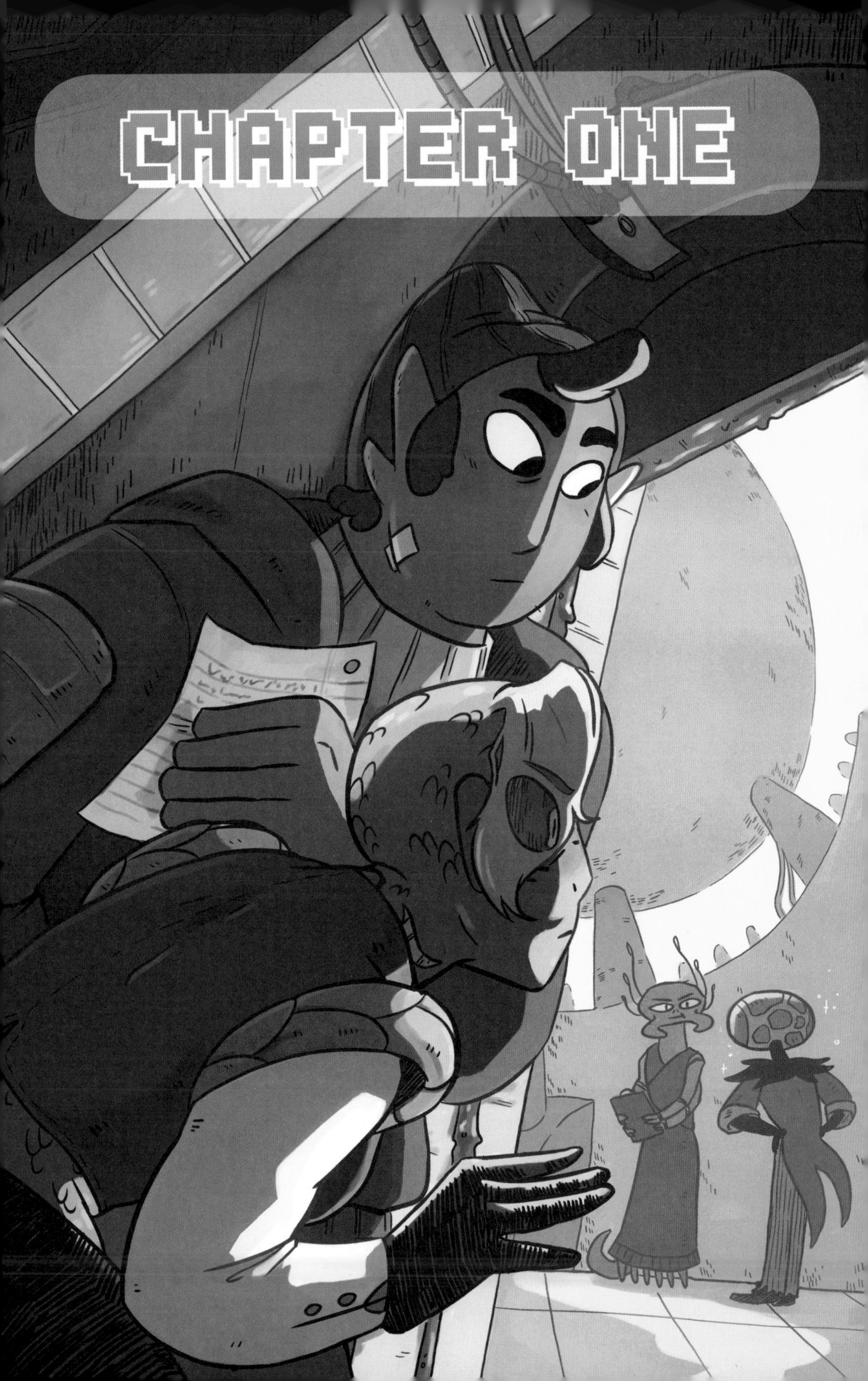
CHAPTER ONE

PREVIOUSLY, ON SPACE BATTLE LUNCHTIME...

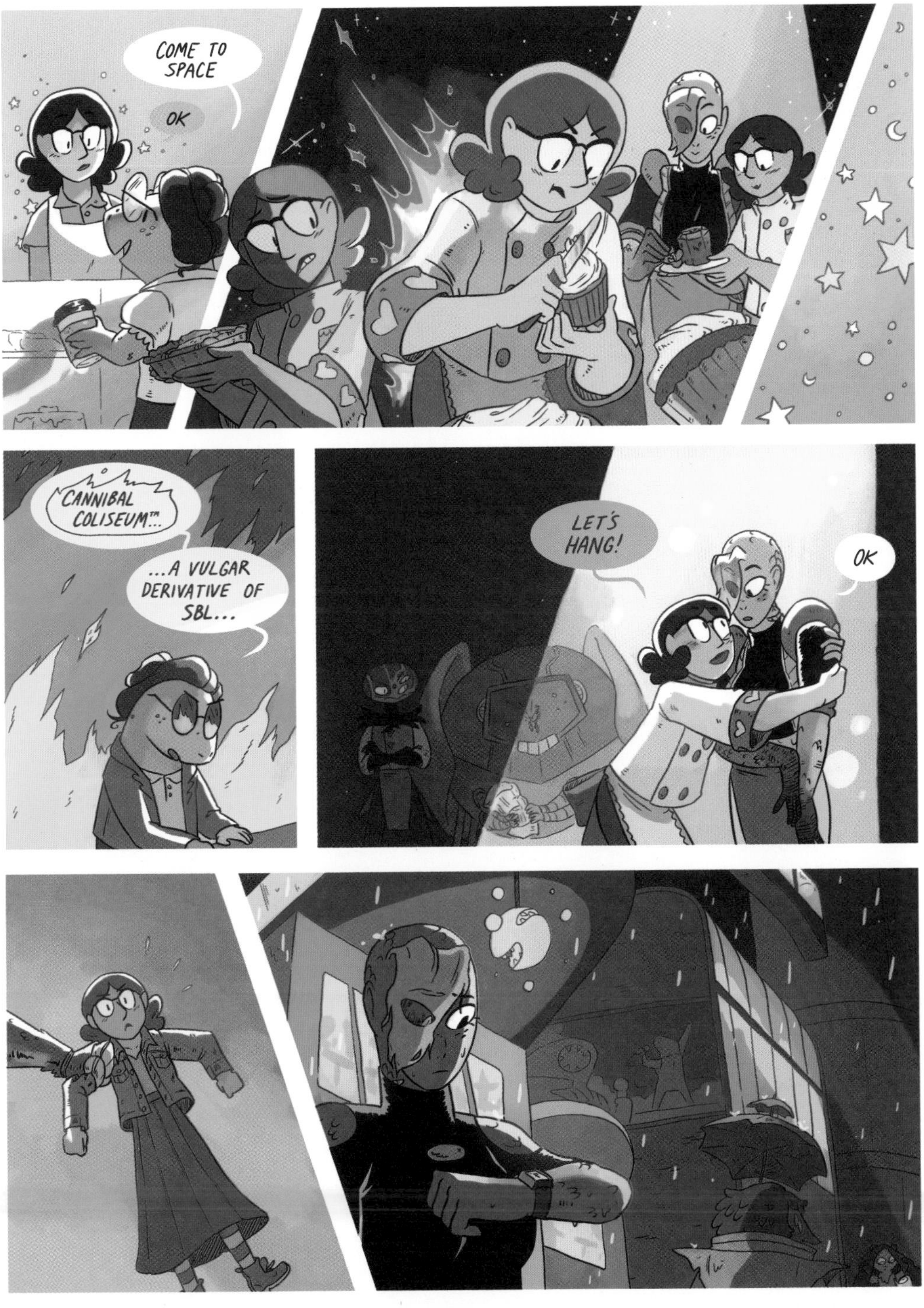
COME TO SPACE
OK
CANNIBAL COLISEUM™...
...A VULGAR DERIVATIVE OF SBL...
LET'S HANG!
OK

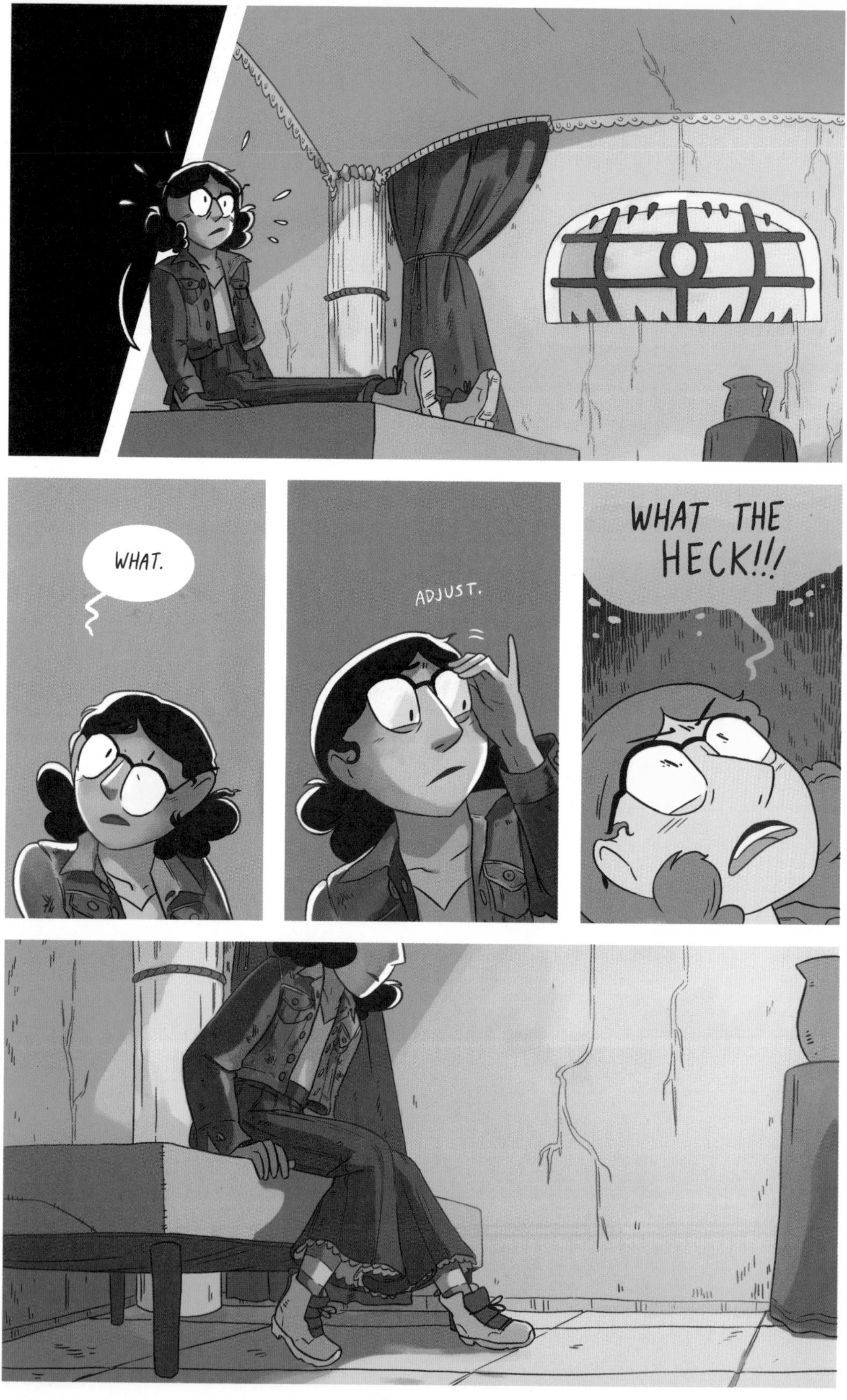
WHAT.
ADJUST.
WHAT THE HECK!!!

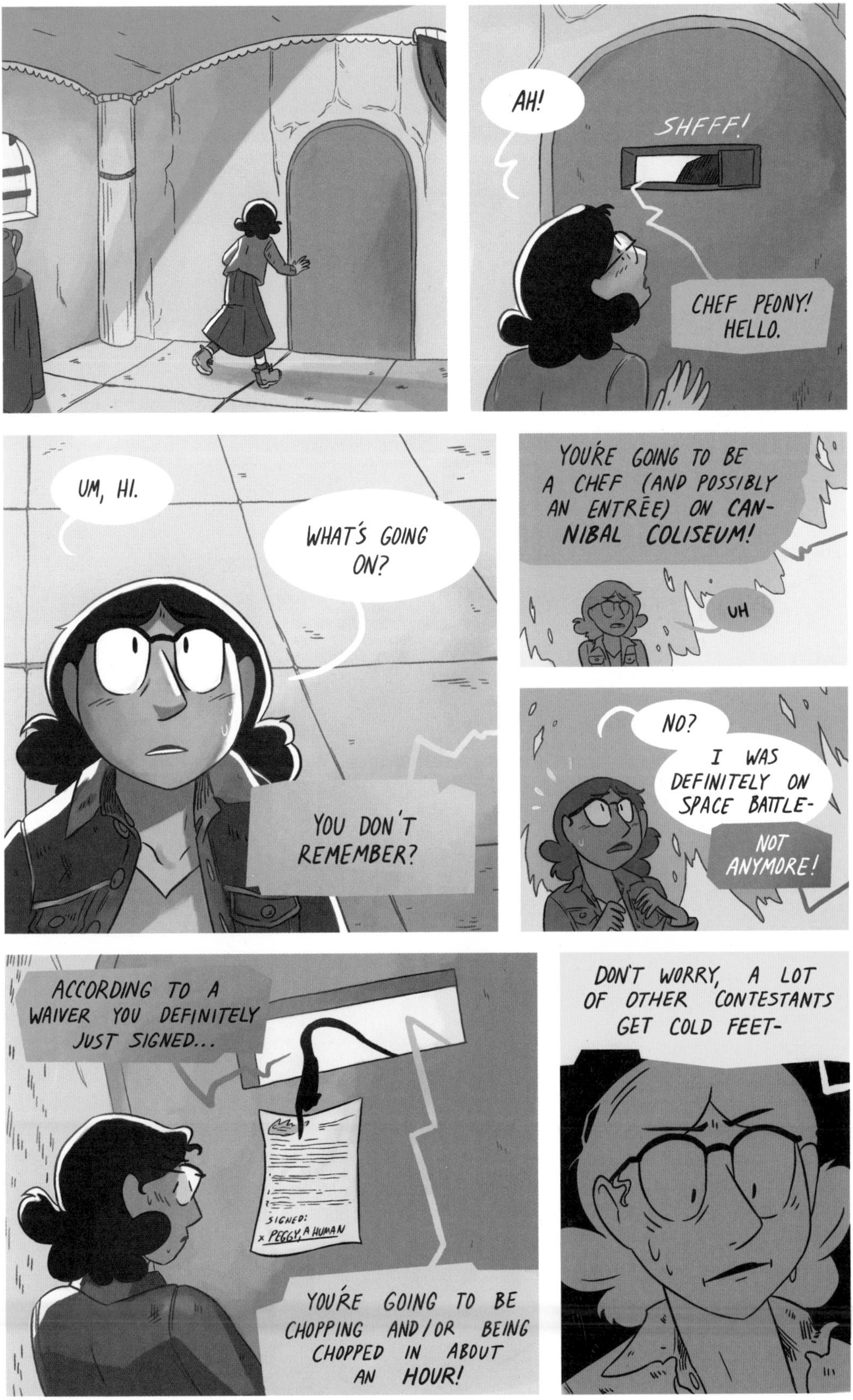
AH!
SHFFF!
CHEF PEONY! HELLO.
UM, HI.
WHAT'S GOING ON?
YOU DON'T REMEMBER?
YOU'RE GOING TO BE A CHEF (AND POSSIBLY AN ENTRÉE) ON CANNIBAL COLISEUM!
UH
NO?
I WAS DEFINITELY ON SPACE BATTLE-
NOT ANYMORE!
ACCORDING TO A WAIVER YOU DEFINITELY JUST SIGNED...
SIGNED:
x PEGGY, A HUMAN
YOU'RE GOING TO BE CHOPPING AND/OR BEING CHOPPED IN ABOUT AN HOUR!
DON'T WORRY, A LOT OF OTHER CONTESTANTS GET COLD FEET-

THIS IS A MISTAKE!

I CAN'T CUT UP AND COOK ANYONE—

NOT WITH THAT ATTITUDE YOU WON'T!

IT'S CALLED CAN-NIBAL COLISEUM, NOT CAN'T-IBAL—

UGH!

WELL, LET US KNOW IF YOU NEED ANYTHING.

I NEED TO NOT BE HERE.

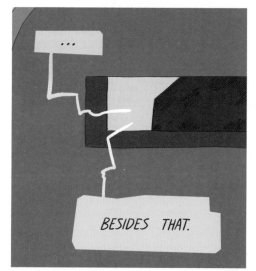

...

BESIDES THAT.

OH!

MY PHONE.

MAYBE I CAN CALL FOR HELP?

BOOP!

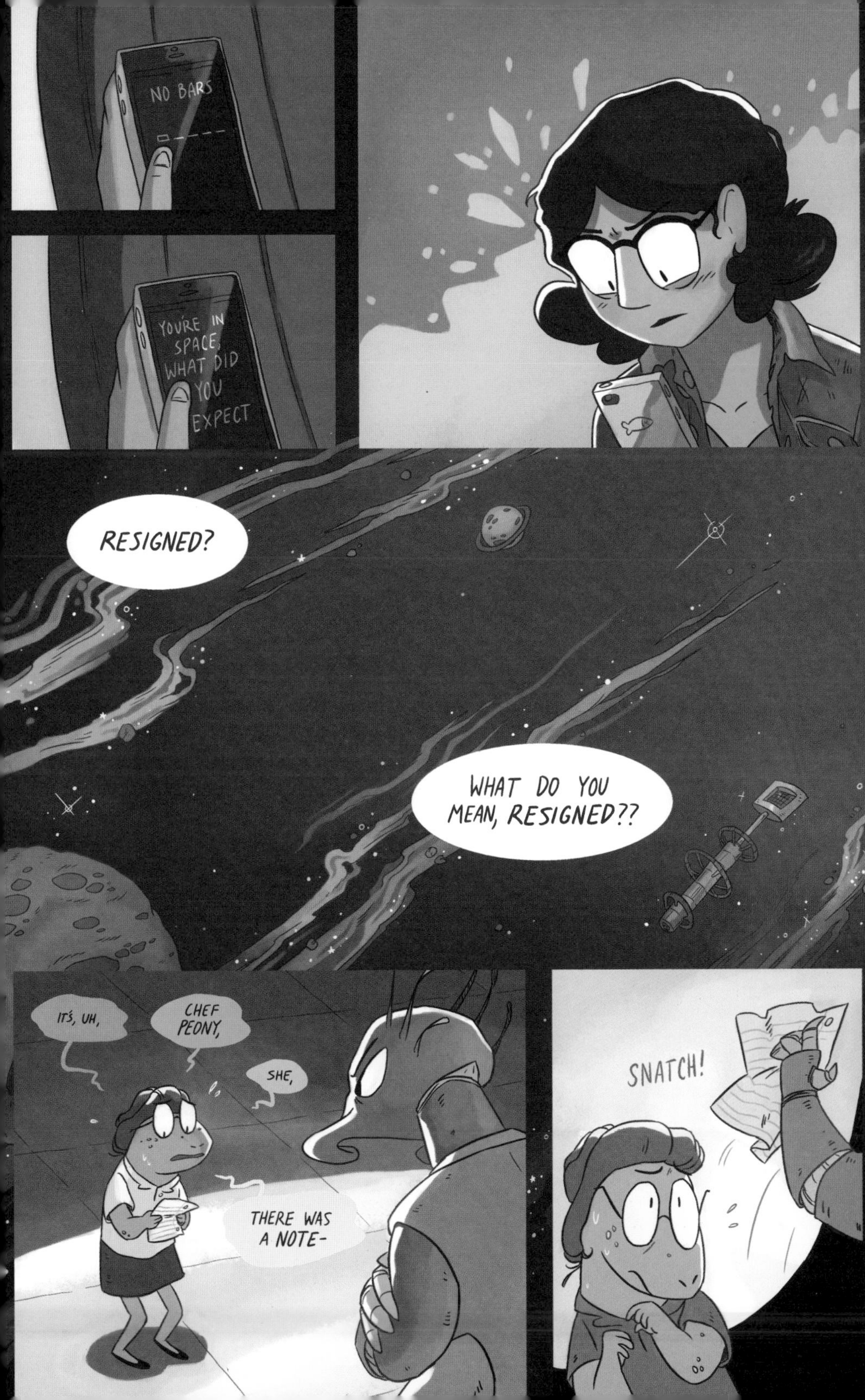
NO BARS
YOU'RE IN SPACE, WHAT DID YOU EXPECT
RESIGNED?
WHAT DO YOU MEAN, RESIGNED??
IT'S, UH,
CHEF PEONY,
SHE,
THERE WAS A NOTE-
SNATCH!

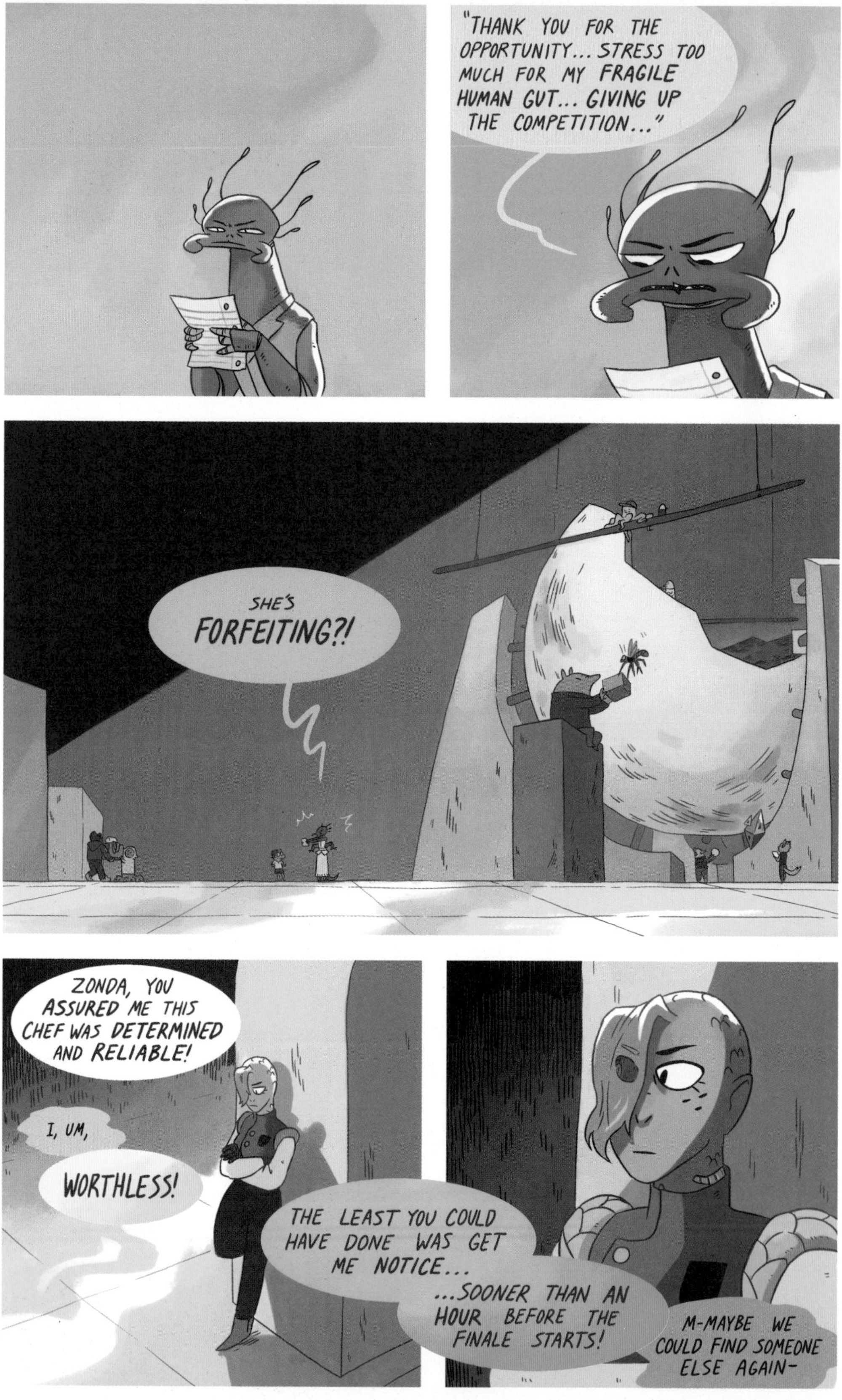
"THANK YOU FOR THE OPPORTUNITY... STRESS TOO MUCH FOR MY FRAGILE HUMAN GUT... GIVING UP THE COMPETITION..."
SHE'S FORFEITING?!
ZONDA, YOU ASSURED ME THIS CHEF WAS DETERMINED AND RELIABLE!
I, UM,
WORTHLESS!
THE LEAST YOU COULD HAVE DONE WAS GET ME NOTICE...
...SOONER THAN AN HOUR BEFORE THE FINALE STARTS!
M-MAYBE WE COULD FIND SOMEONE ELSE AGAIN-

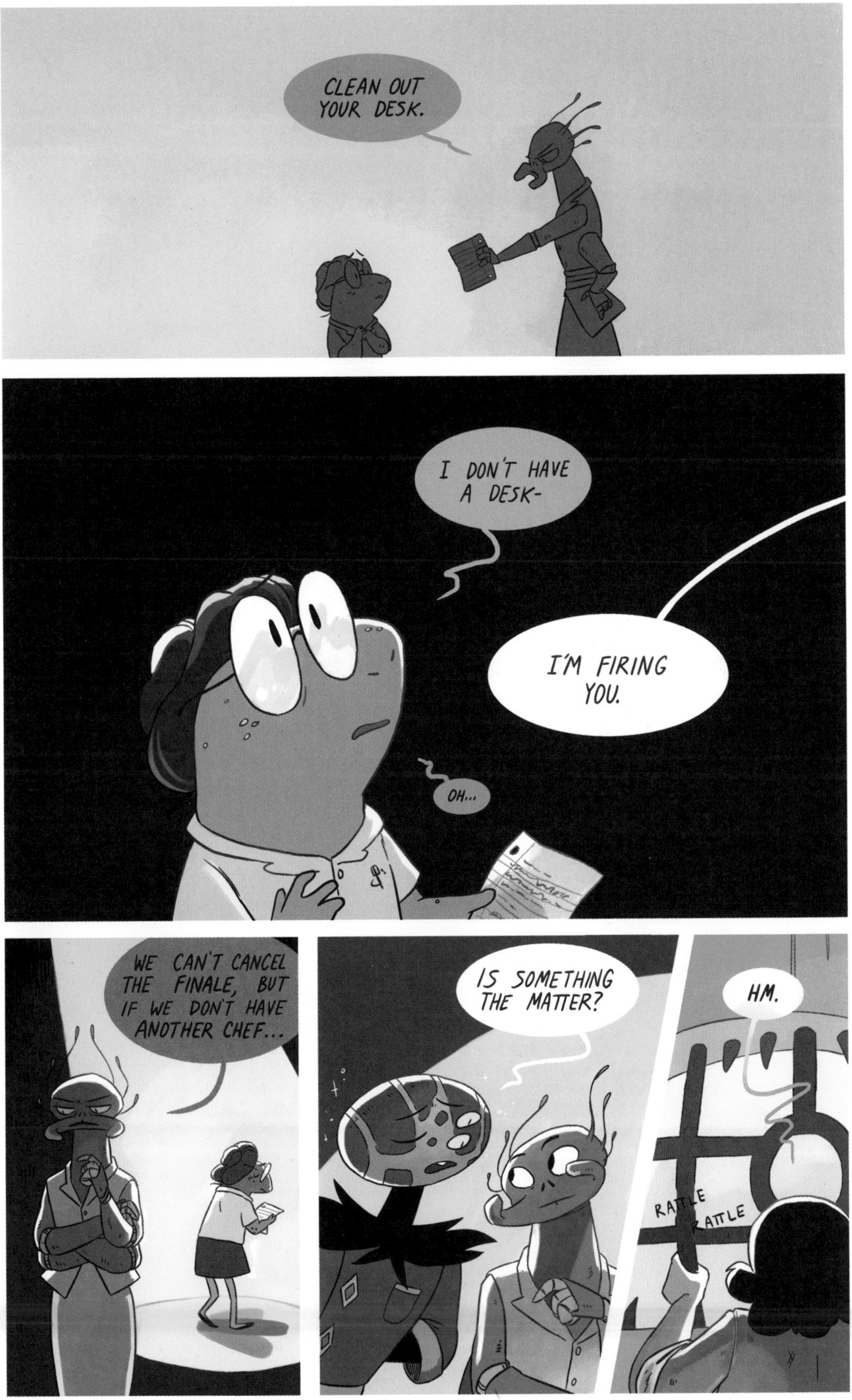
CLEAN OUT YOUR DESK.
I DON'T HAVE A DESK-
I'M FIRING YOU.
OH...
WE CAN'T CANCEL THE FINALE, BUT IF WE DON'T HAVE ANOTHER CHEF...
IS SOMETHING THE MATTER?
HM.
RATTLE
RATTLE

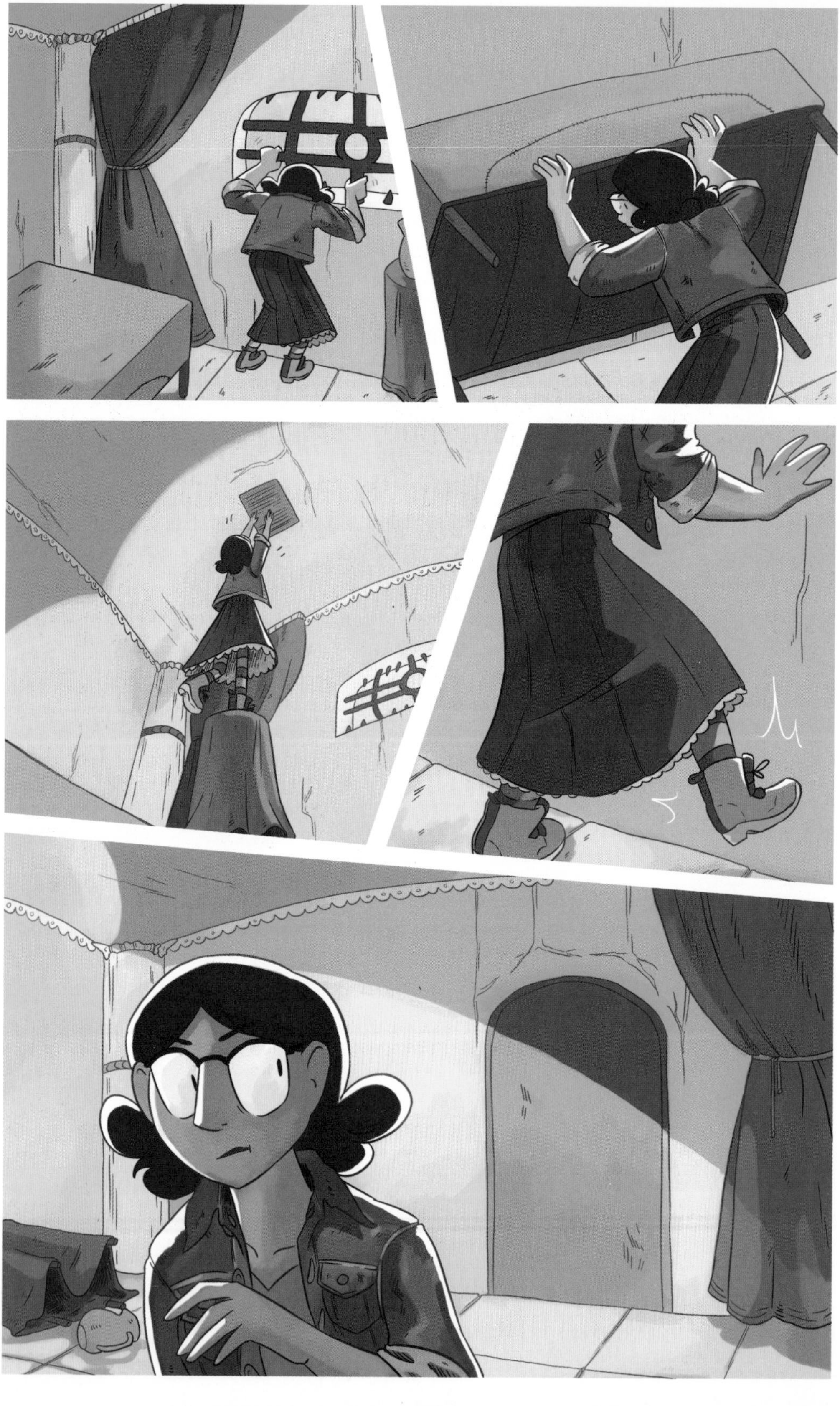

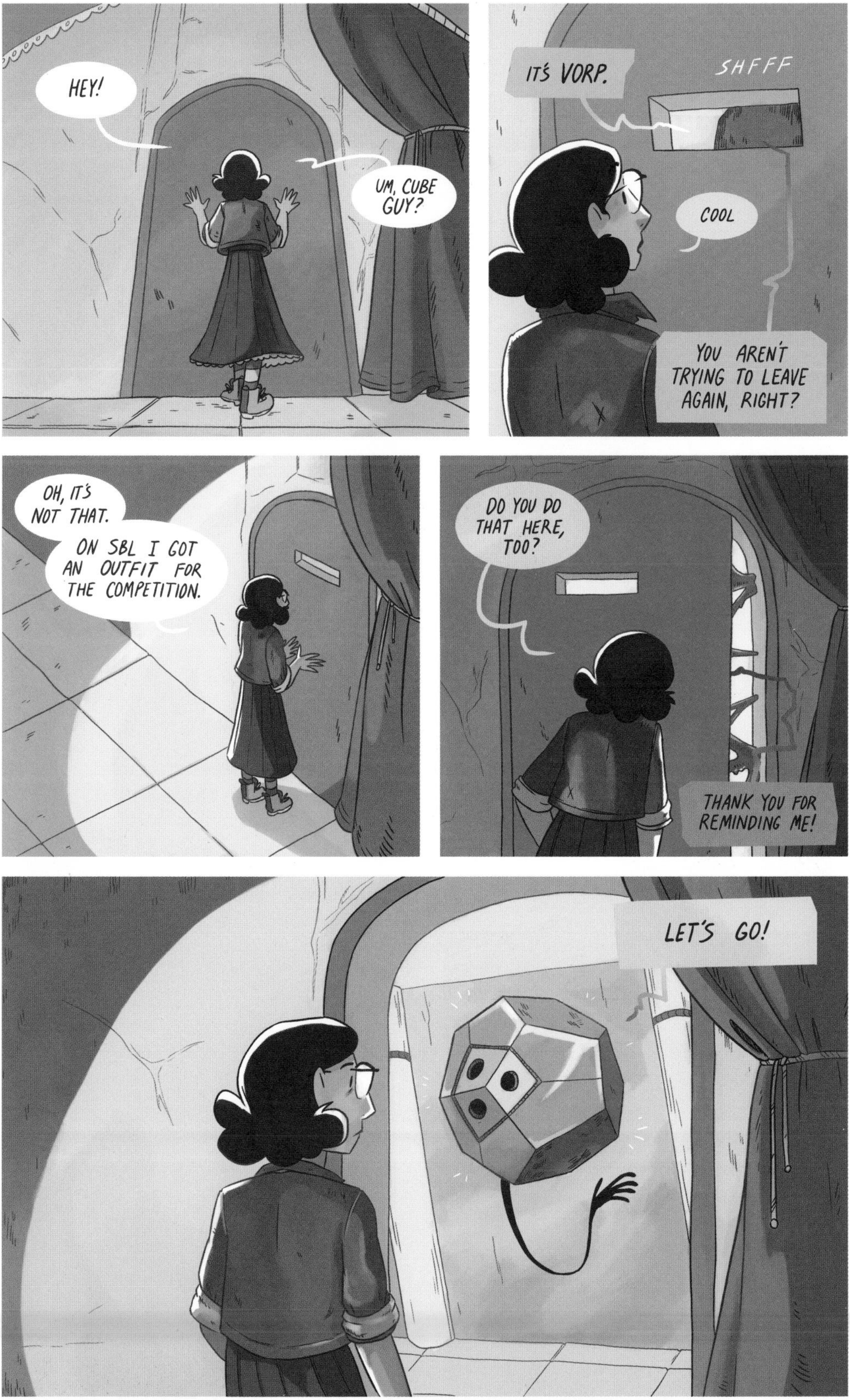
HEY!
UM, CUBE GUY?
IT'S VORP.
SHFFF
COOL
YOU AREN'T TRYING TO LEAVE AGAIN, RIGHT?
OH, IT'S NOT THAT.
ON SBL I GOT AN OUTFIT FOR THE COMPETITION.
DO YOU DO THAT HERE, TOO?
THANK YOU FOR REMINDING ME!
LET'S GO!

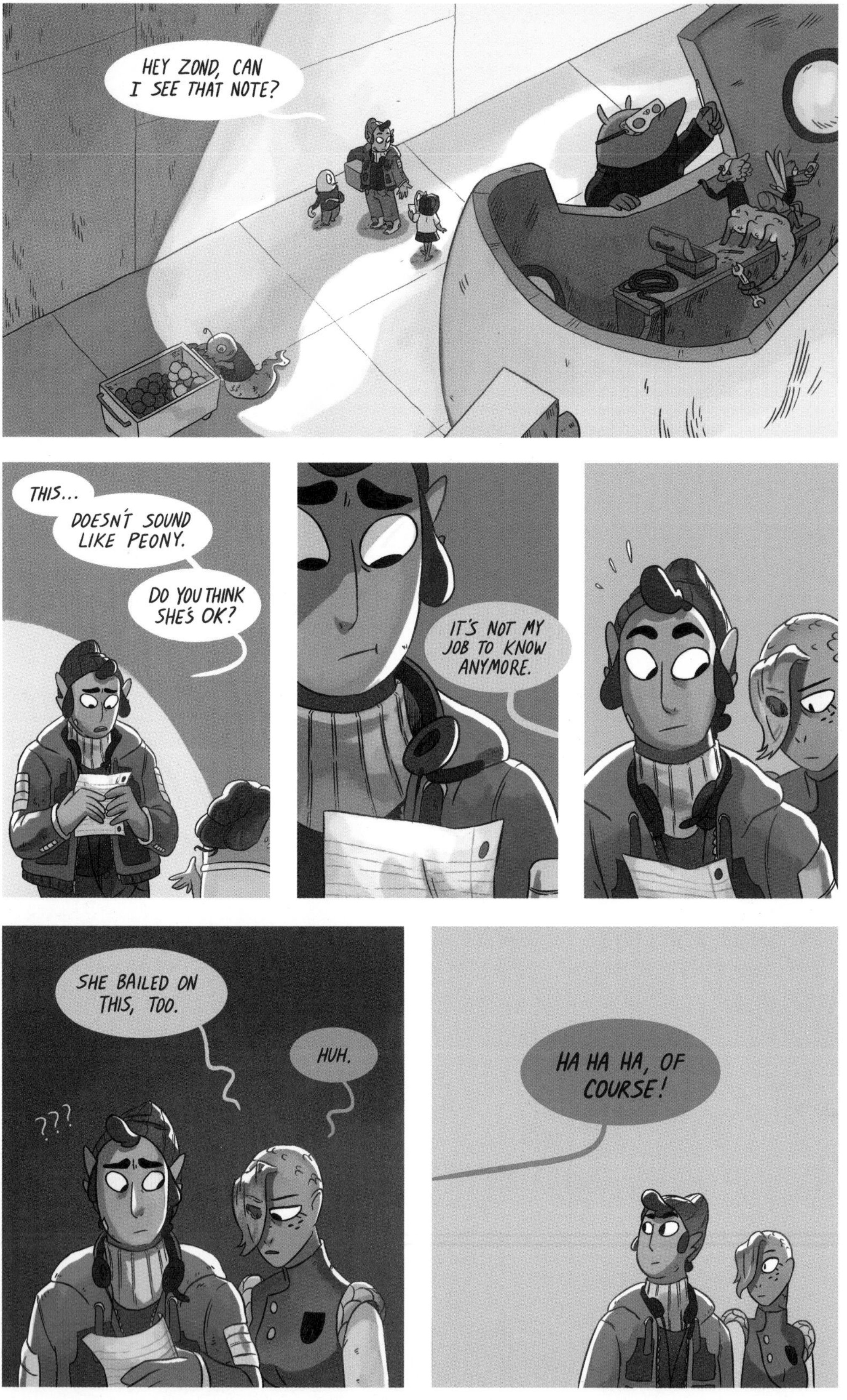
HEY ZOND, CAN I SEE THAT NOTE?
THIS...
DOESN'T SOUND LIKE PEONY.
DO YOU THINK SHE'S OK?
IT'S NOT MY JOB TO KNOW ANYMORE.
SHE BAILED ON THIS, TOO.
HUH.
???
HA HA HA, OF COURSE!

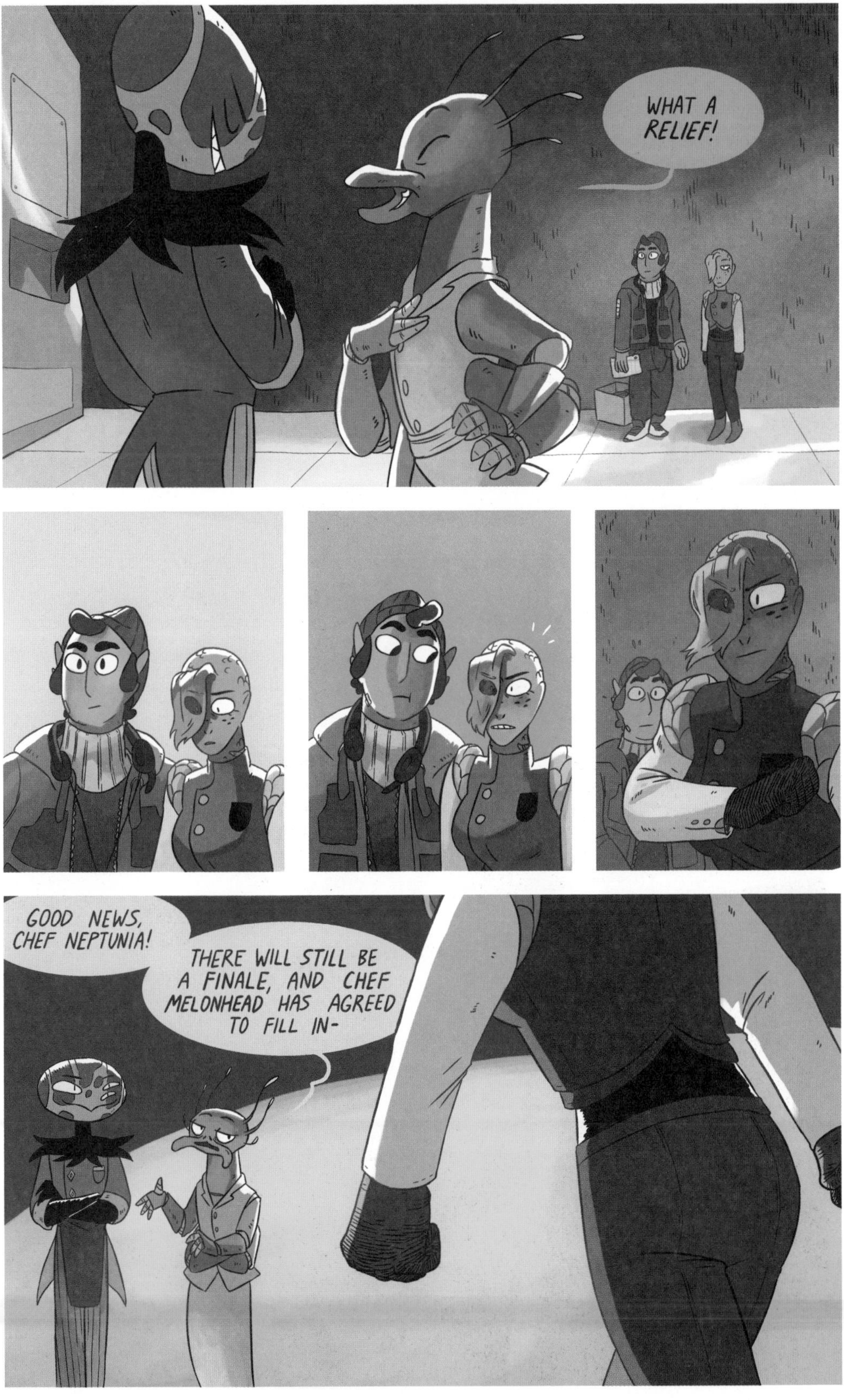
WHAT A RELIEF!
GOOD NEWS, CHEF NEPTUNIA!
THERE WILL STILL BE A FINALE, AND CHEF MELONHEAD HAS AGREED TO FILL IN-

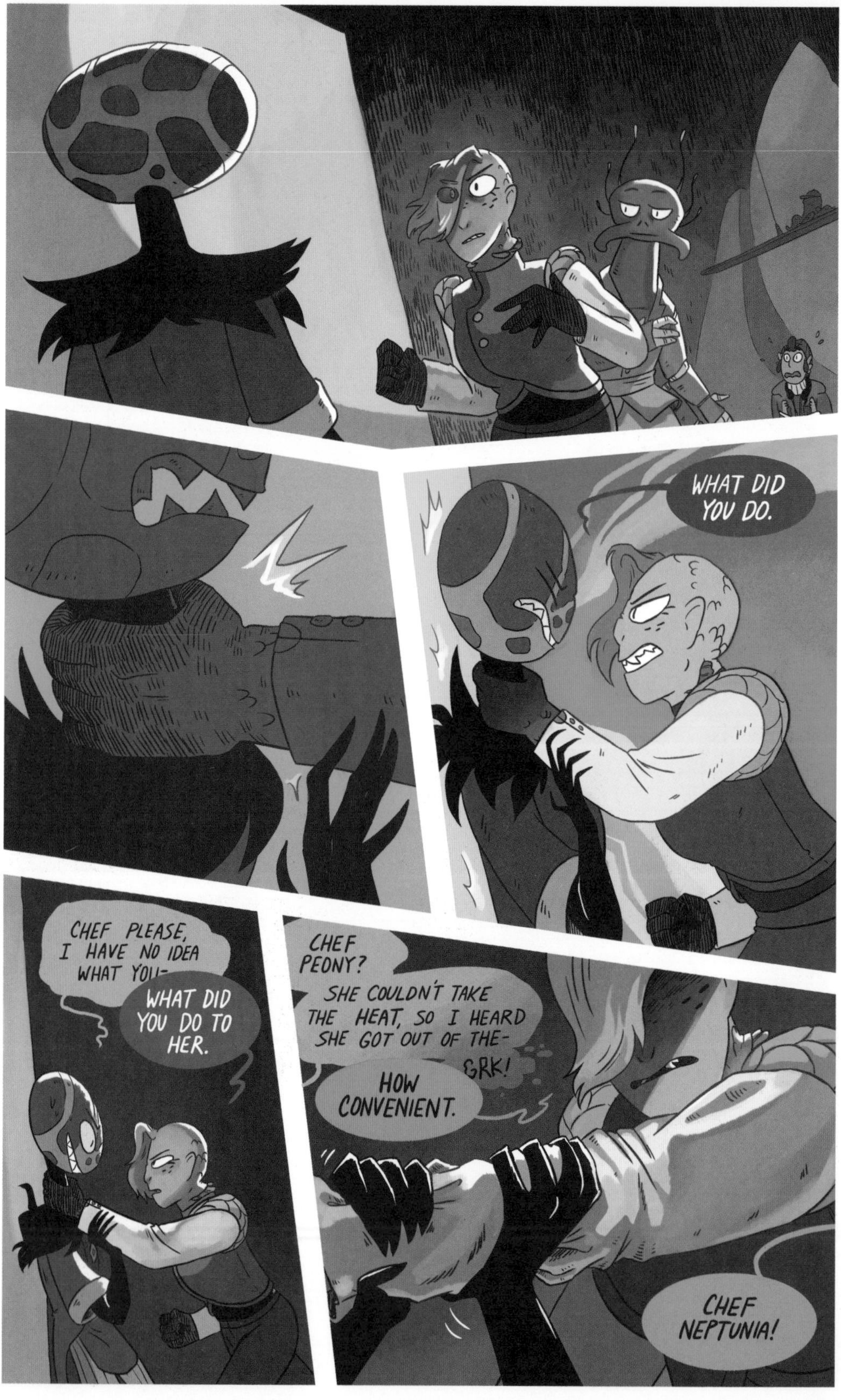
WHAT DID YOU DO.
CHEF PLEASE, I HAVE NO IDEA WHAT YOU-
WHAT DID YOU DO TO HER.
CHEF PEONY?
SHE COULDN'T TAKE THE HEAT, SO I HEARD SHE GOT OUT OF THE-
GRK!
HOW CONVENIENT.
CHEF NEPTUNIA!

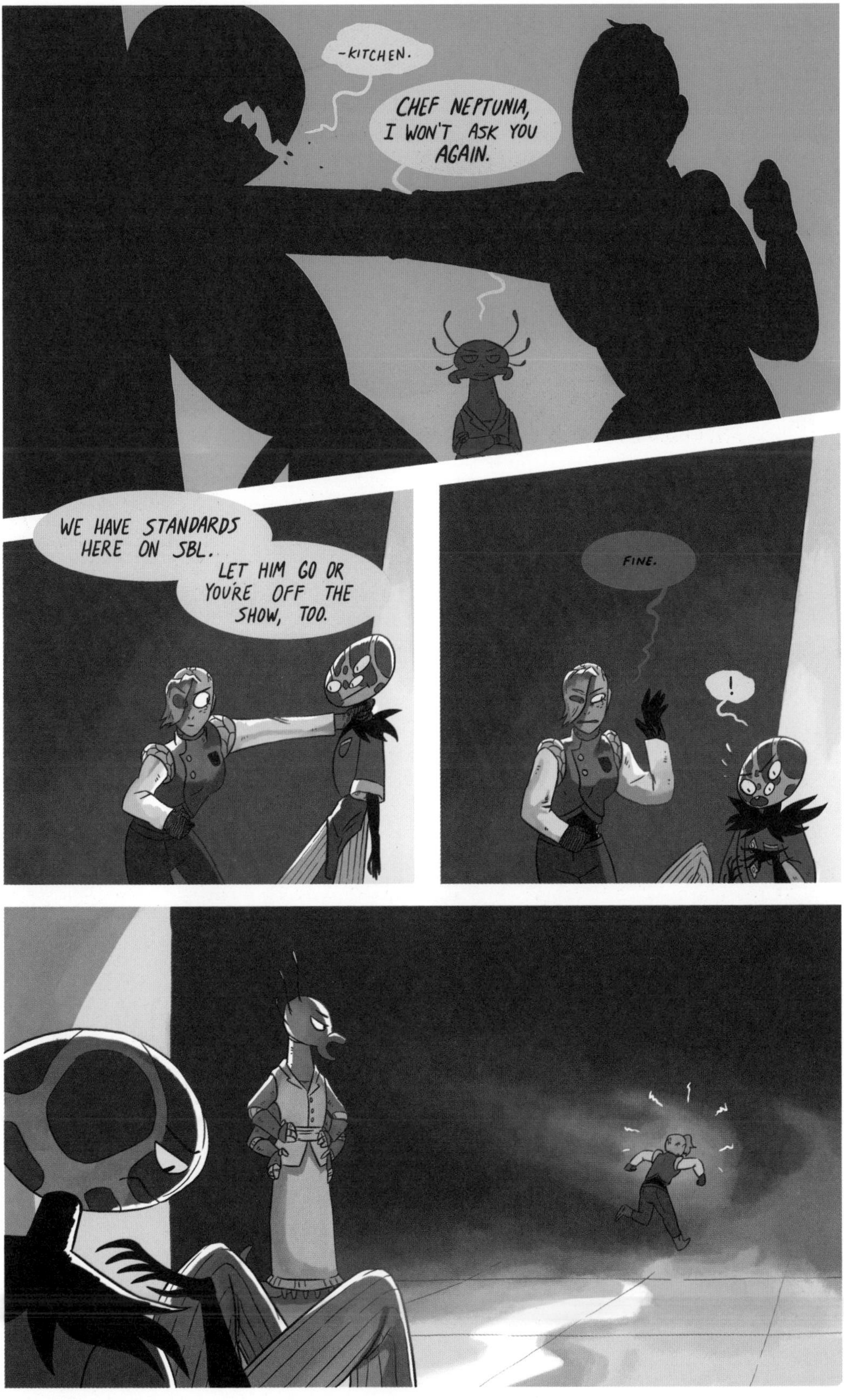
-KITCHEN.
CHEF NEPTUNIA, I WON'T ASK YOU AGAIN.
WE HAVE STANDARDS HERE ON SBL.
LET HIM GO OR YOU'RE OFF THE SHOW, TOO.
FINE.
!

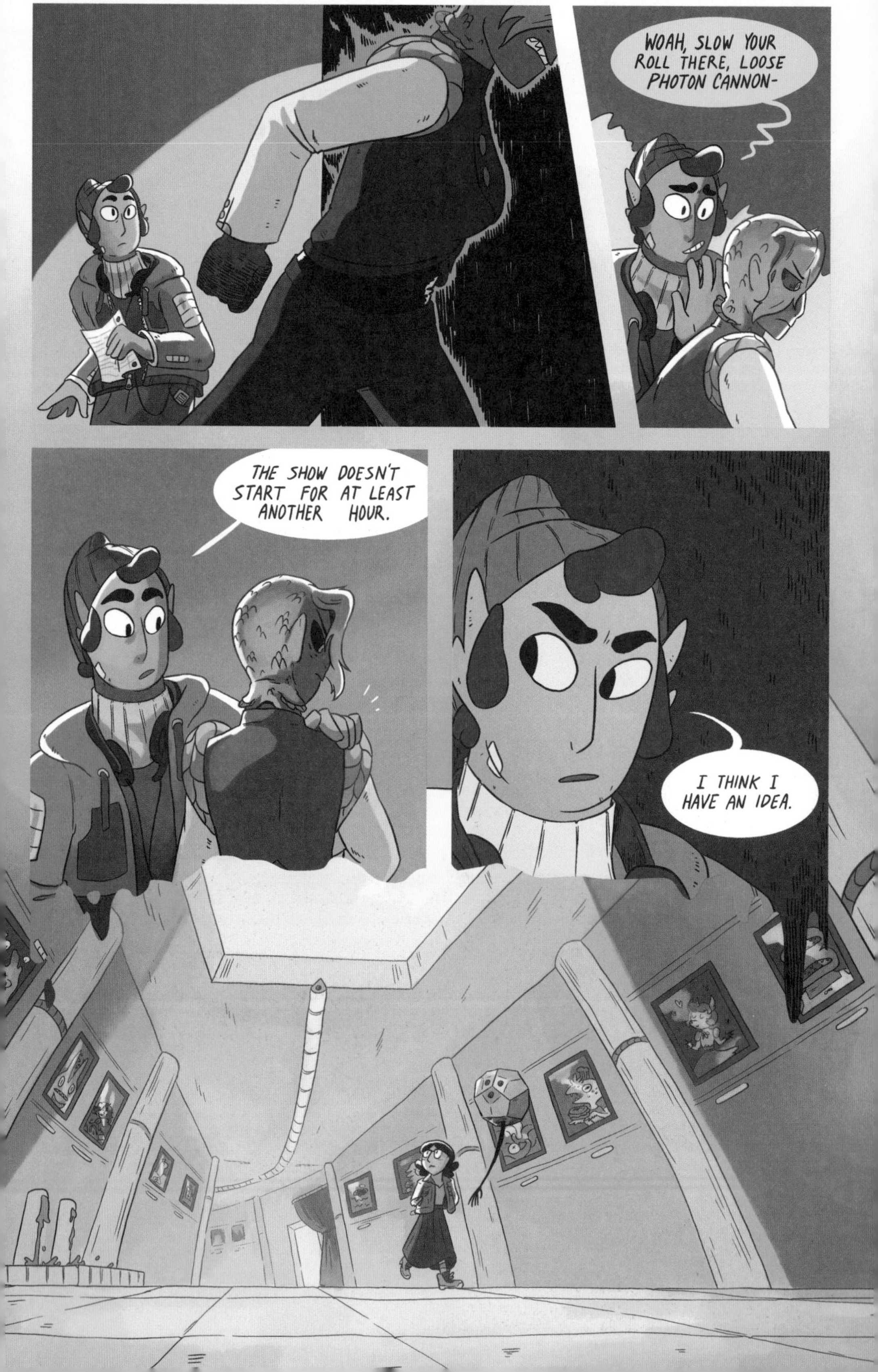
WOAH, SLOW YOUR ROLL THERE, LOOSE PHOTON CANNON-
THE SHOW DOESN'T START FOR AT LEAST ANOTHER HOUR.
I THINK I HAVE AN IDEA.

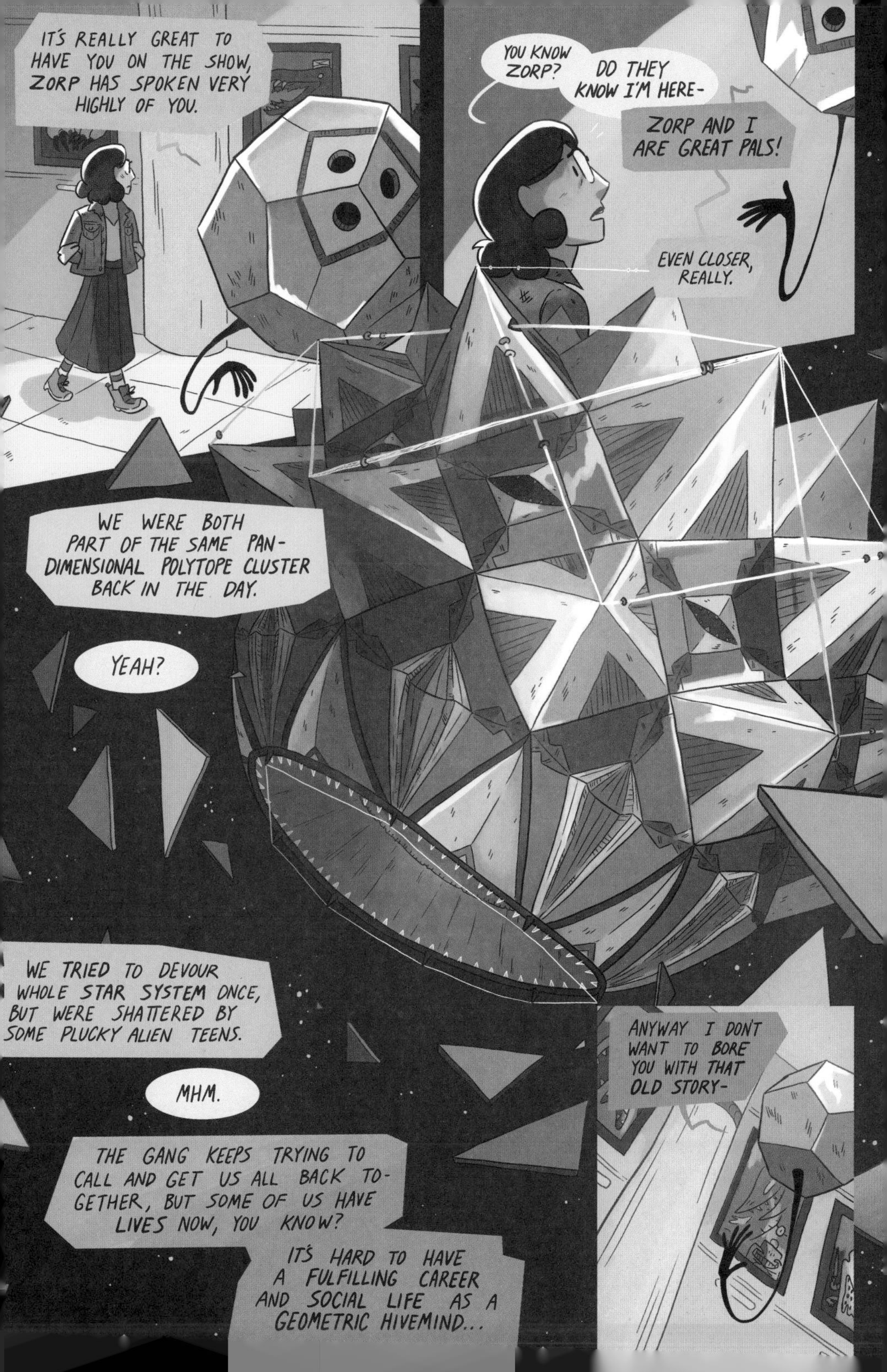
IT'S REALLY GREAT TO HAVE YOU ON THE SHOW, ZORP HAS SPOKEN VERY HIGHLY OF YOU.
YOU KNOW ZORP?
DO THEY KNOW I'M HERE-
ZORP AND I ARE GREAT PALS!
EVEN CLOSER, REALLY.
WE WERE BOTH PART OF THE SAME PAN-DIMENSIONAL POLYTOPE CLUSTER BACK IN THE DAY.
YEAH?
WE TRIED TO DEVOUR WHOLE STAR SYSTEM ONCE, BUT WERE SHATTERED BY SOME PLUCKY ALIEN TEENS.
MHM.
THE GANG KEEPS TRYING TO CALL AND GET US ALL BACK TO-GETHER, BUT SOME OF US HAVE LIVES NOW, YOU KNOW?
IT'S HARD TO HAVE A FULFILLING CAREER AND SOCIAL LIFE AS A GEOMETRIC HIVEMIND...
ANYWAY I DON'T WANT TO BORE YOU WITH THAT OLD STORY-

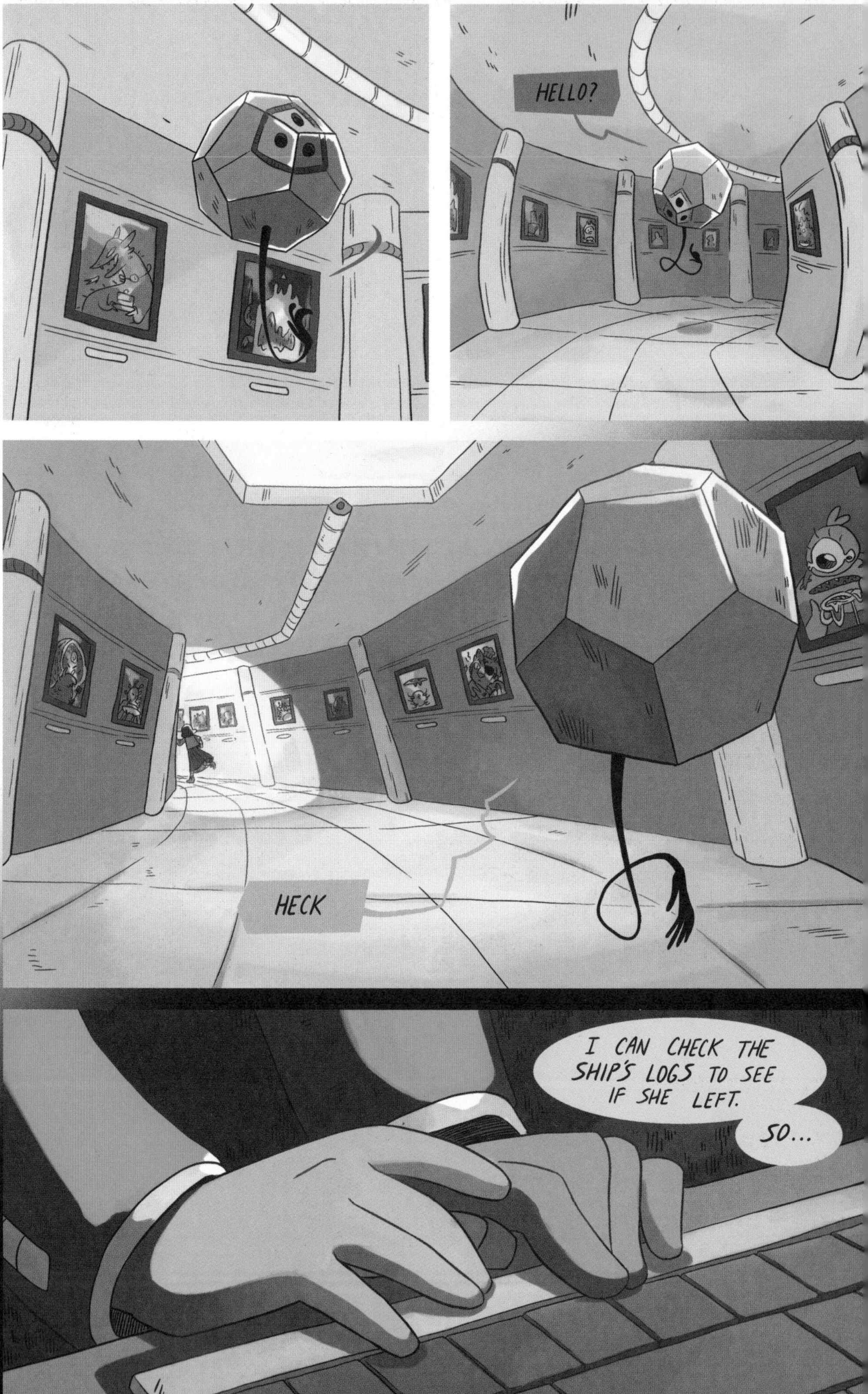
HELLO?
HECK
I CAN CHECK THE SHIP'S LOGS TO SEE IF SHE LEFT.
SO...

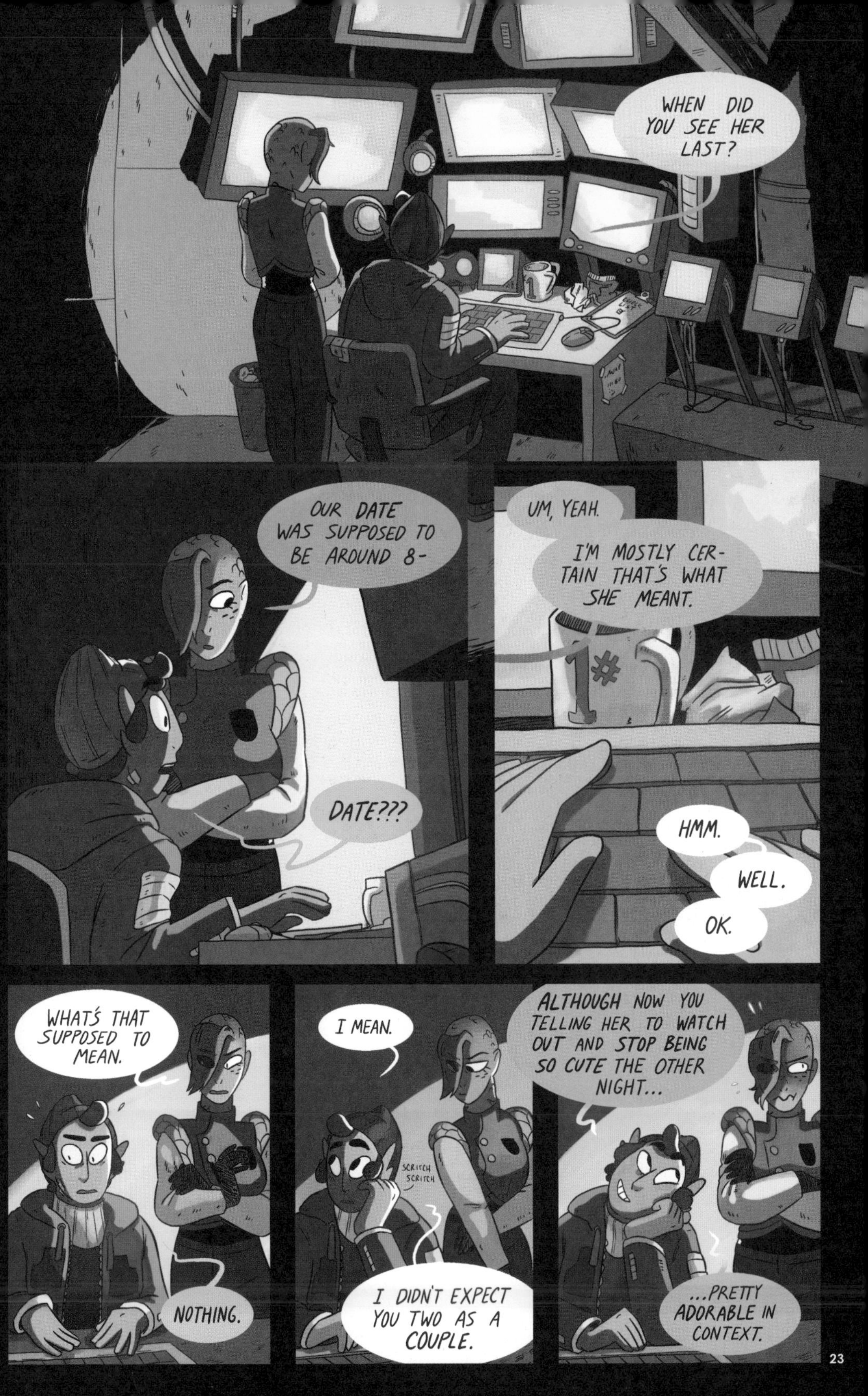
WHEN DID YOU SEE HER LAST?
OUR DATE WAS SUPPOSED TO BE AROUND 8-
DATE???
UM, YEAH.
I'M MOSTLY CERTAIN THAT'S WHAT SHE MEANT.
HMM.
WELL.
OK.
WHAT'S THAT SUPPOSED TO MEAN.
NOTHING.
I MEAN.
SCRITCH SCRITCH
I DIDN'T EXPECT YOU TWO AS A COUPLE.
ALTHOUGH NOW YOU TELLING HER TO WATCH OUT AND STOP BEING SO CUTE THE OTHER NIGHT...
...PRETTY ADORABLE IN CONTEXT.

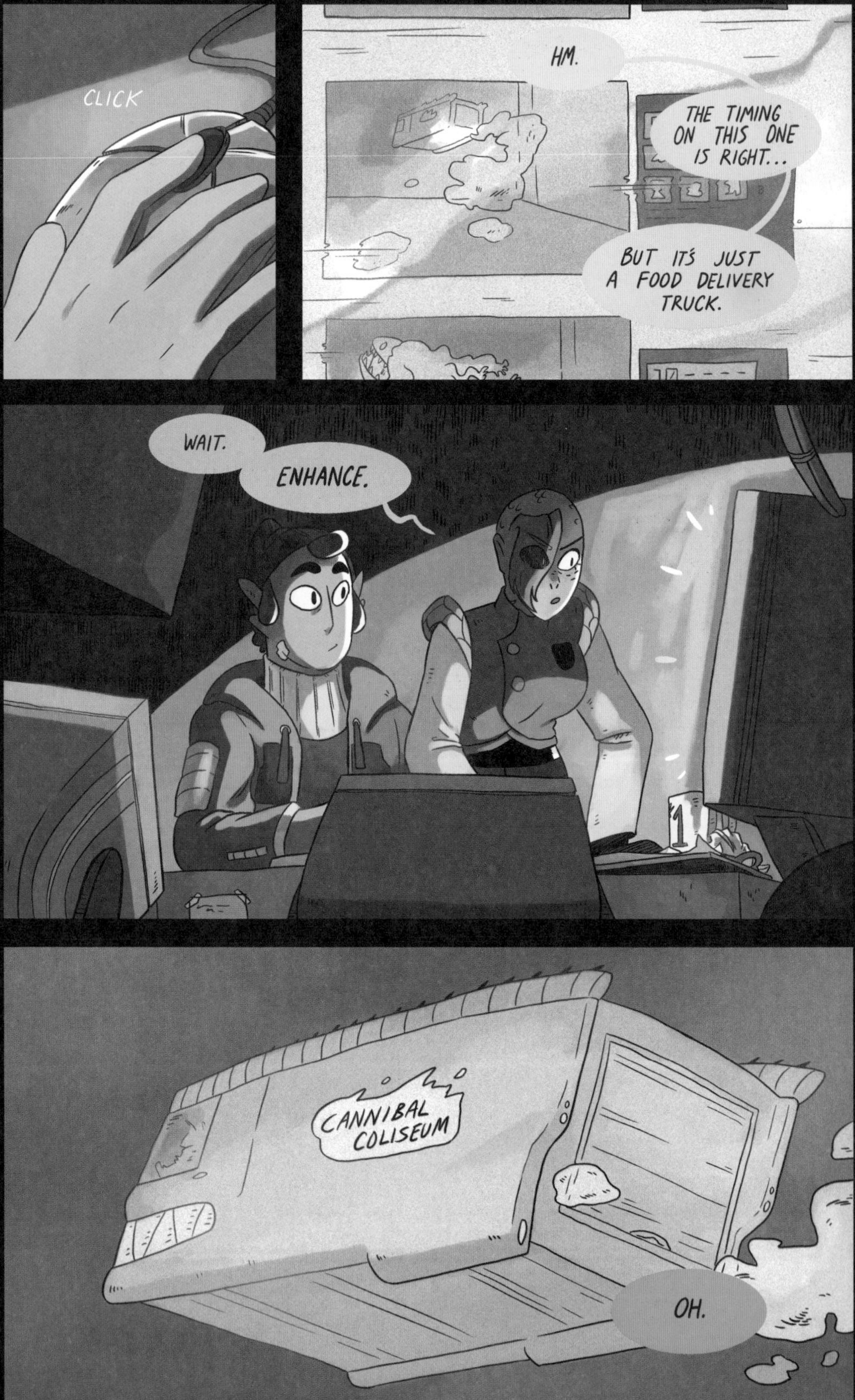
CLICK
HM.
THE TIMING ON THIS ONE IS RIGHT...
BUT IT'S JUST A FOOD DELIVERY TRUCK.
WAIT.
ENHANCE.
CANNIBAL COLISEUM
OH.

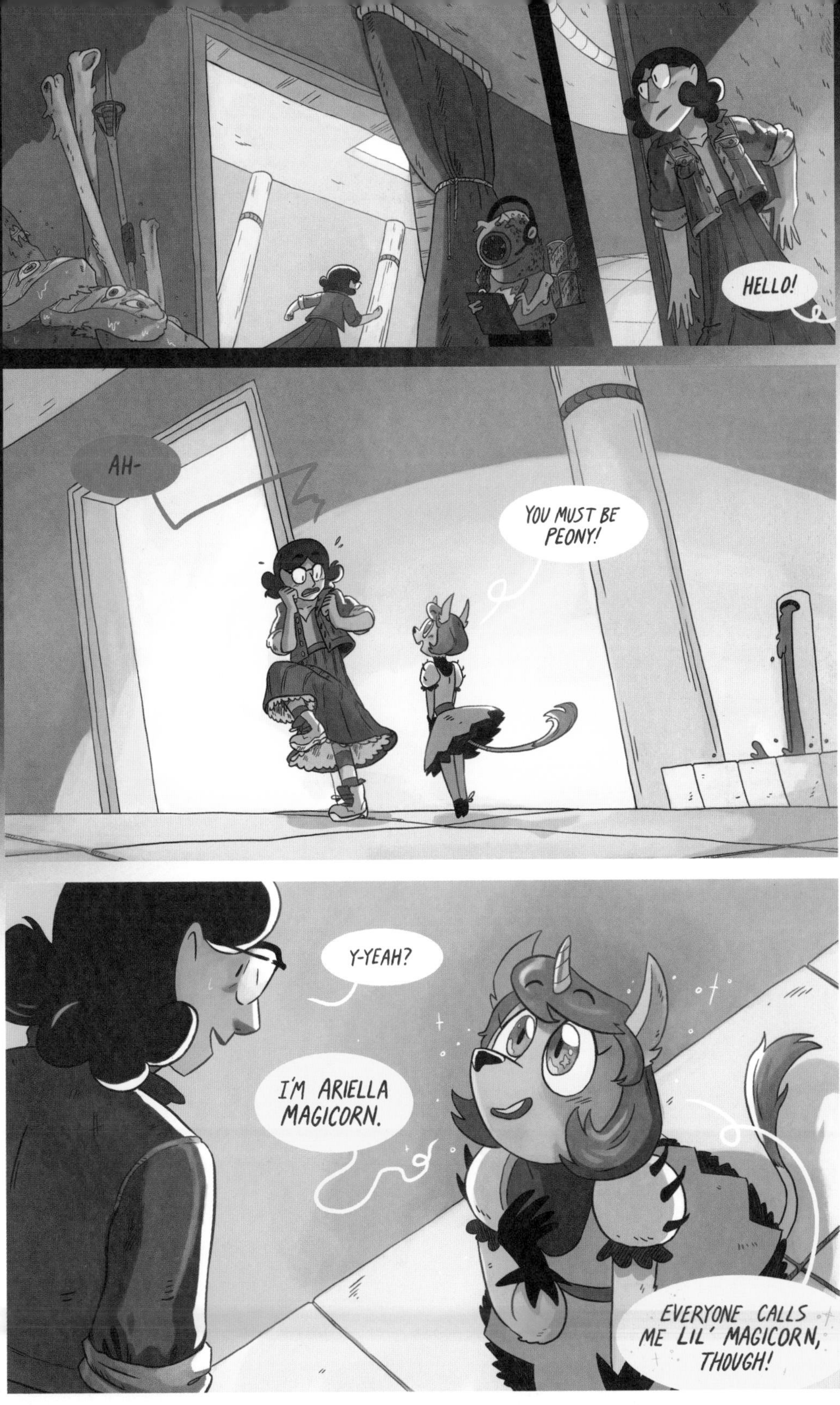
HELLO!
AH-
YOU MUST BE PEONY!
Y-YEAH?
I'M ARIELLA MAGICORN.
EVERYONE CALLS ME LIL' MAGICORN, THOUGH!

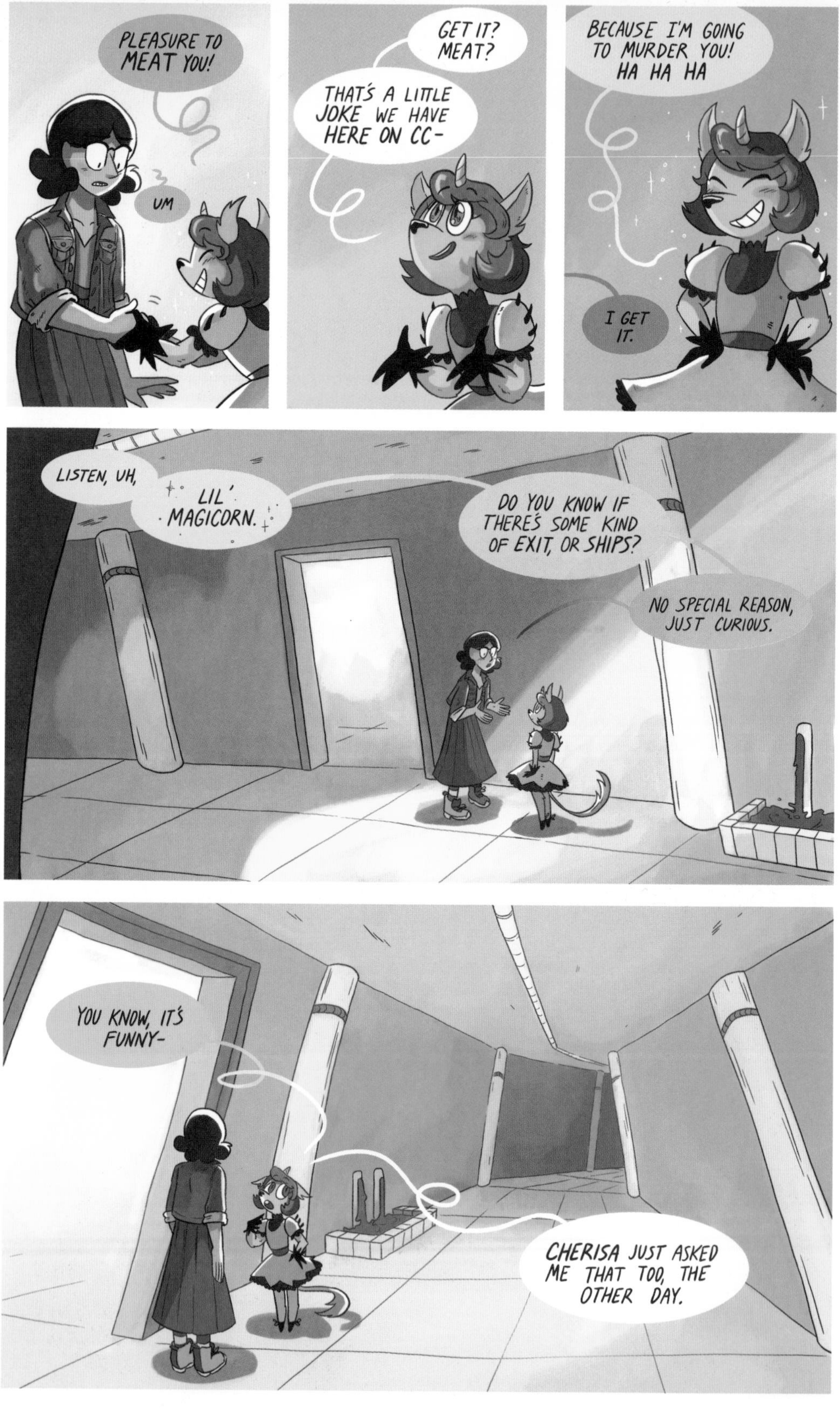
PLEASURE TO MEAT YOU!
UM
GET IT? MEAT?
THAT'S A LITTLE JOKE WE HAVE HERE ON CC-
BECAUSE I'M GOING TO MURDER YOU! HA HA HA
I GET IT.
LISTEN, UH,
LIL' MAGICORN.
DO YOU KNOW IF THERE'S SOME KIND OF EXIT, OR SHIPS?
NO SPECIAL REASON, JUST CURIOUS.
YOU KNOW, IT'S FUNNY-
CHERISA JUST ASKED ME THAT TOO, THE OTHER DAY.

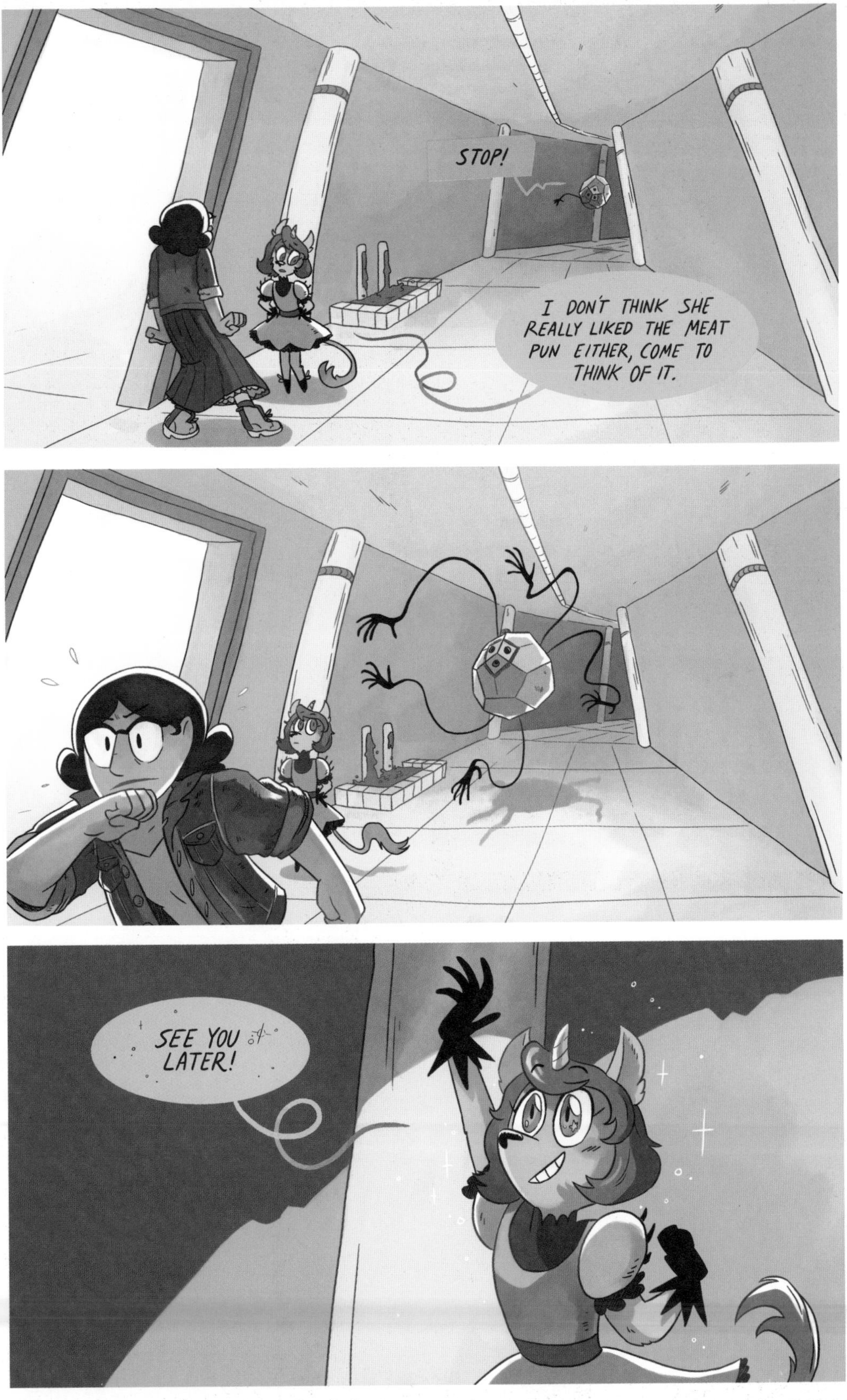
STOP!
I DON'T THINK SHE REALLY LIKED THE MEAT PUN EITHER, COME TO THINK OF IT.
SEE YOU LATER!

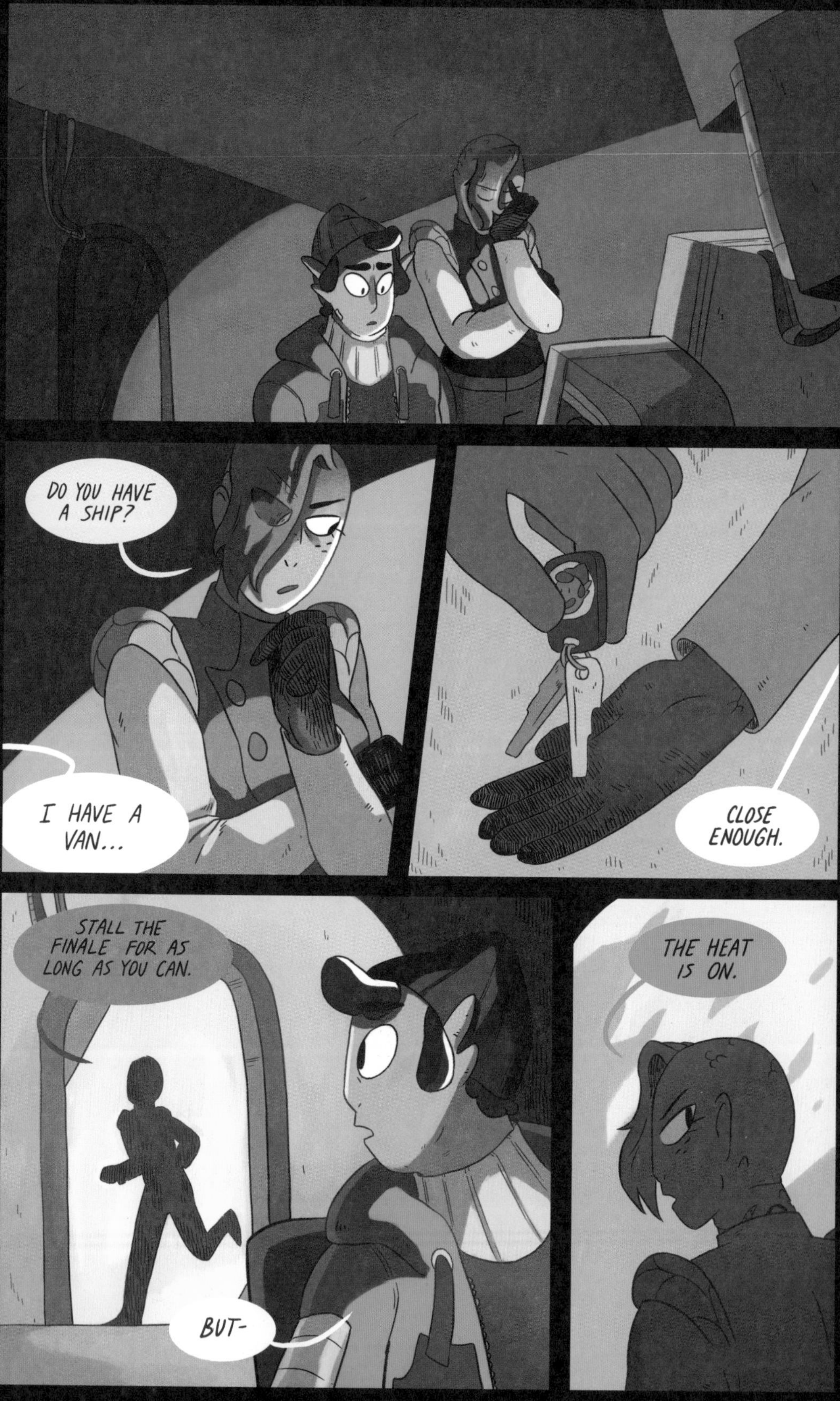
DO YOU HAVE A SHIP?
I HAVE A VAN...
CLOSE ENOUGH.
STALL THE FINALE FOR AS LONG AS YOU CAN.
BUT-
THE HEAT IS ON.

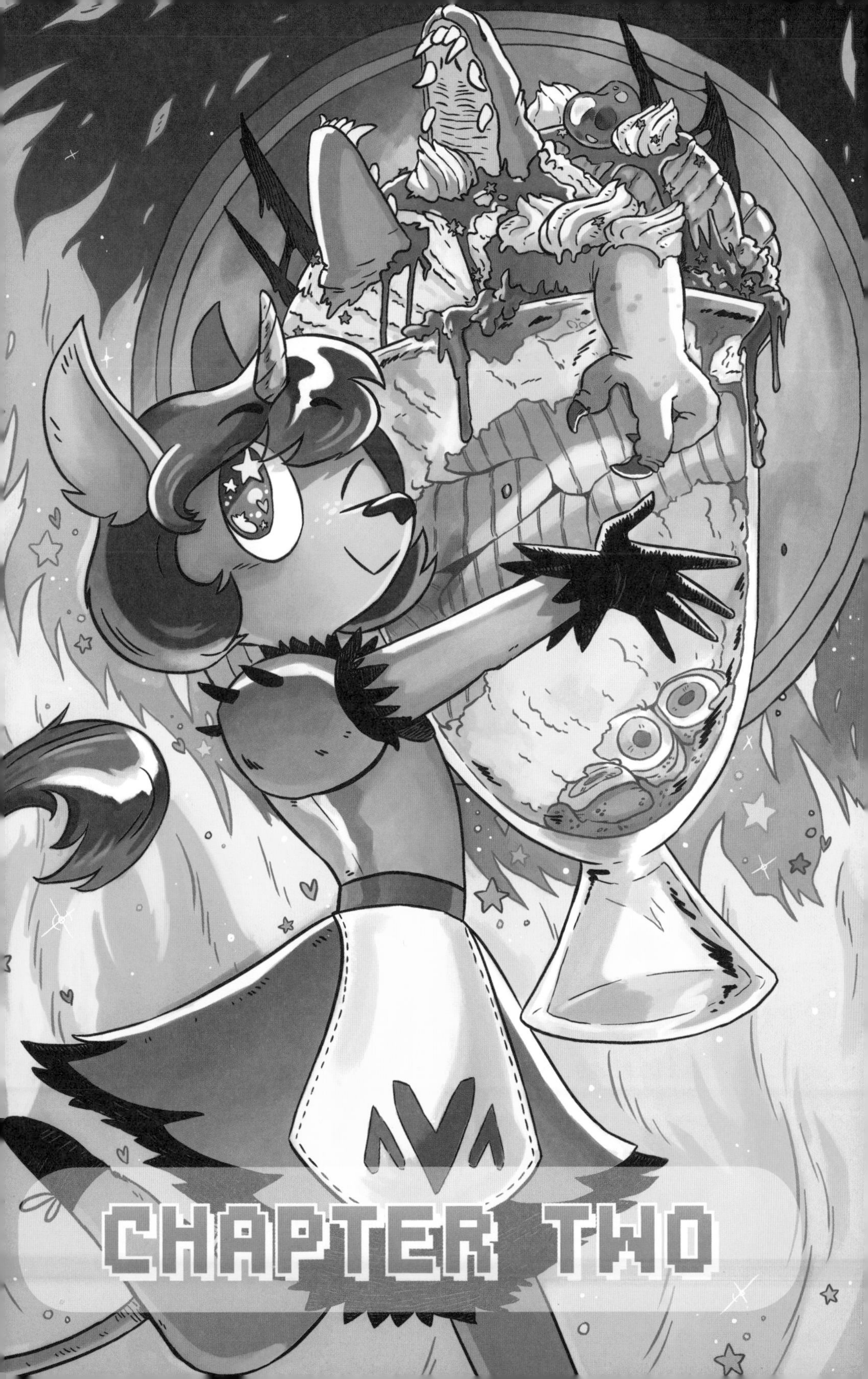

CHAPTER TWO

PREVIOUSLY ON CANNIBAL COLISEUM...

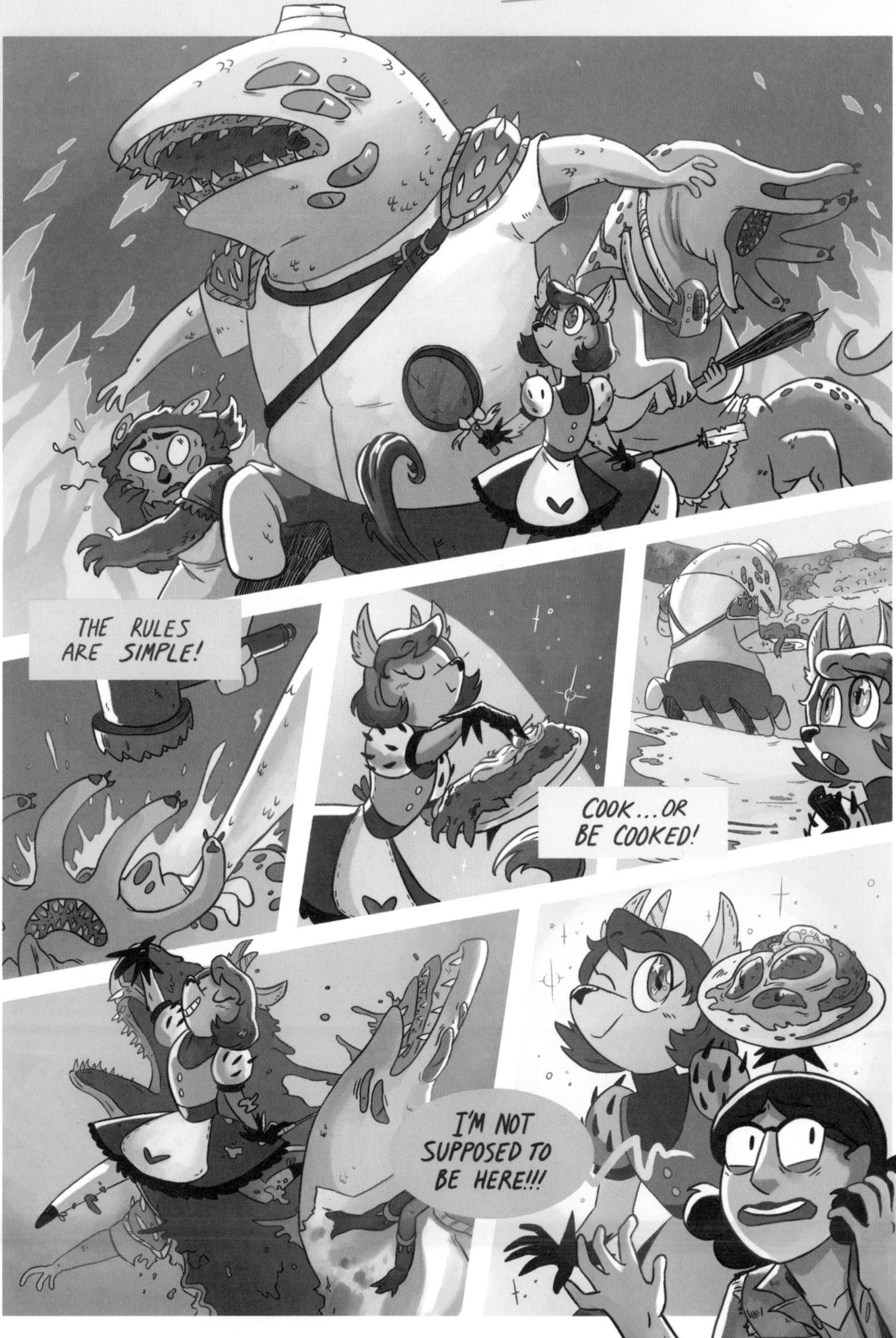
THE RULES ARE SIMPLE!
COOK... OR BE COOKED!
I'M NOT SUPPOSED TO BE HERE!!!

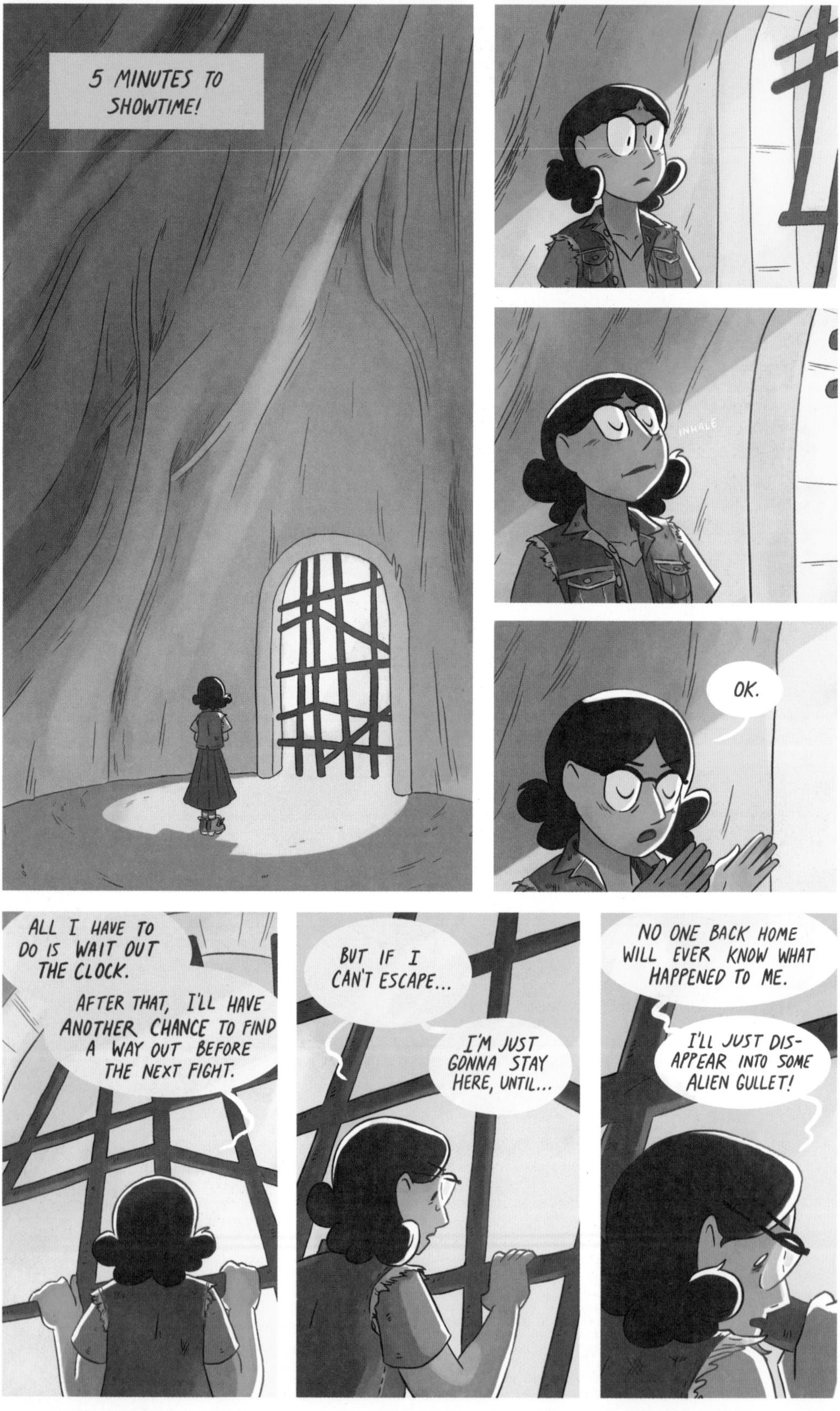
5 MINUTES TO SHOWTIME!
INHALE
OK.
ALL I HAVE TO DO IS WAIT OUT THE CLOCK.
AFTER THAT, I'LL HAVE ANOTHER CHANCE TO FIND A WAY OUT BEFORE THE NEXT FIGHT.
BUT IF I CAN'T ESCAPE...
I'M JUST GONNA STAY HERE, UNTIL...
NO ONE BACK HOME WILL EVER KNOW WHAT HAPPENED TO ME.
I'LL JUST DIS-APPEAR INTO SOME ALIEN GULLET!

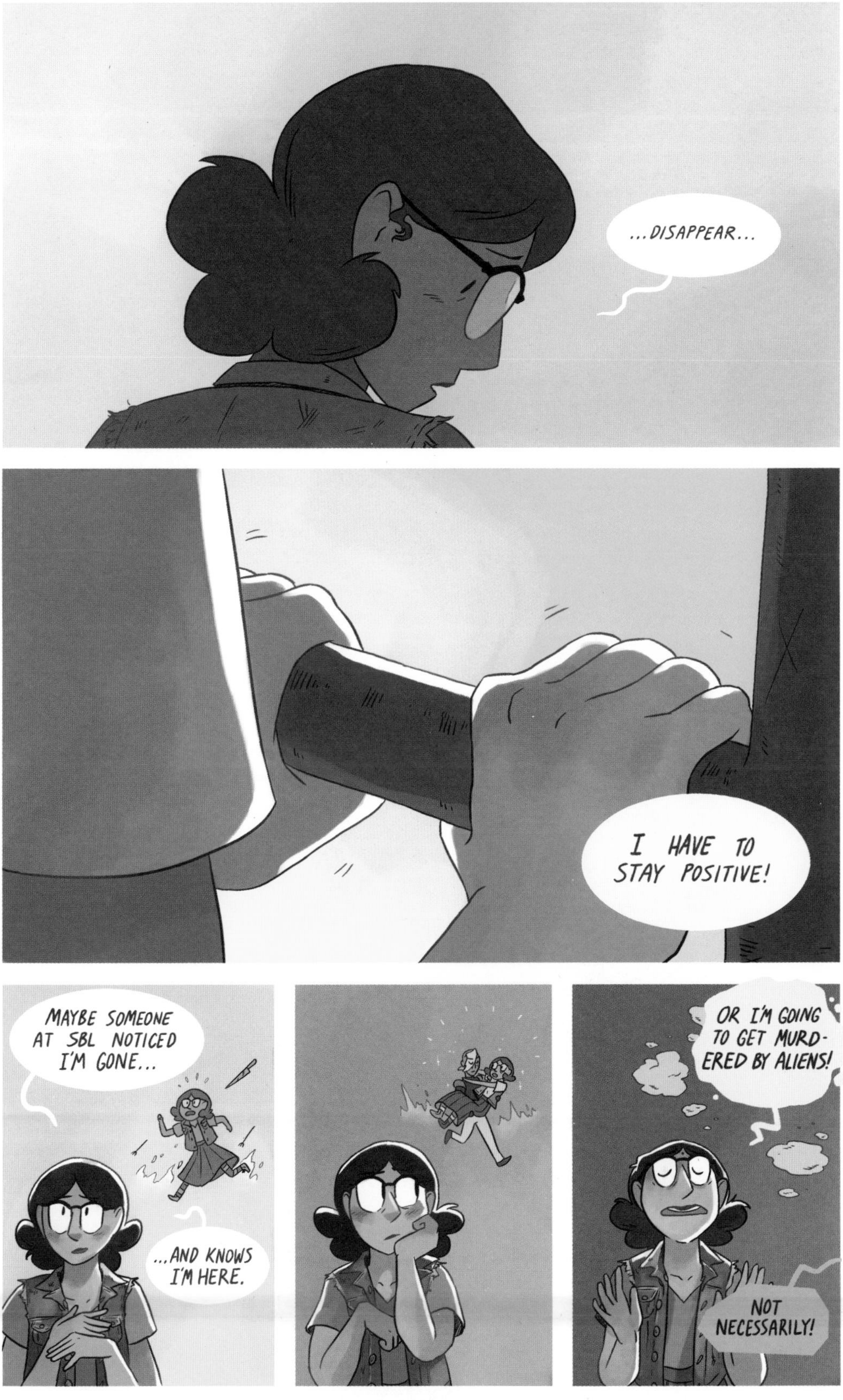
...DISAPPEAR...
I HAVE TO STAY POSITIVE!
MAYBE SOMEONE AT SBL NOTICED I'M GONE...
...AND KNOWS I'M HERE.
OR I'M GOING TO GET MURD-ERED BY ALIENS!
NOT NECESSARILY!

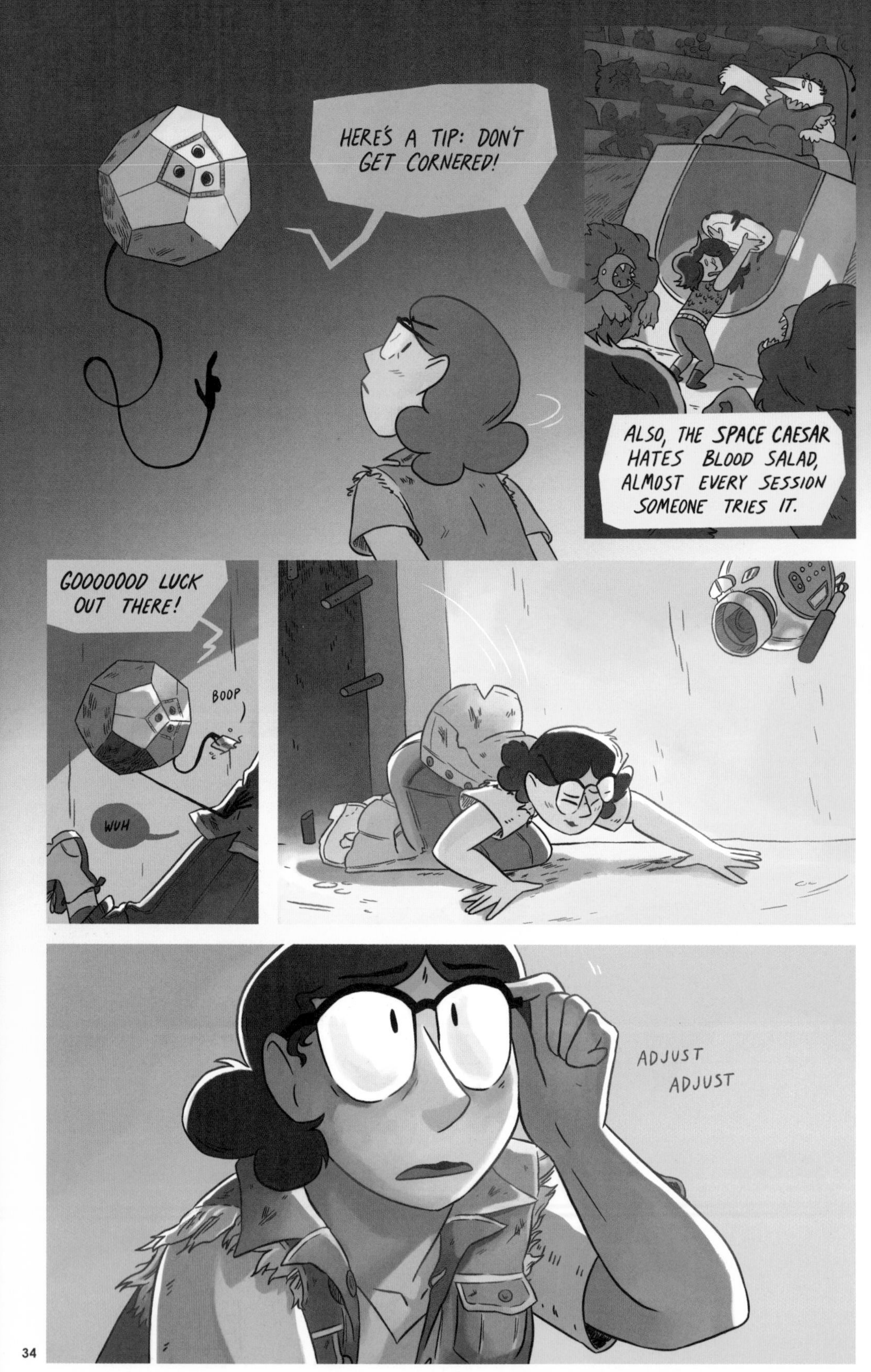
HERE'S A TIP: DON'T GET CORNERED!
ALSO, THE SPACE CAESAR HATES BLOOD SALAD, ALMOST EVERY SESSION SOMEONE TRIES IT.
GOOOOOOD LUCK OUT THERE!
BOOP
WUH
ADJUST
ADJUST

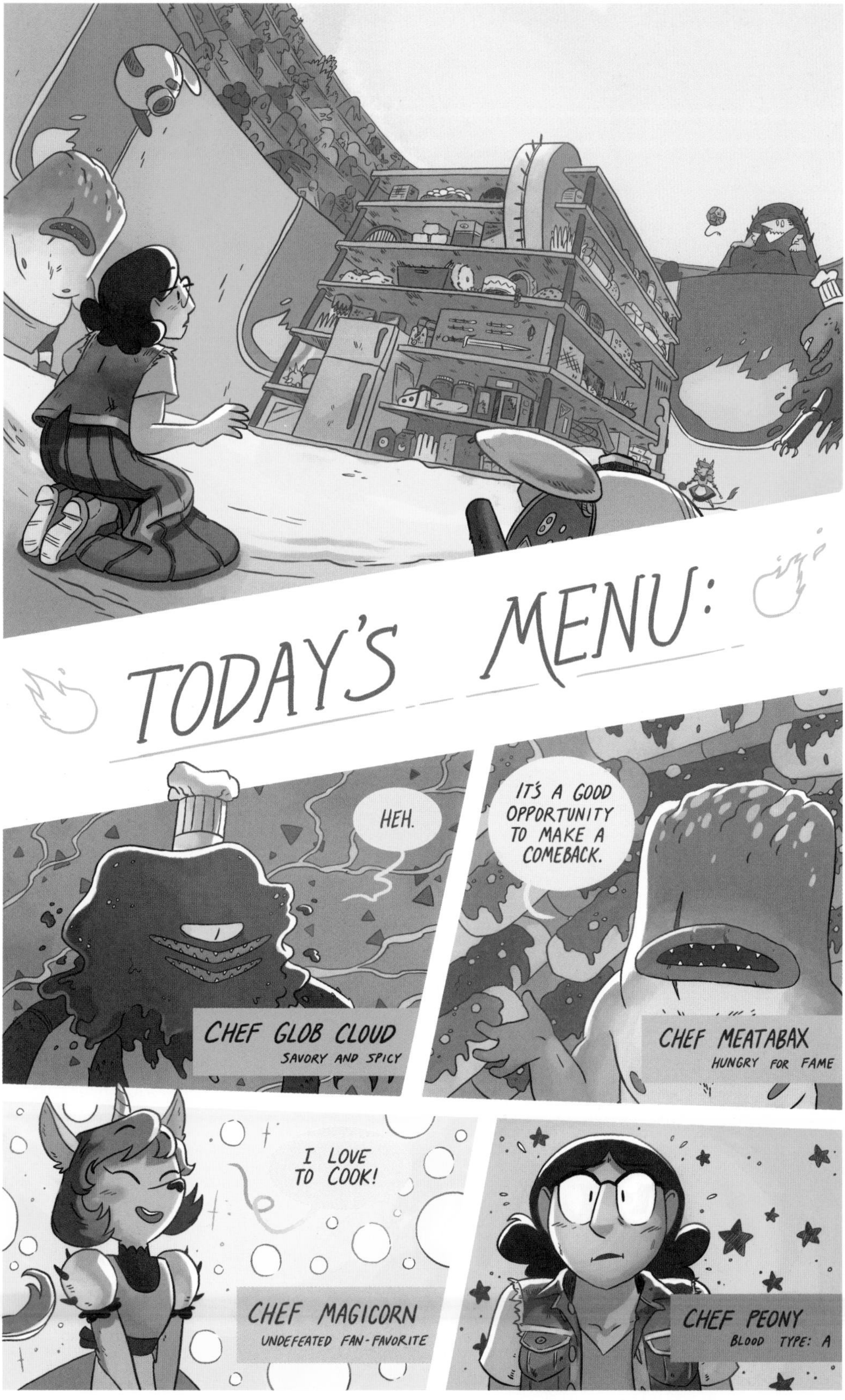
TODAY'S MENU:
HEH.
CHEF GLOB CLOUD
SAVORY AND SPICY
IT'S A GOOD OPPORTUNITY TO MAKE A COMEBACK.
CHEF MEATABAX
HUNGRY FOR FAME
I LOVE TO COOK!
CHEF MAGICORN
UNDEFEATED FAN-FAVORITE
CHEF PEONY
BLOOD TYPE: A

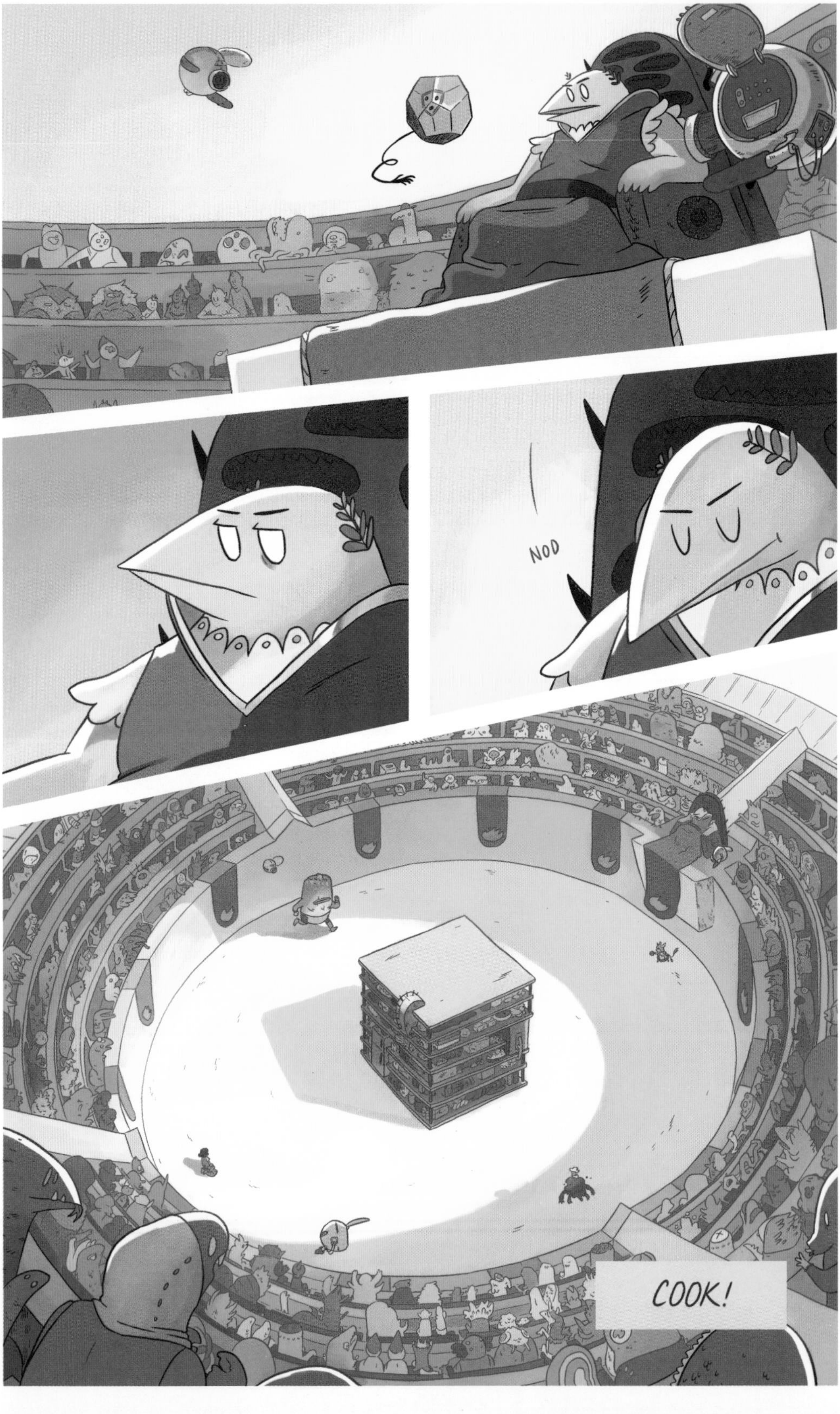
NOD
COOK!

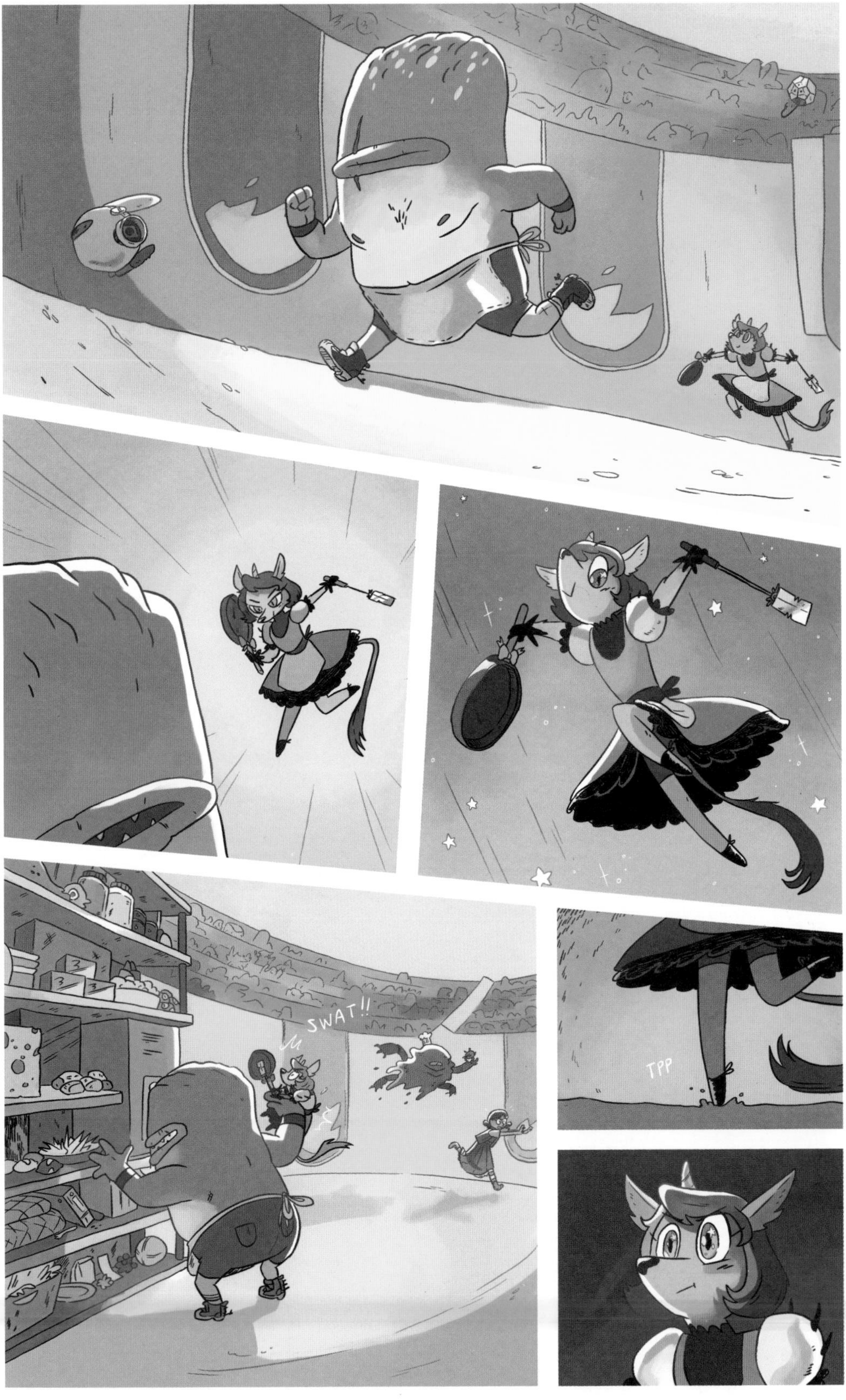
SWAT!!
TPP

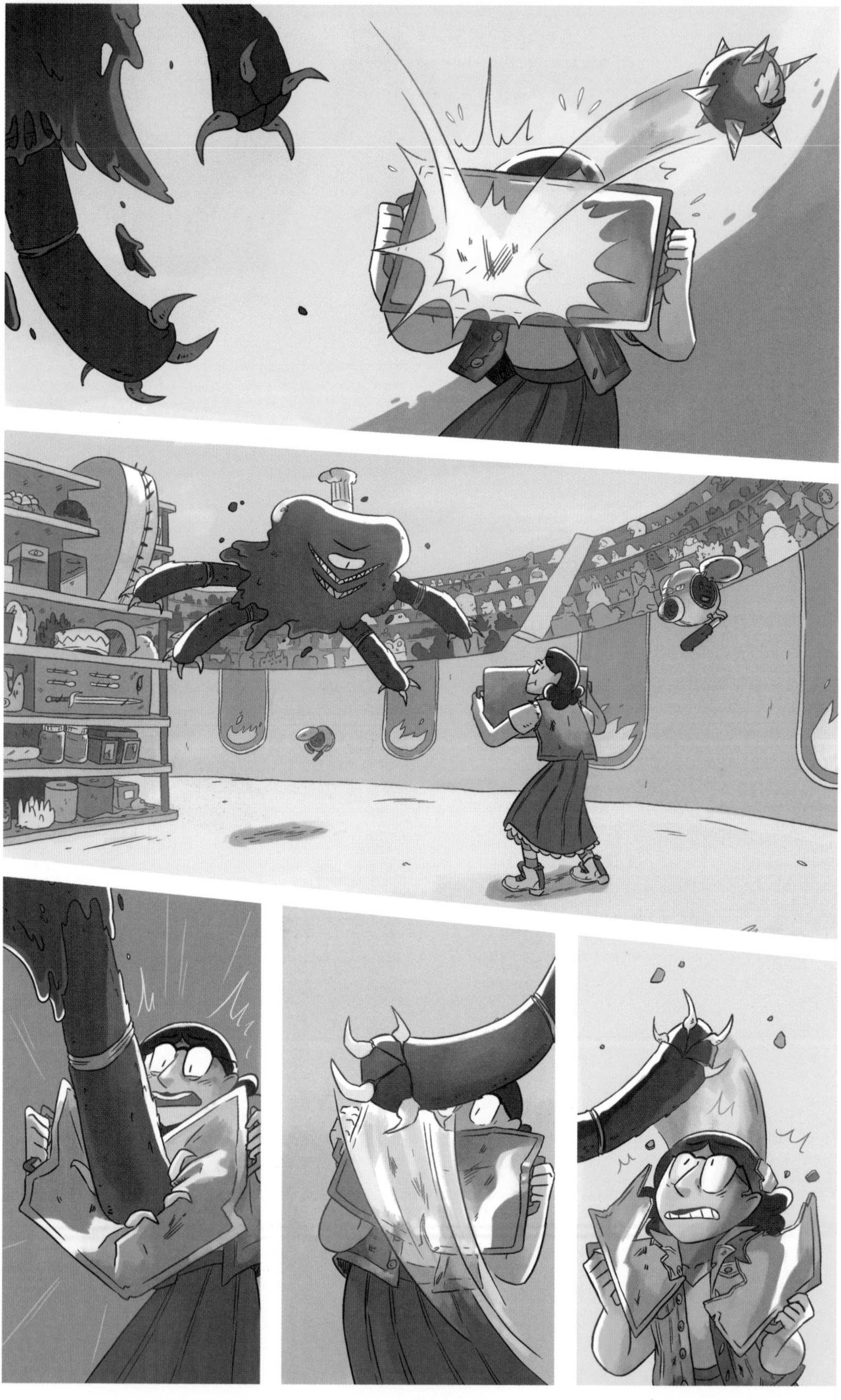

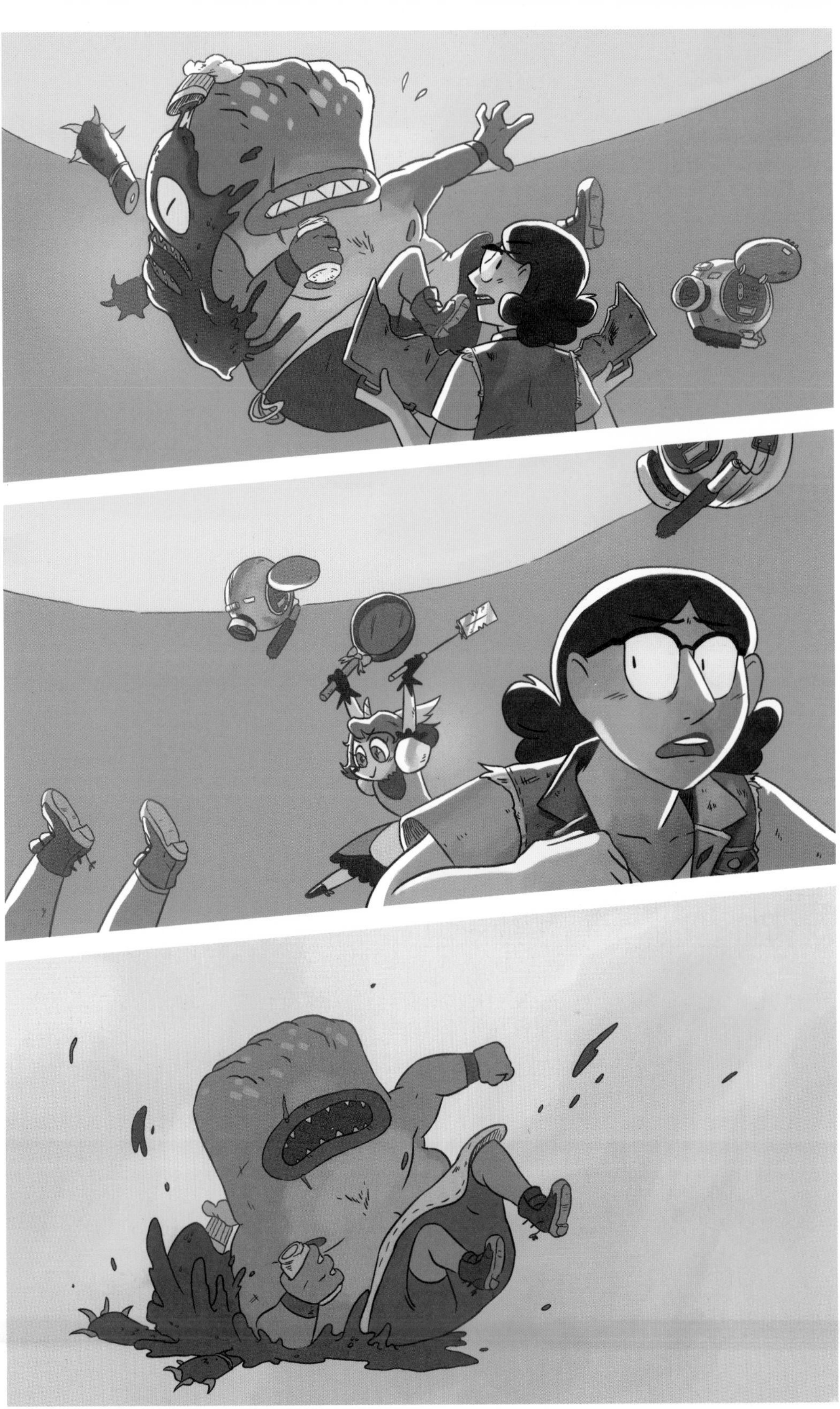

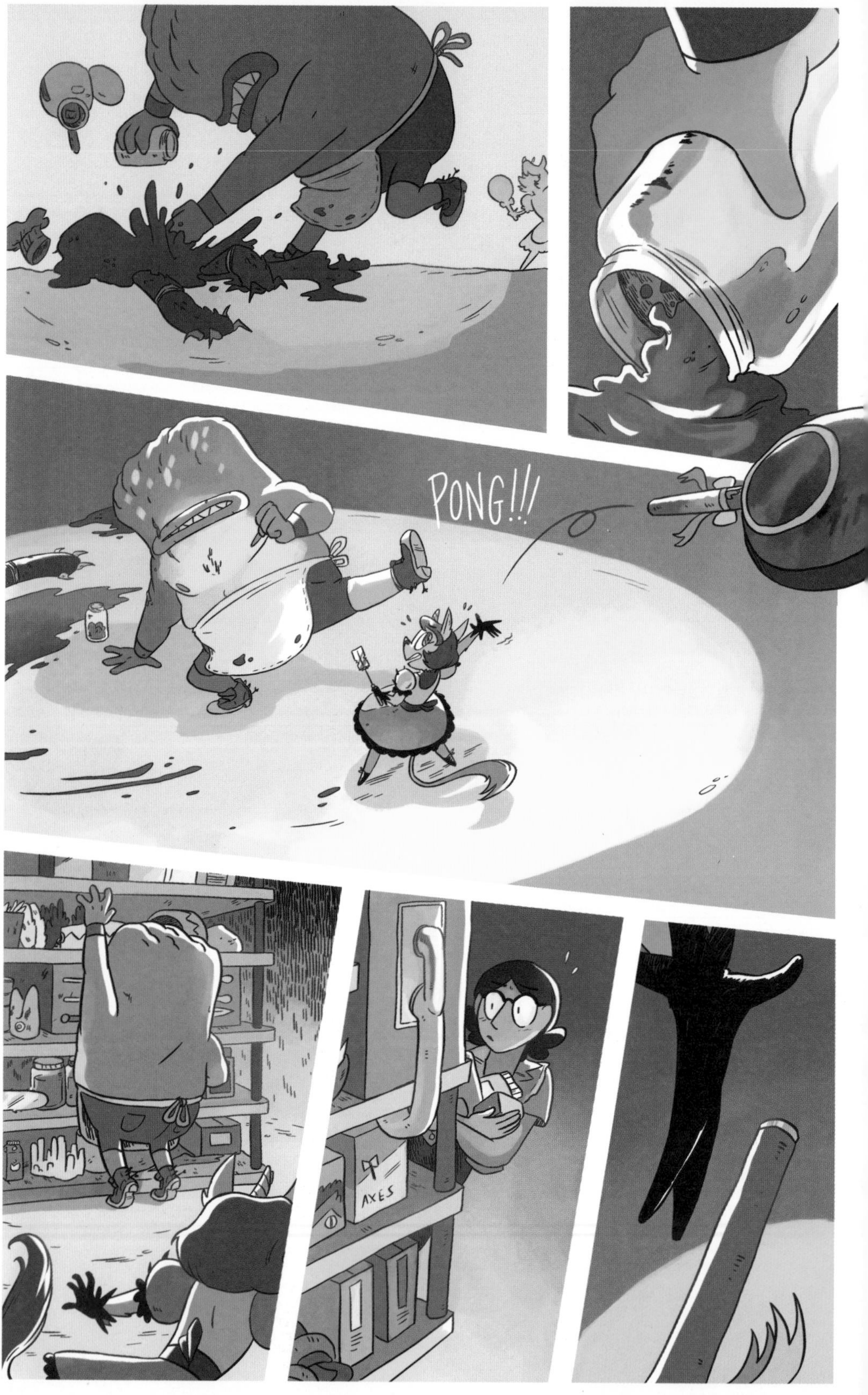
PONG!!!
AXES

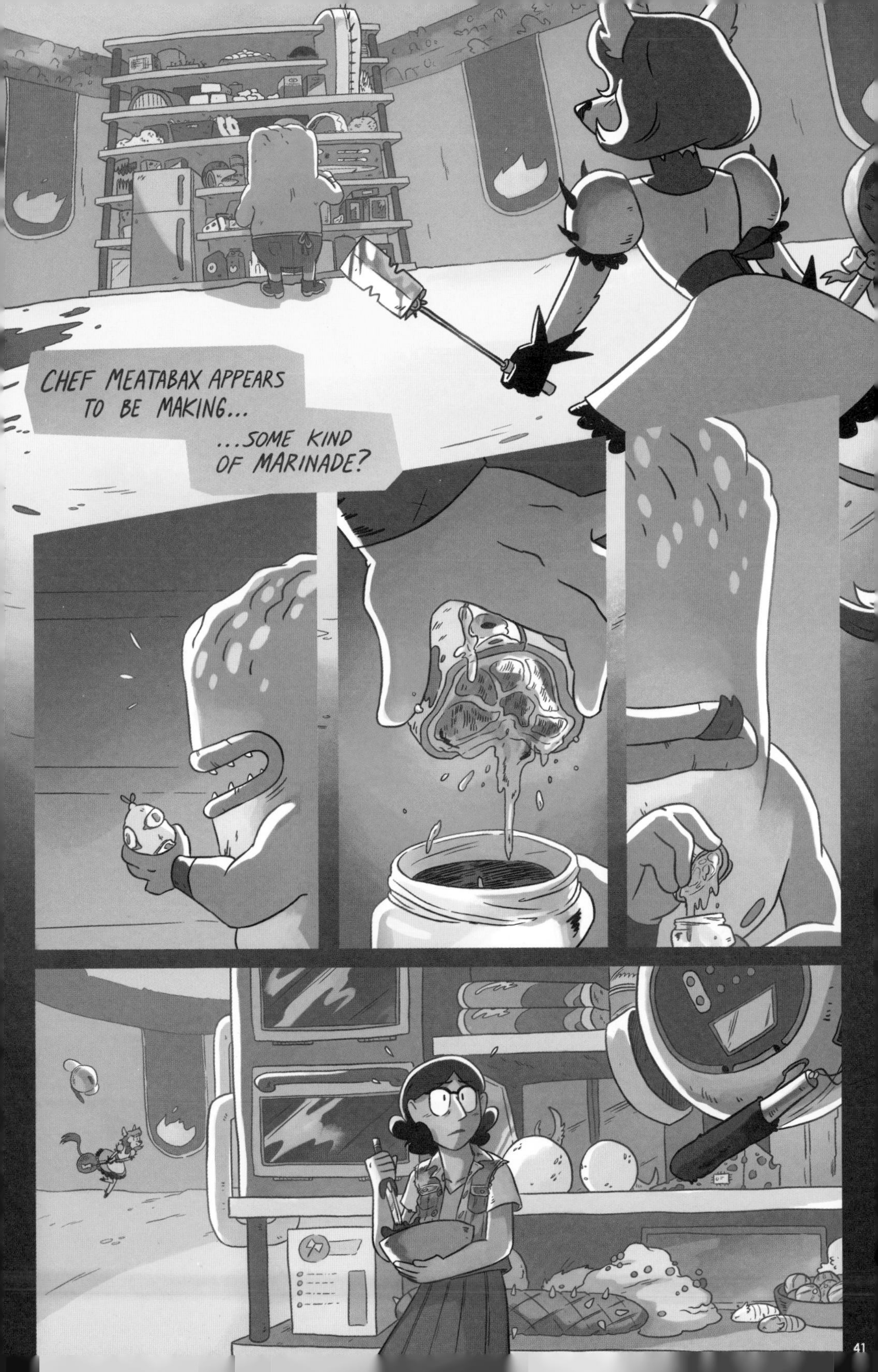
CHEF MEATABAX APPEARS TO BE MAKING...
...SOME KIND OF MARINADE?

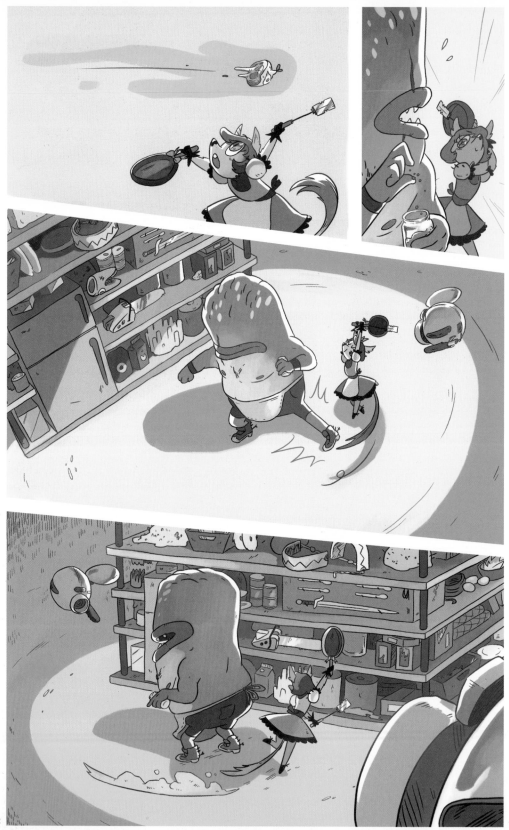

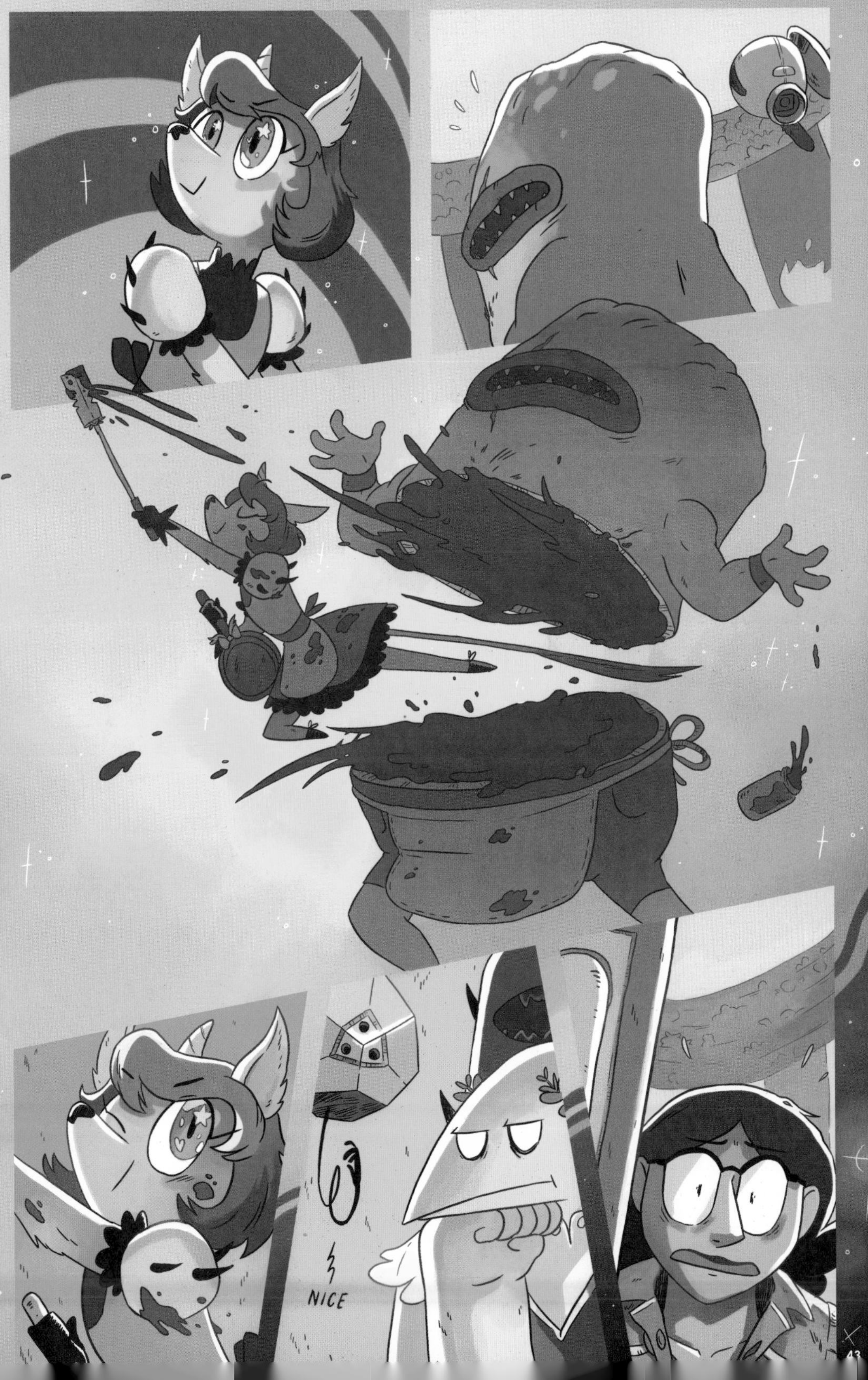
NICE

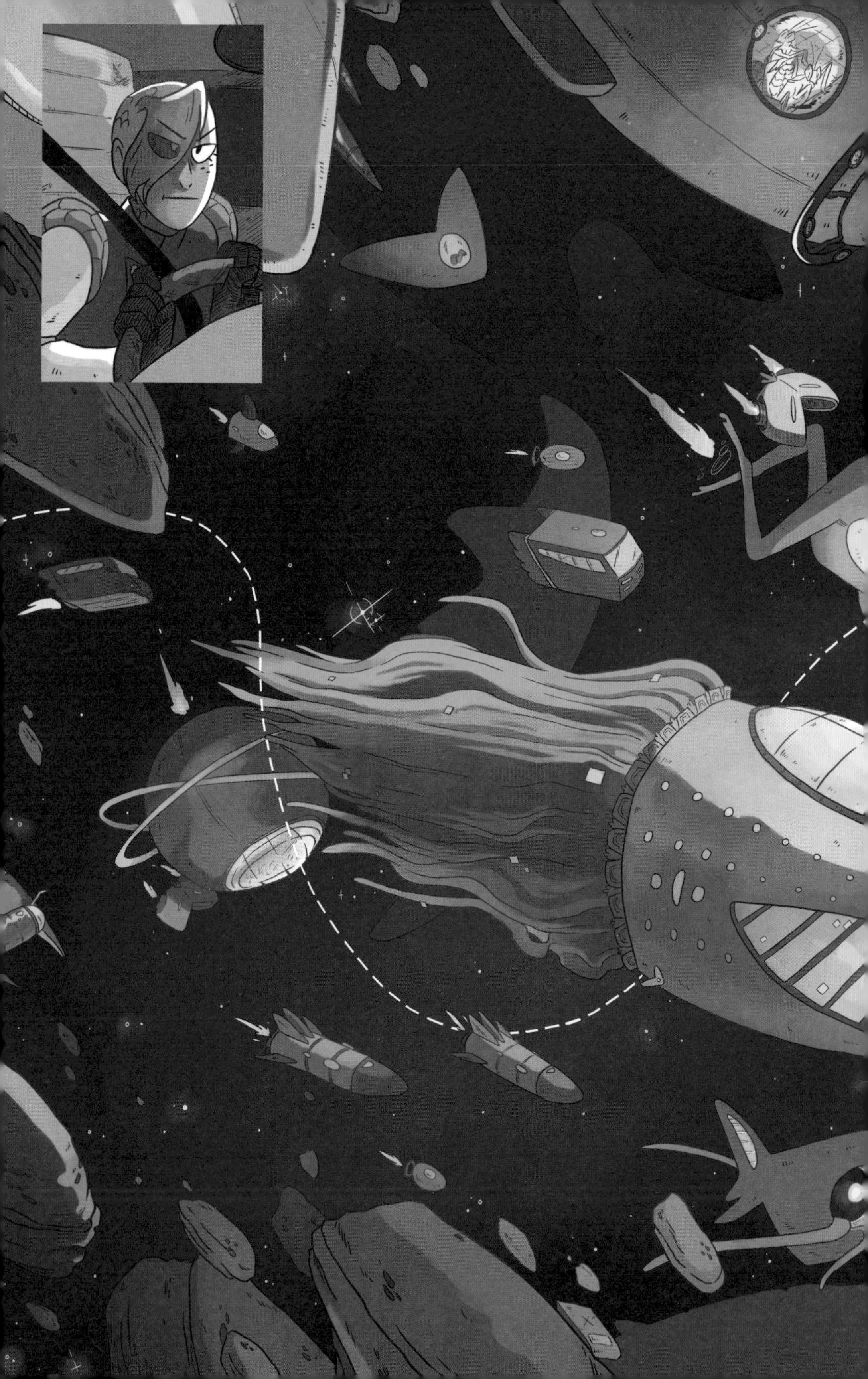

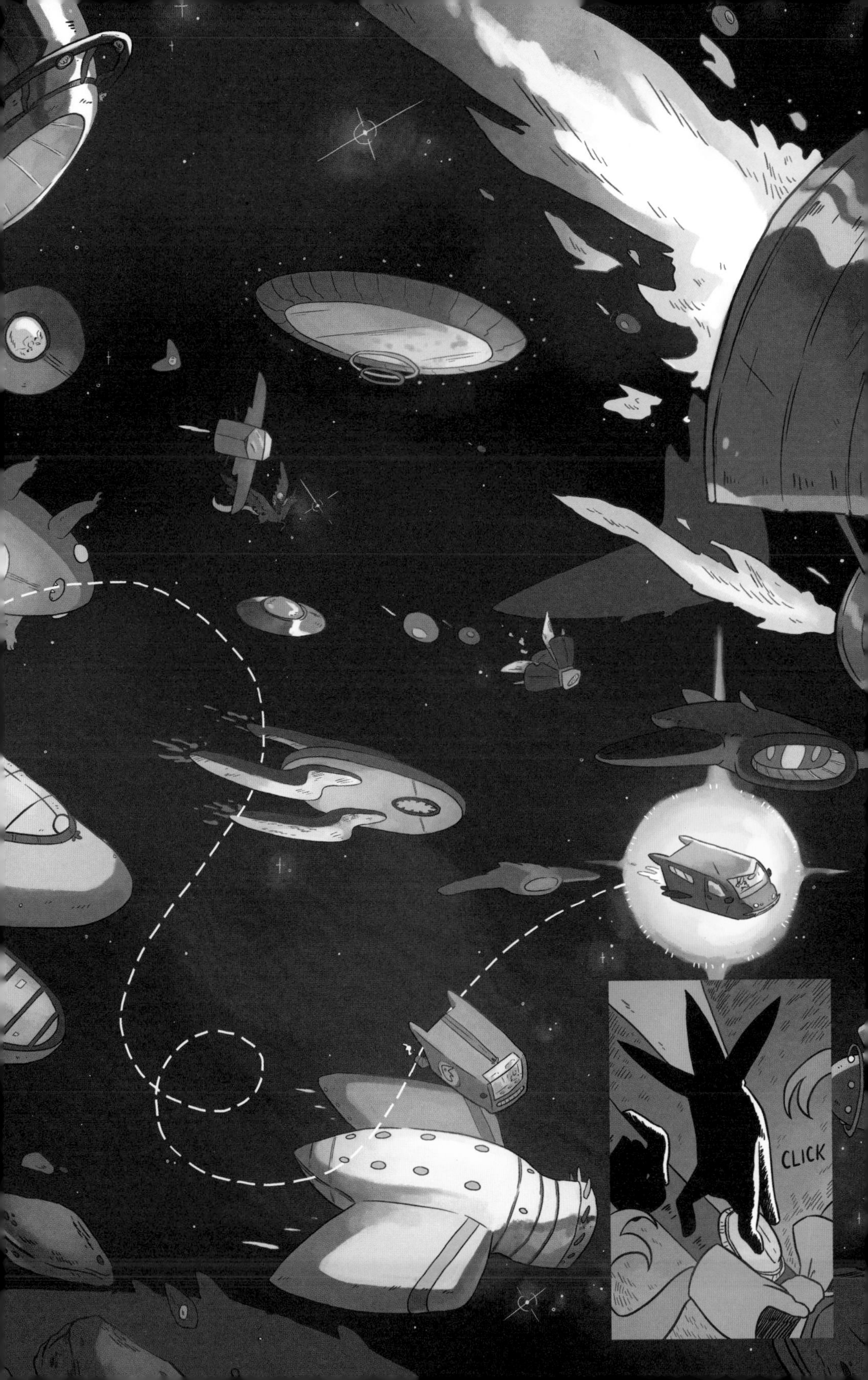
CLICK

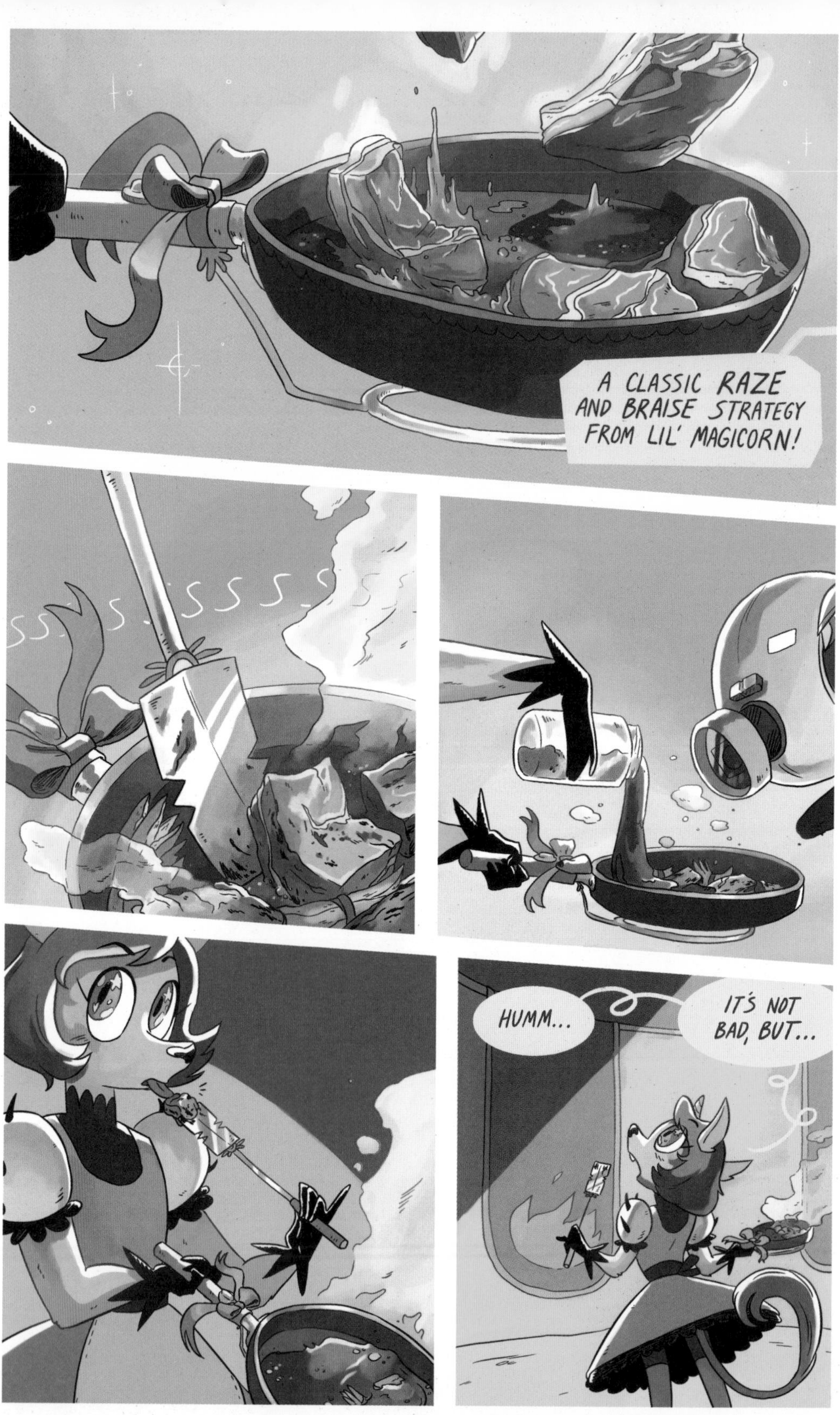
A CLASSIC RAZE AND BRAISE STRATEGY FROM LIL' MAGICORN!
SSSSSSSSS
HUMM...
IT'S NOT BAD, BUT...

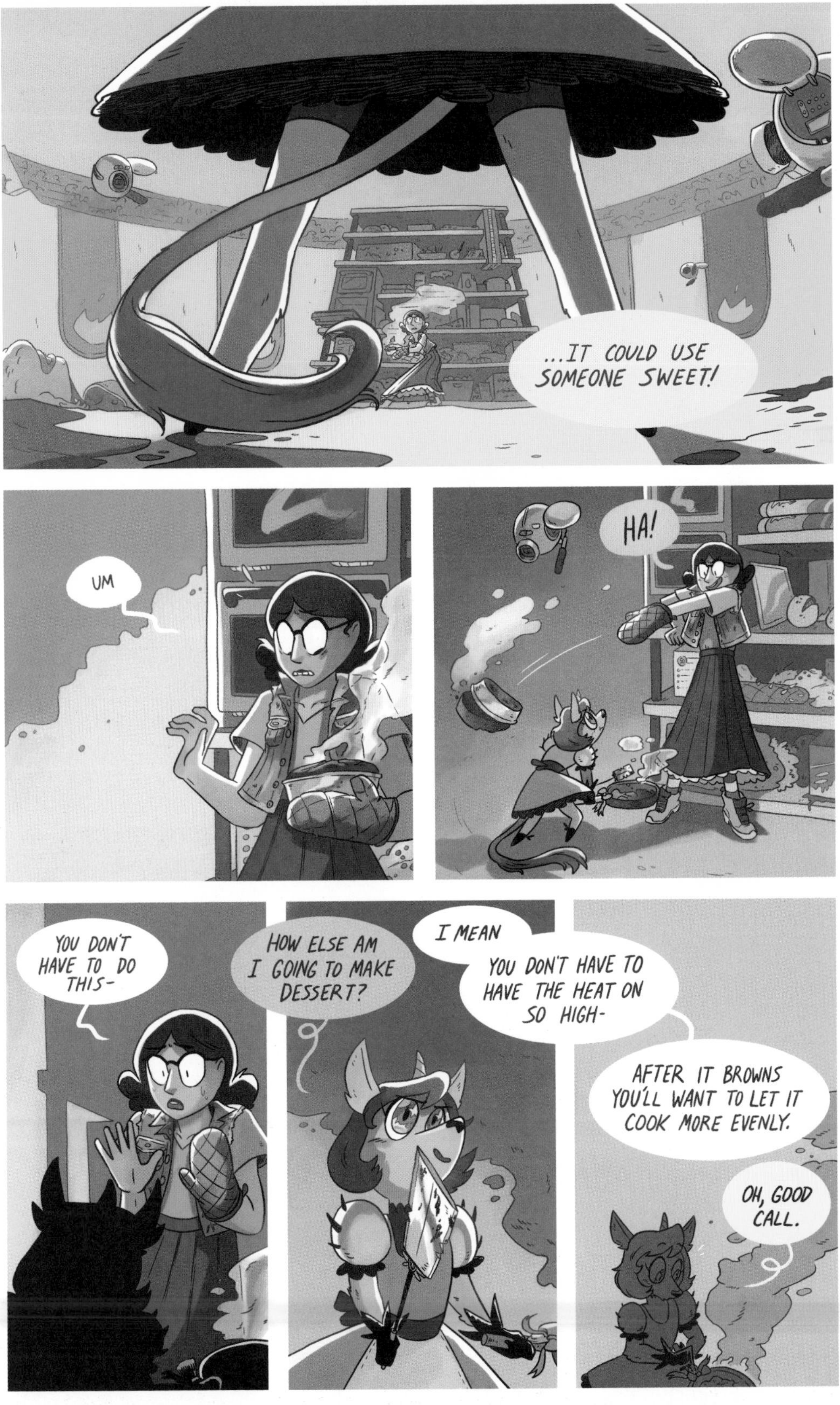
...IT COULD USE SOMEONE SWEET!
UM
HA!
YOU DON'T HAVE TO DO THIS-
HOW ELSE AM I GOING TO MAKE DESSERT?
I MEAN
YOU DON'T HAVE TO HAVE THE HEAT ON SO HIGH-
AFTER IT BROWNS YOU'LL WANT TO LET IT COOK MORE EVENLY.
OH, GOOD CALL.

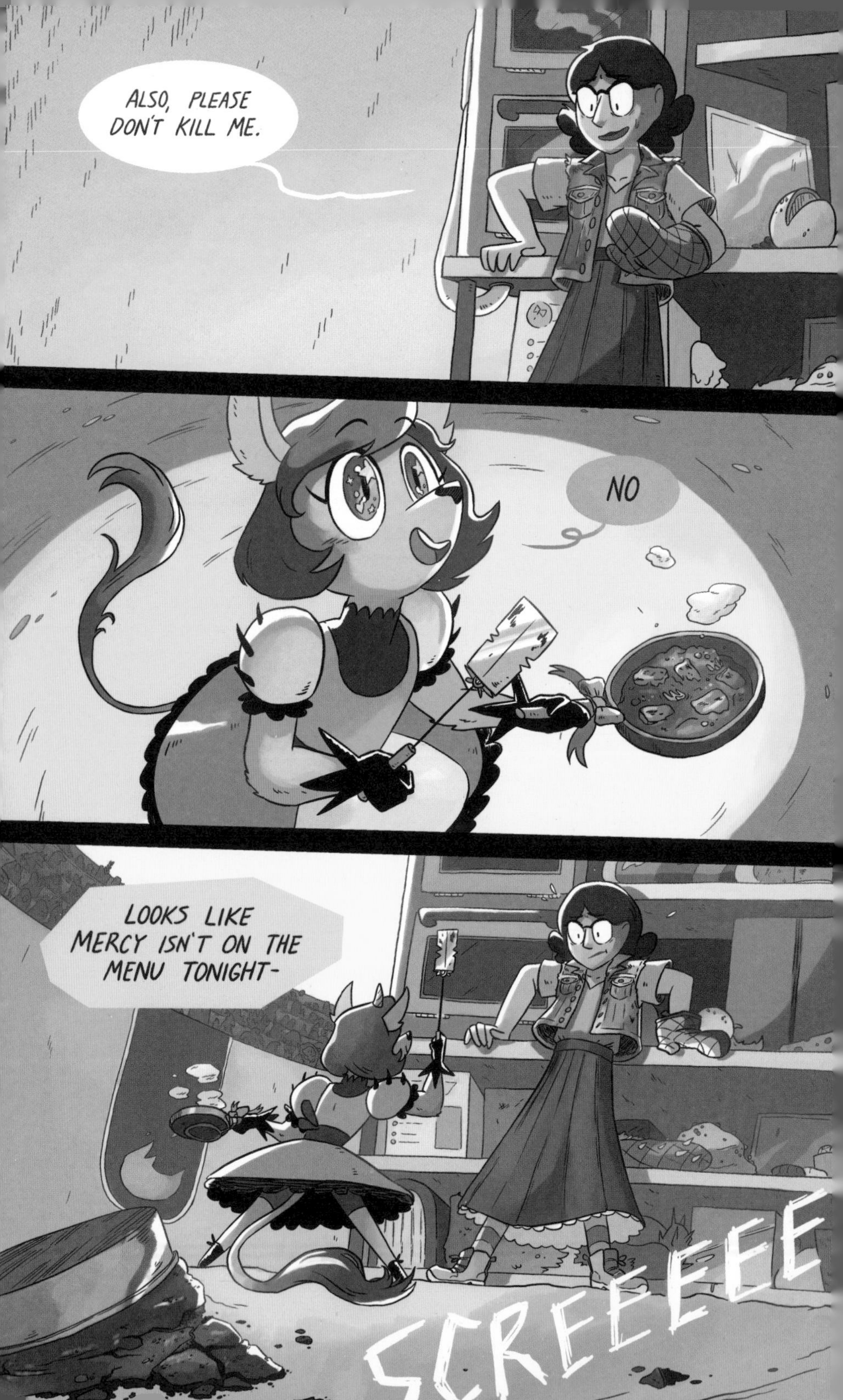
ALSO, PLEASE DON'T KILL ME.
NO
LOOKS LIKE MERCY ISN'T ON THE MENU TONIGHT-
SCREEEEEE

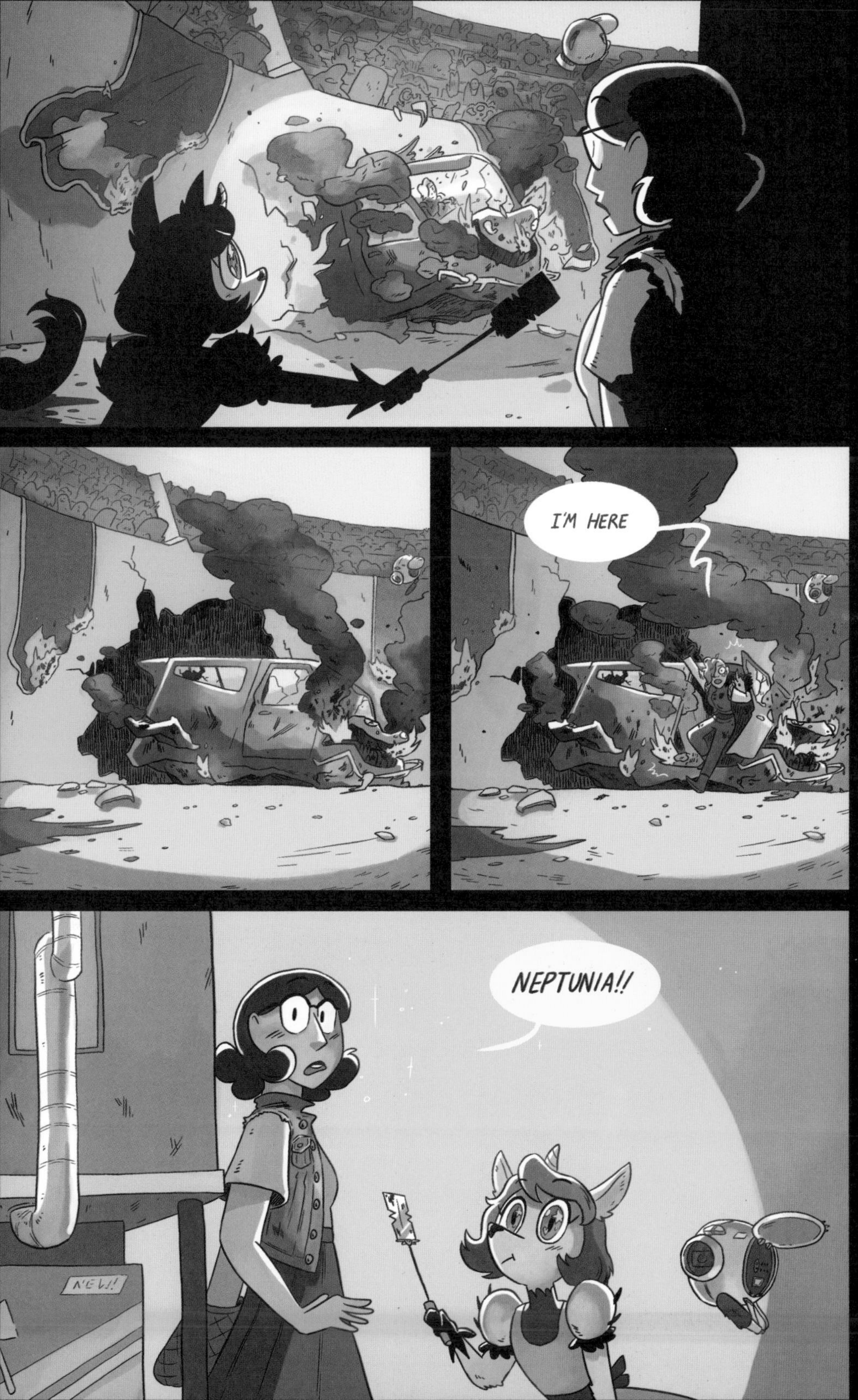
I'M HERE
NEPTUNIA!!
NEW!

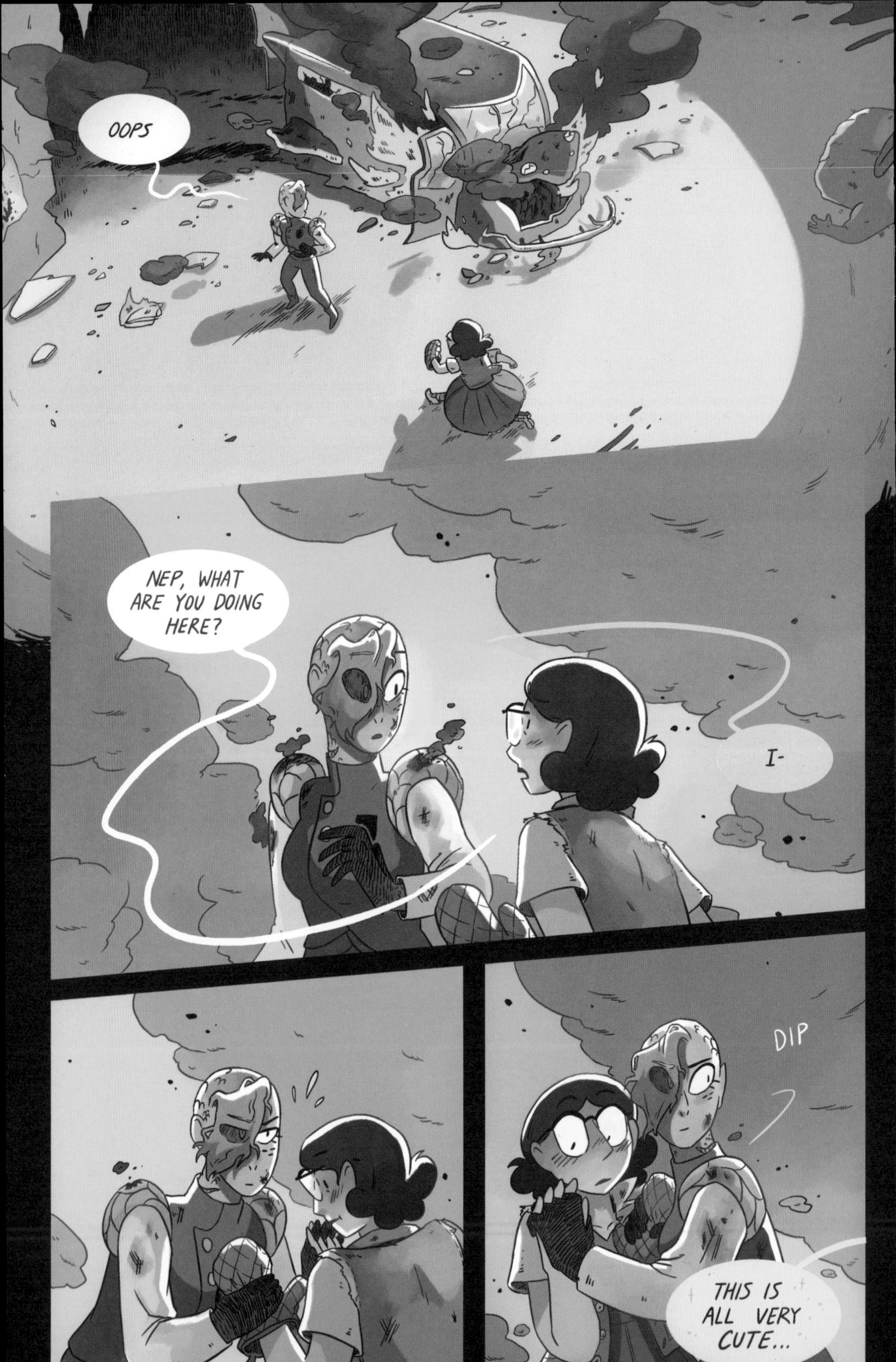

OOPS
NEP, WHAT ARE YOU DOING HERE?
I-
DIP
THIS IS ALL VERY CUTE...

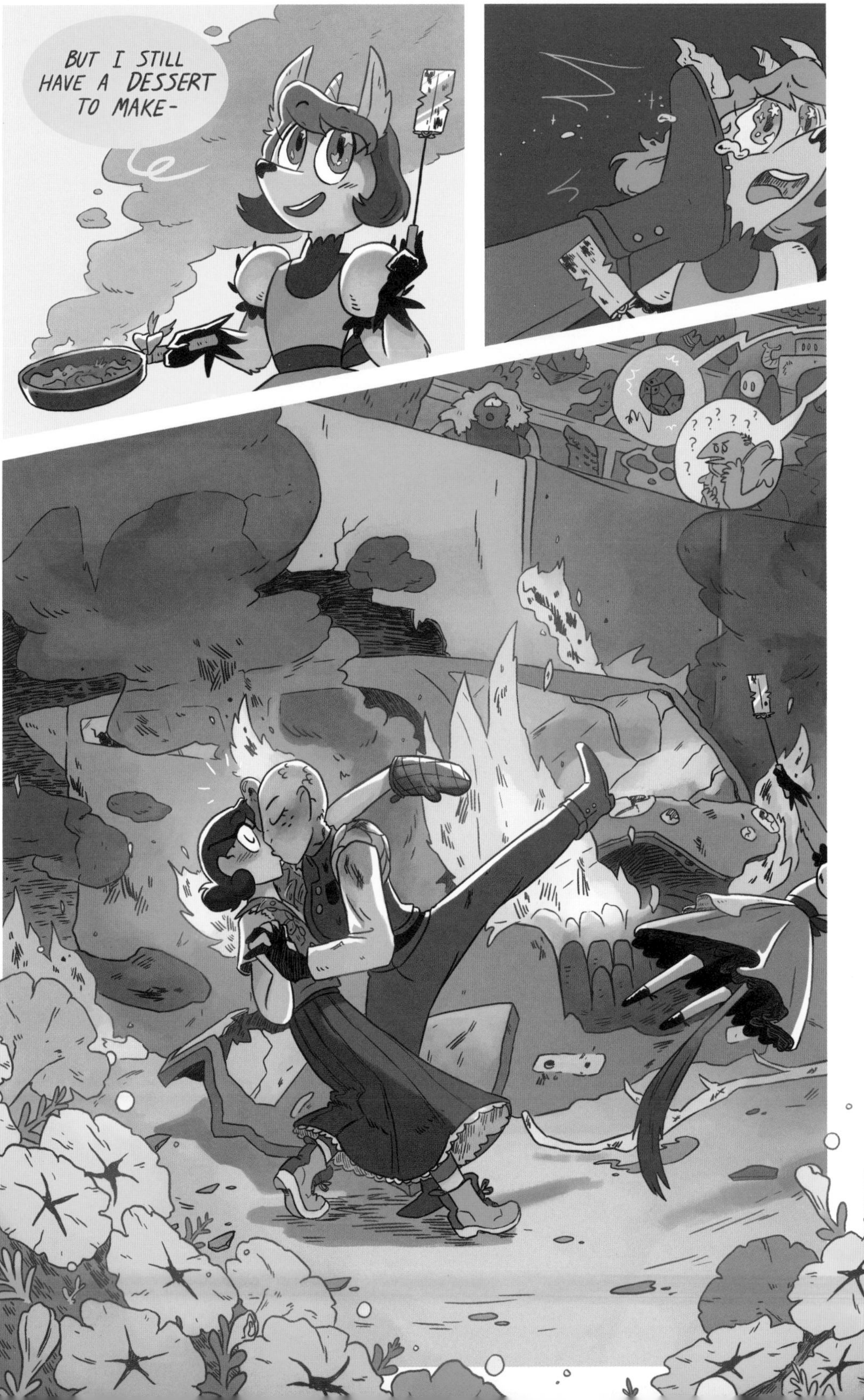
BUT I STILL HAVE A DESSERT TO MAKE-

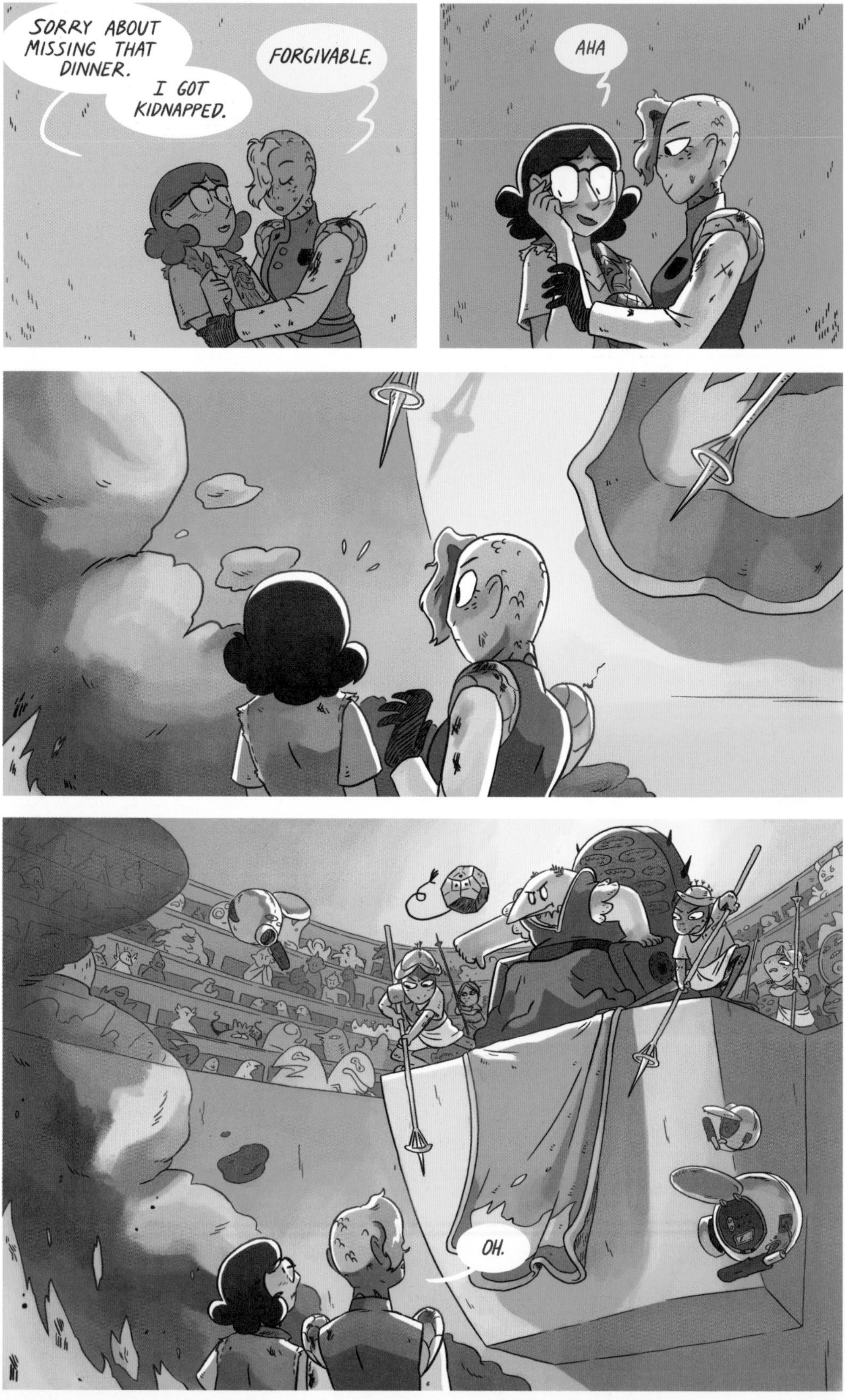
SORRY ABOUT MISSING THAT DINNER.
I GOT KIDNAPPED.
FORGIVABLE.
AHA
OH.

CHAPTER THREE

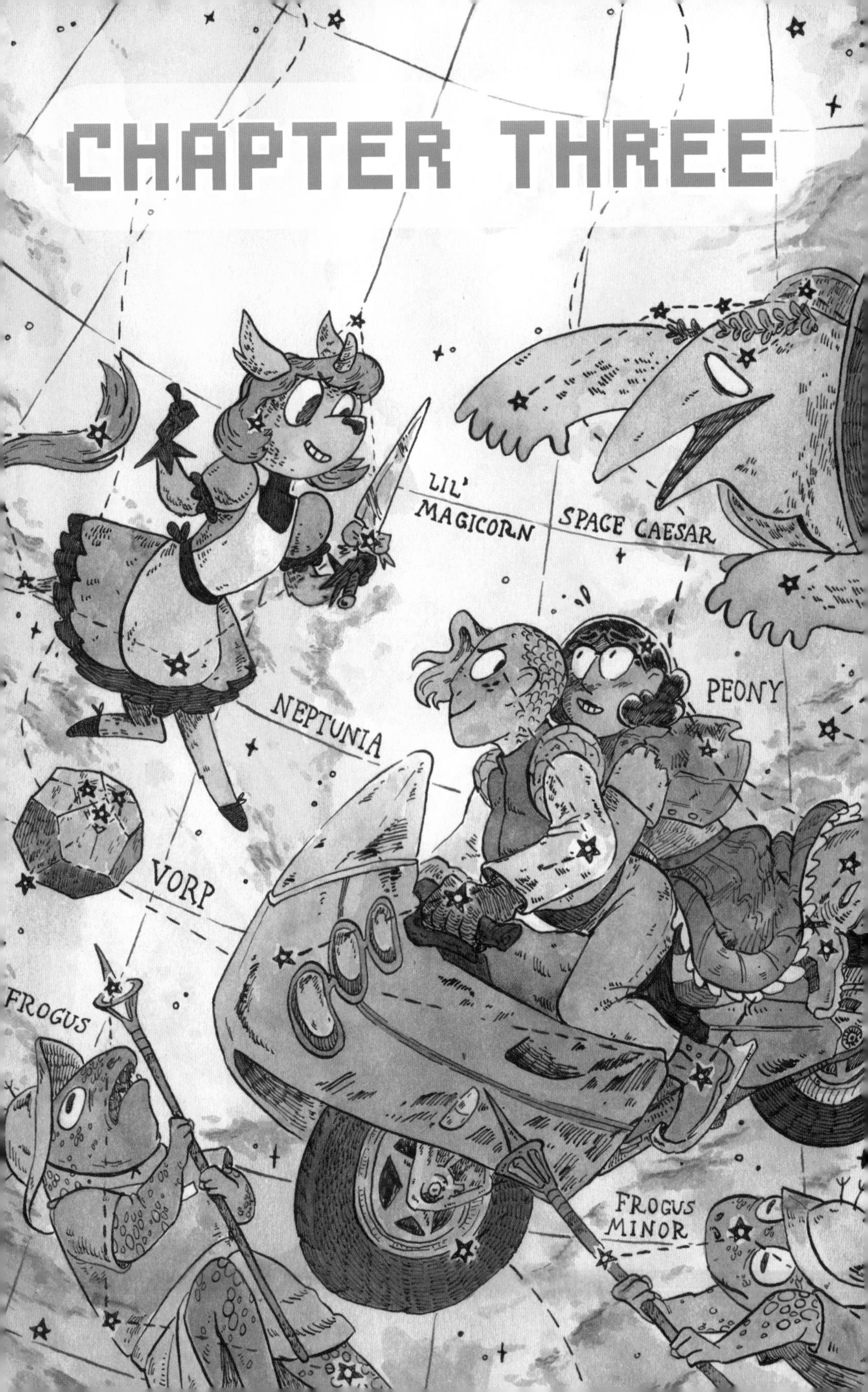
LIL'
MAGICORN
SPACE CAESAR
PEONY
NEPTUNIA
VORP
FROGUS
FROGUS
MINOR

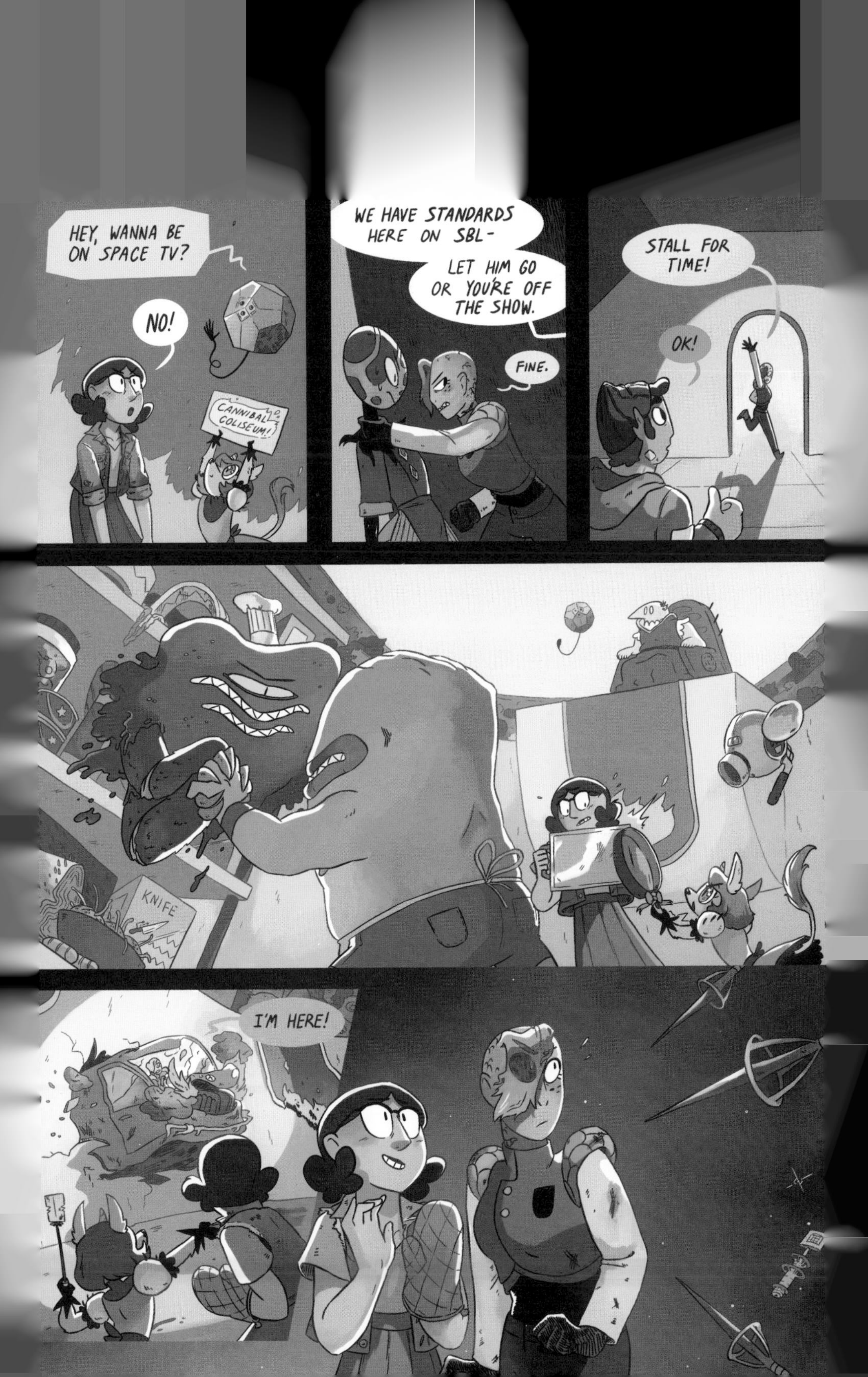
HEY, WANNA BE ON SPACE TV?
NO!
CANNIBAL COLISEUM!
WE HAVE STANDARDS HERE ON SBL-
LET HIM GO OR YOU'RE OFF THE SHOW.
FINE.
STALL FOR TIME!
OK!
KNIFE
I'M HERE!

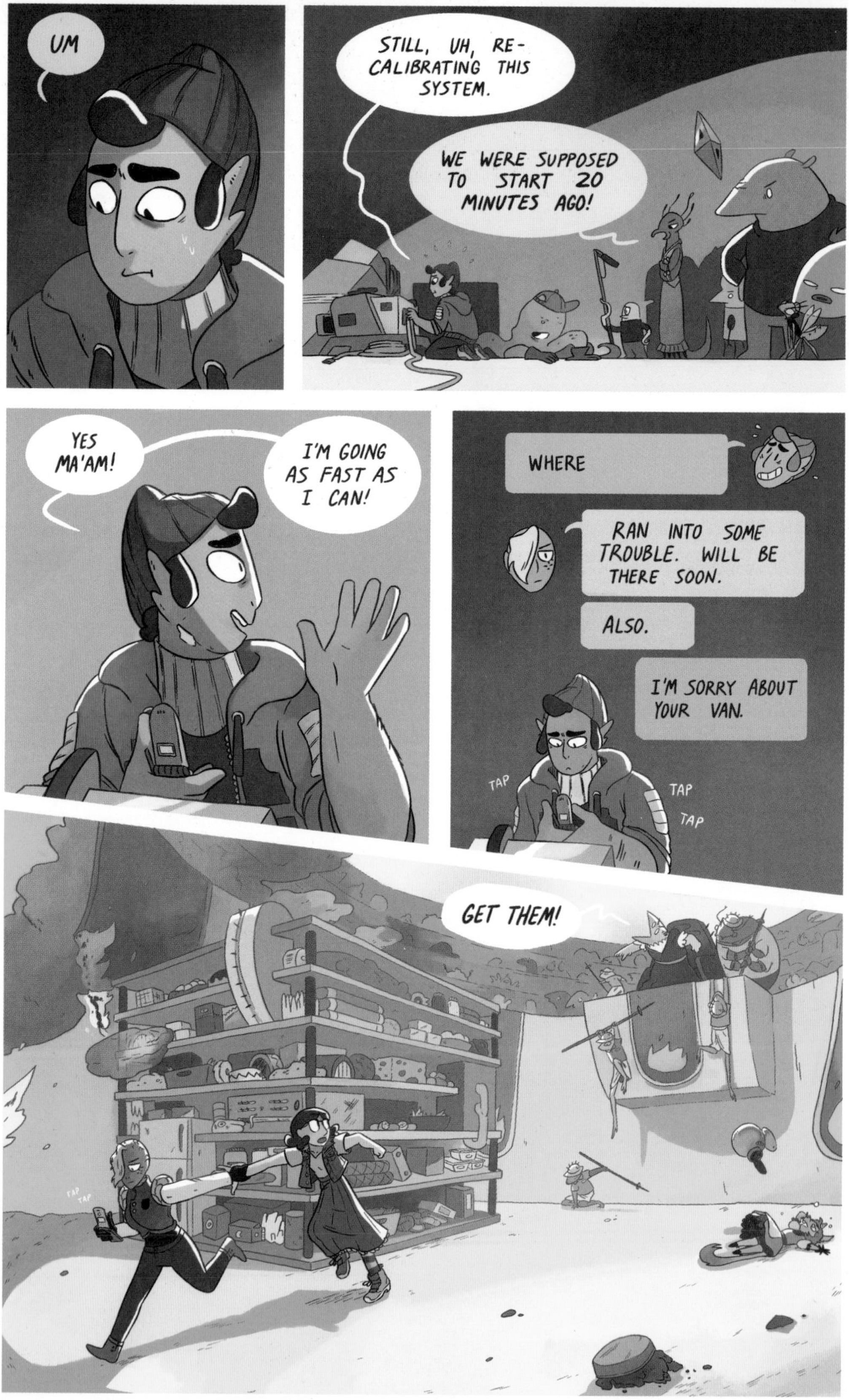
UM
STILL, UH, RE-CALIBRATING THIS SYSTEM.
WE WERE SUPPOSED TO START 20 MINUTES AGO!
YES MA'AM!
I'M GOING AS FAST AS I CAN!
WHERE
RAN INTO SOME TROUBLE. WILL BE THERE SOON.
ALSO.
I'M SORRY ABOUT YOUR VAN.
TAP
TAP
TAP
GET THEM!
TAP TAP

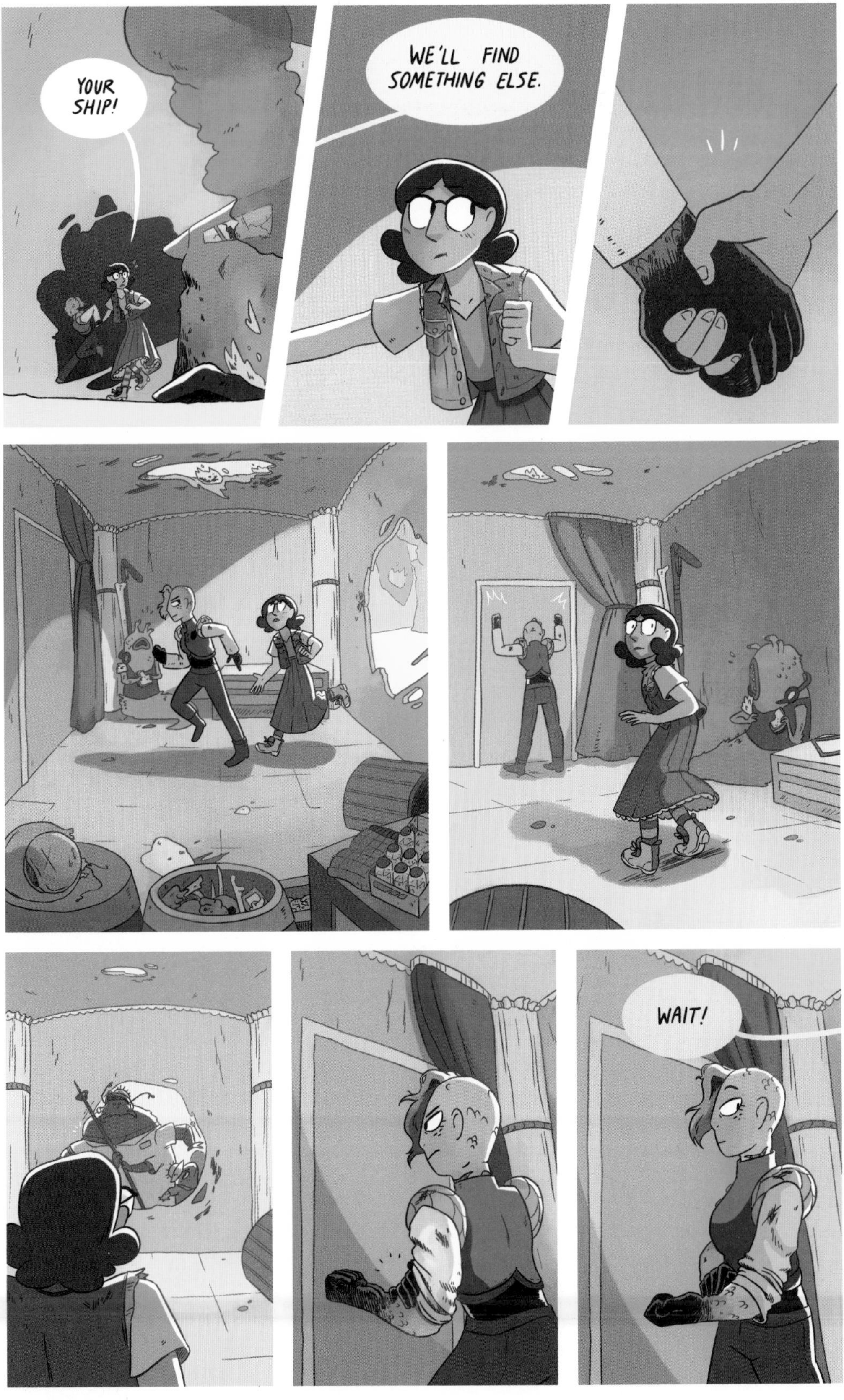

YOUR SHIP!
WE'LL FIND SOMETHING ELSE.
WAIT!

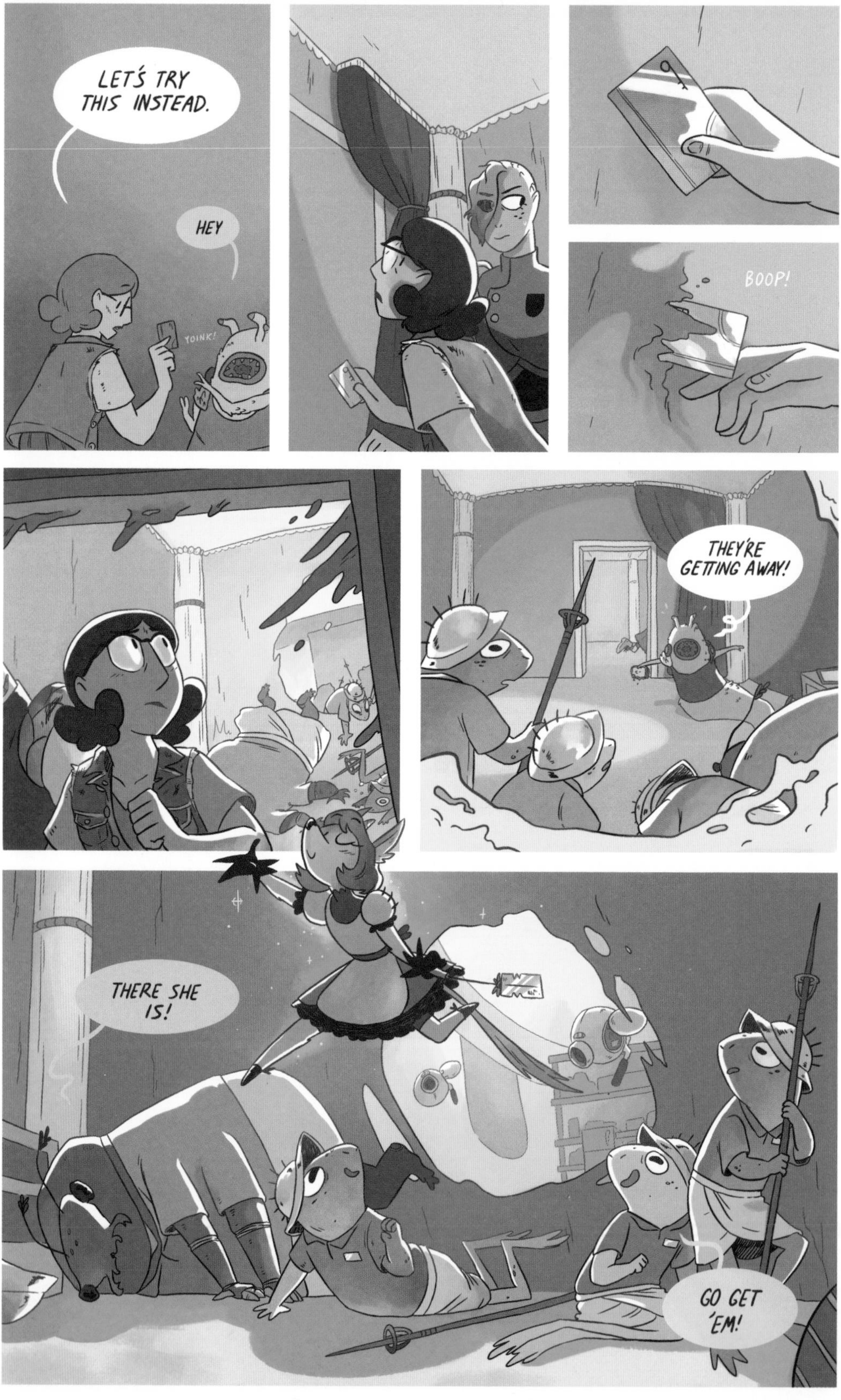
LET'S TRY THIS INSTEAD.
HEY
YOINK!
BOOP!
THEY'RE GETTING AWAY!
THERE SHE IS!
GO GET 'EM!

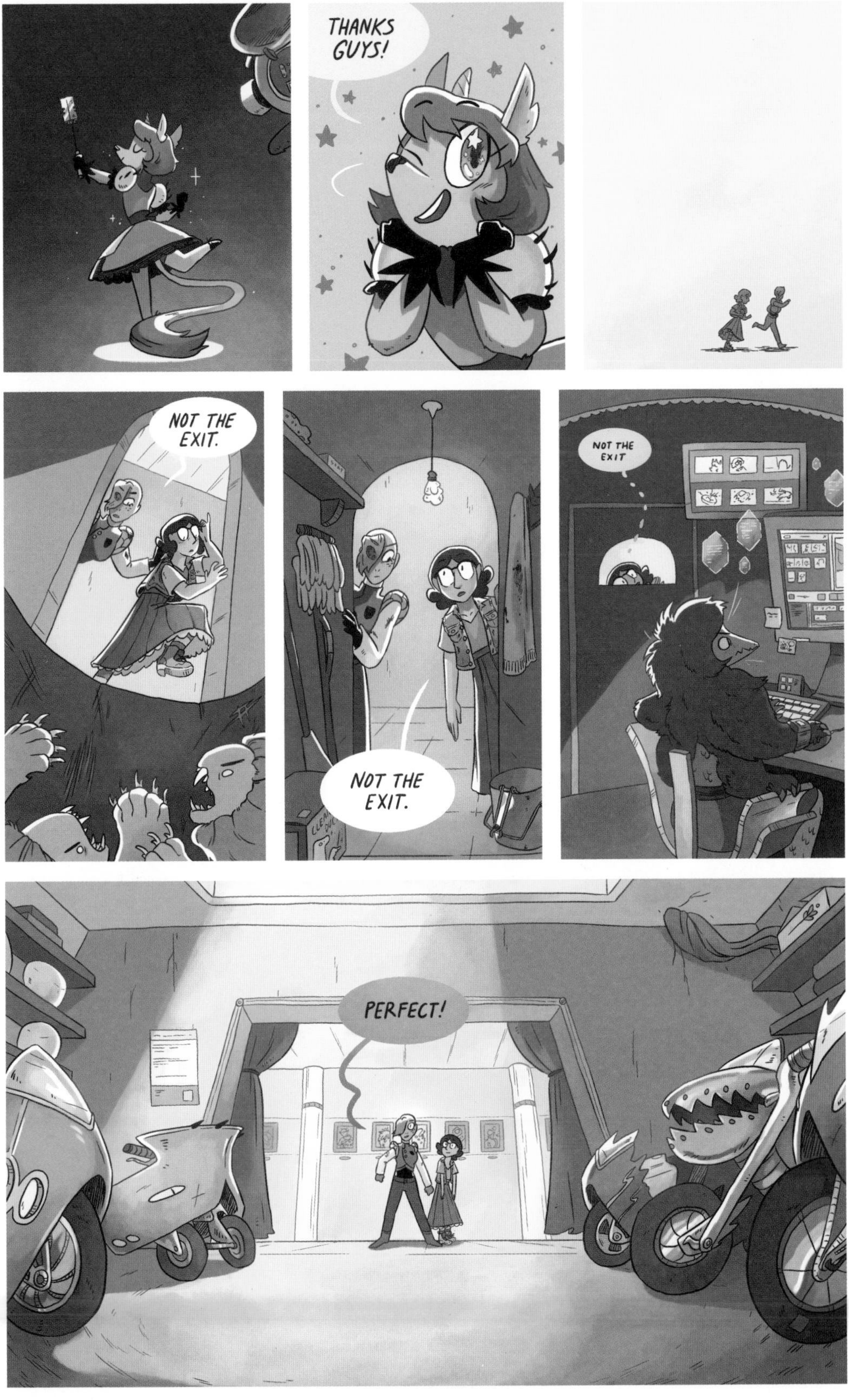
THANKS GUYS!
NOT THE EXIT.
NOT THE EXIT.
NOT THE EXIT
PERFECT!

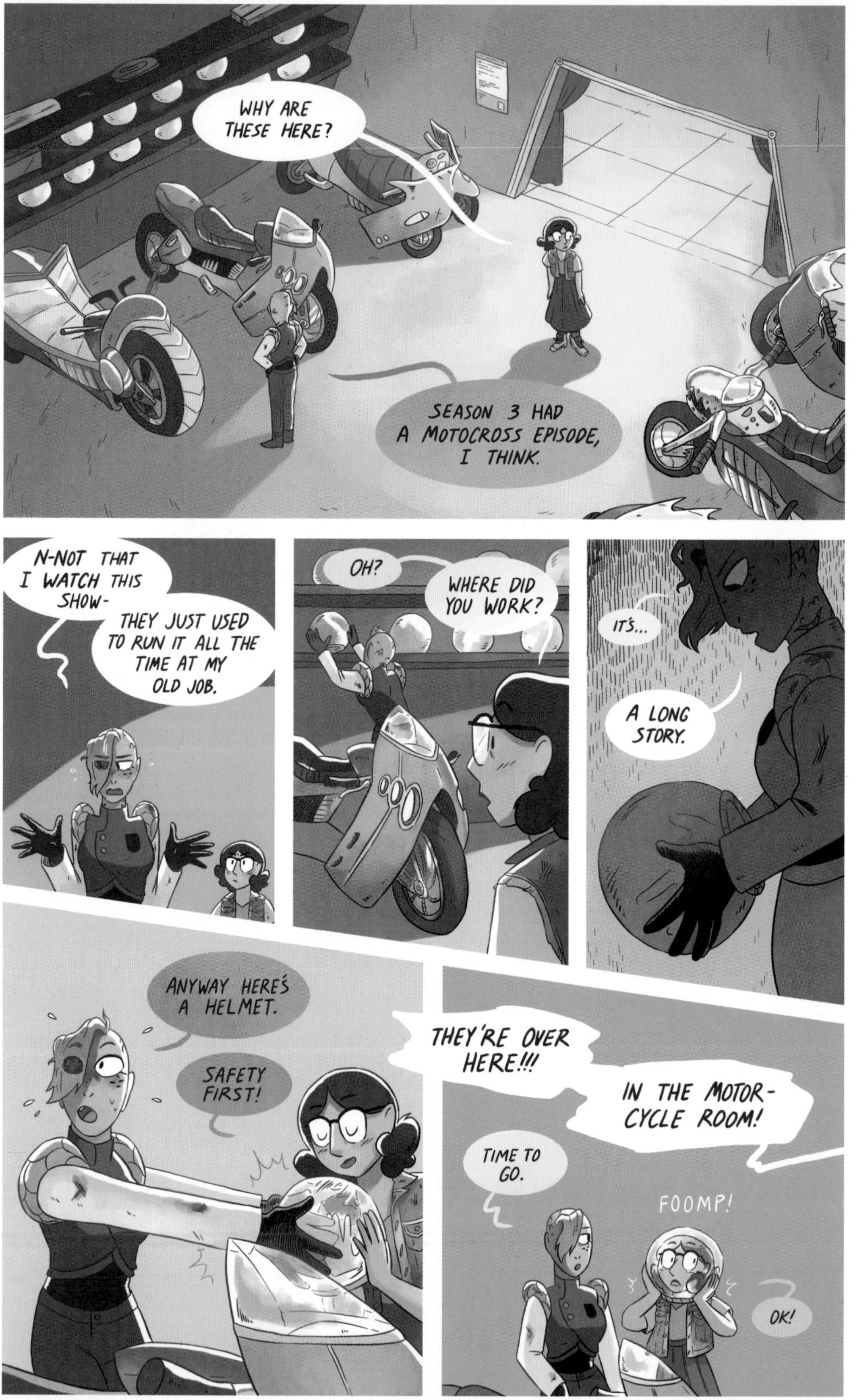
WHY ARE THESE HERE?
SEASON 3 HAD A MOTOCROSS EPISODE, I THINK.
N-NOT THAT I WATCH THIS SHOW-
THEY JUST USED TO RUN IT ALL THE TIME AT MY OLD JOB.
OH?
WHERE DID YOU WORK?
IT'S...
A LONG STORY.
ANYWAY HERE'S A HELMET.
SAFETY FIRST!
THEY'RE OVER HERE!!!
IN THE MOTOR-CYCLE ROOM!
TIME TO GO.
FOOMP!
OK!

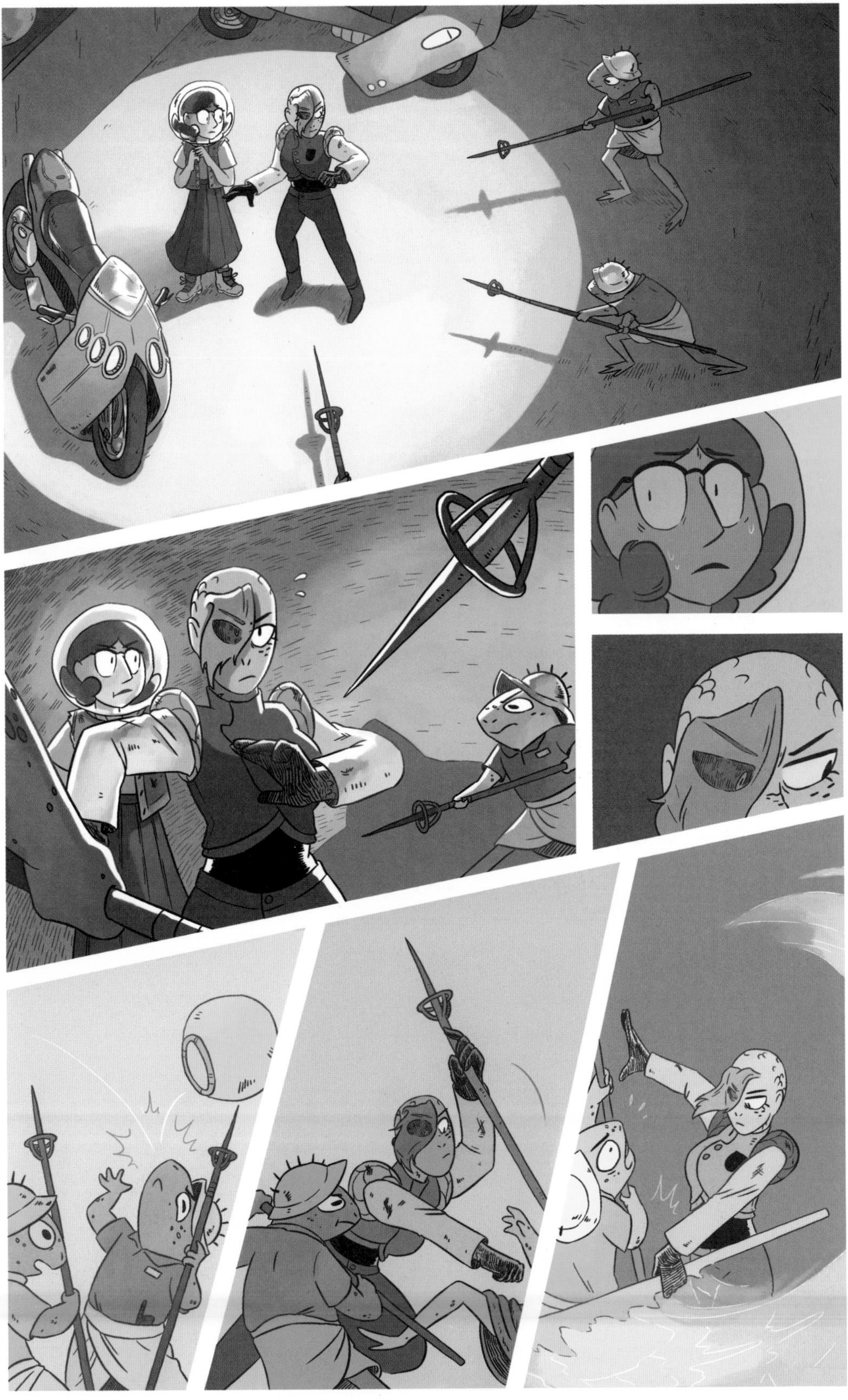

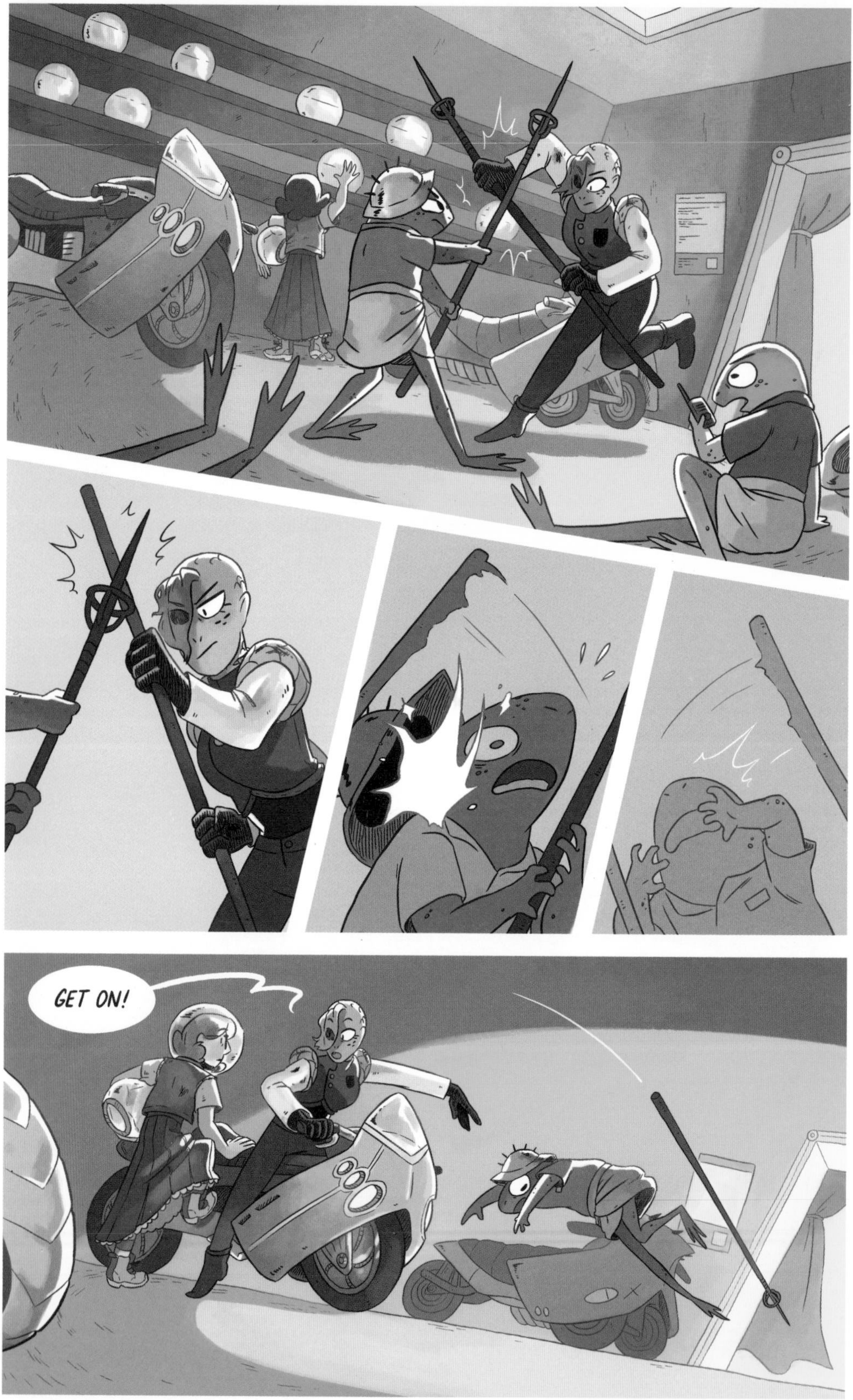
GET ON!

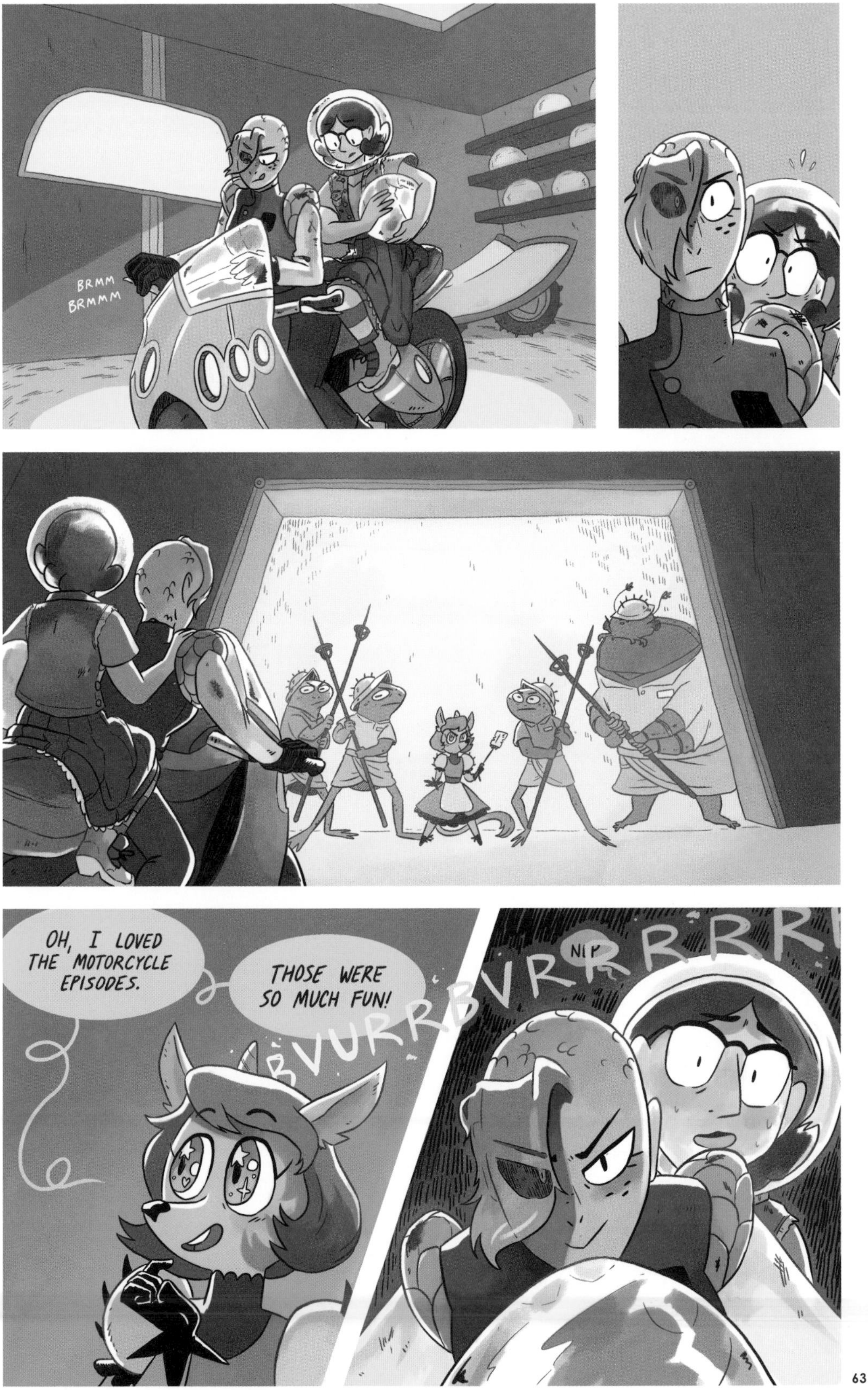
BRMM
BRMMM
OH, I LOVED THE MOTORCYCLE EPISODES.
THOSE WERE SO MUCH FUN!
BVURRBVRRRRRR
NIP

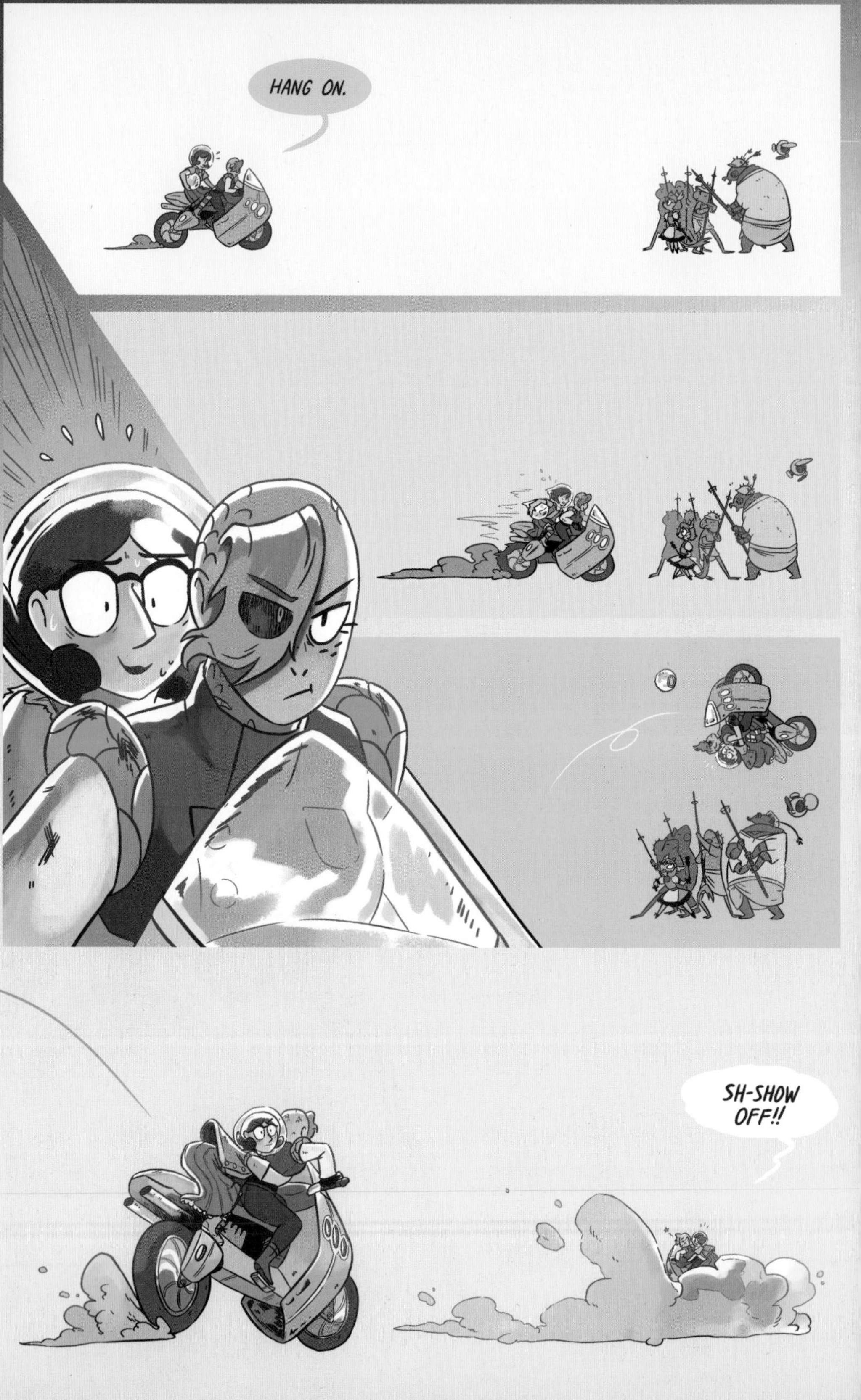
HANG ON.
SH-SHOW OFF!!

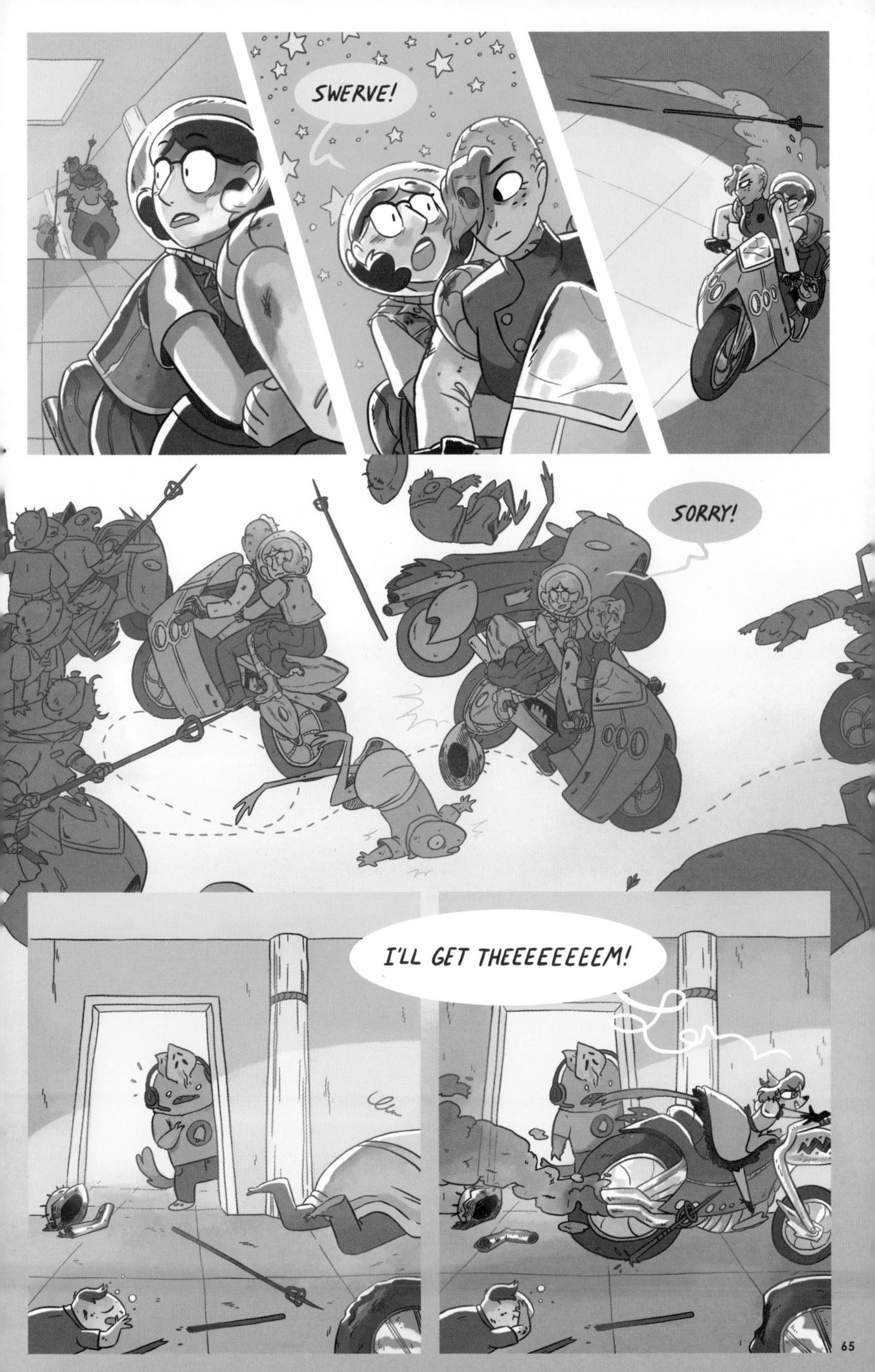
SWERVE!
SORRY!
I'LL GET THEEEEEEEEM!

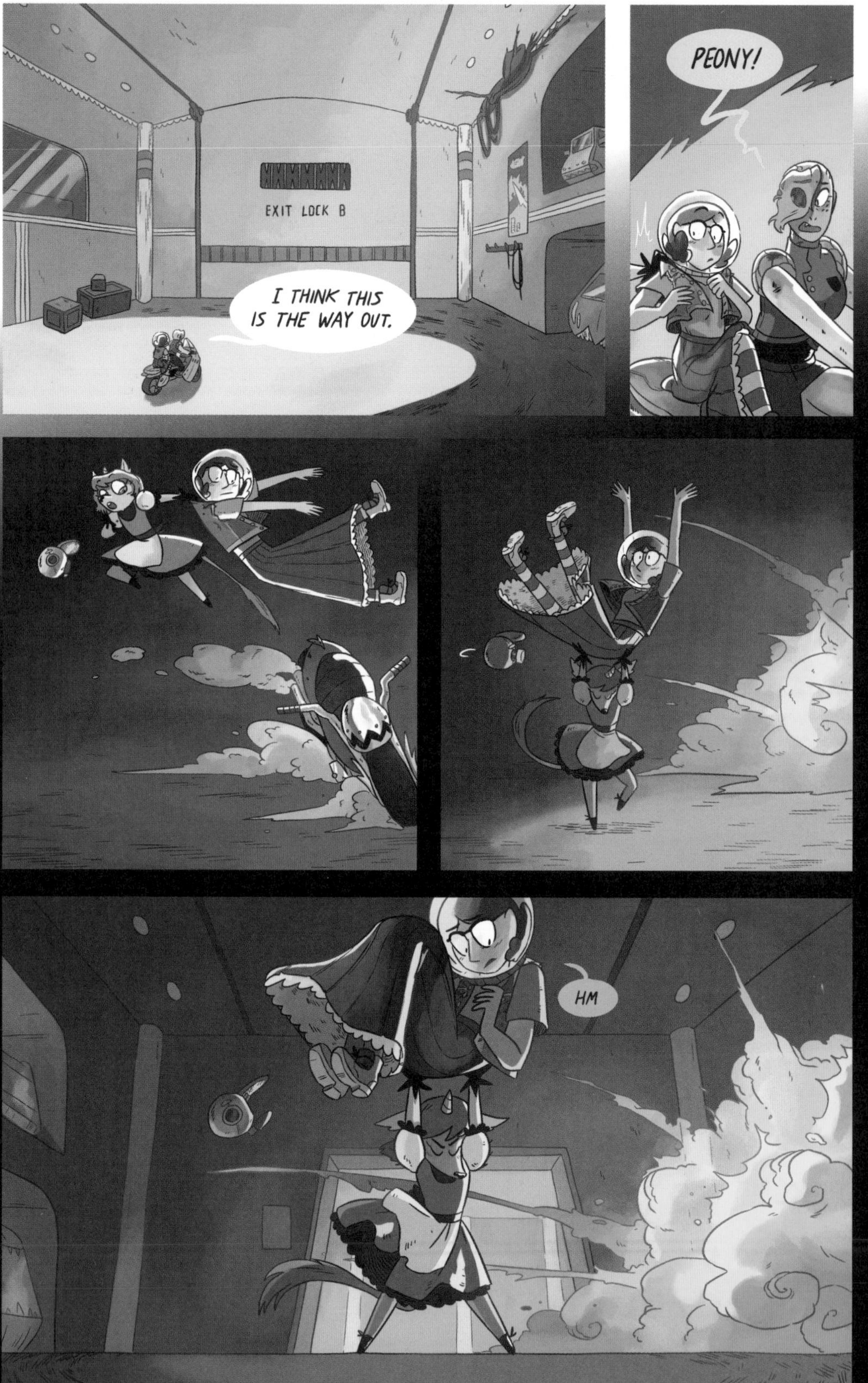
EXIT LOCK B
I THINK THIS IS THE WAY OUT.
PEONY!
HM

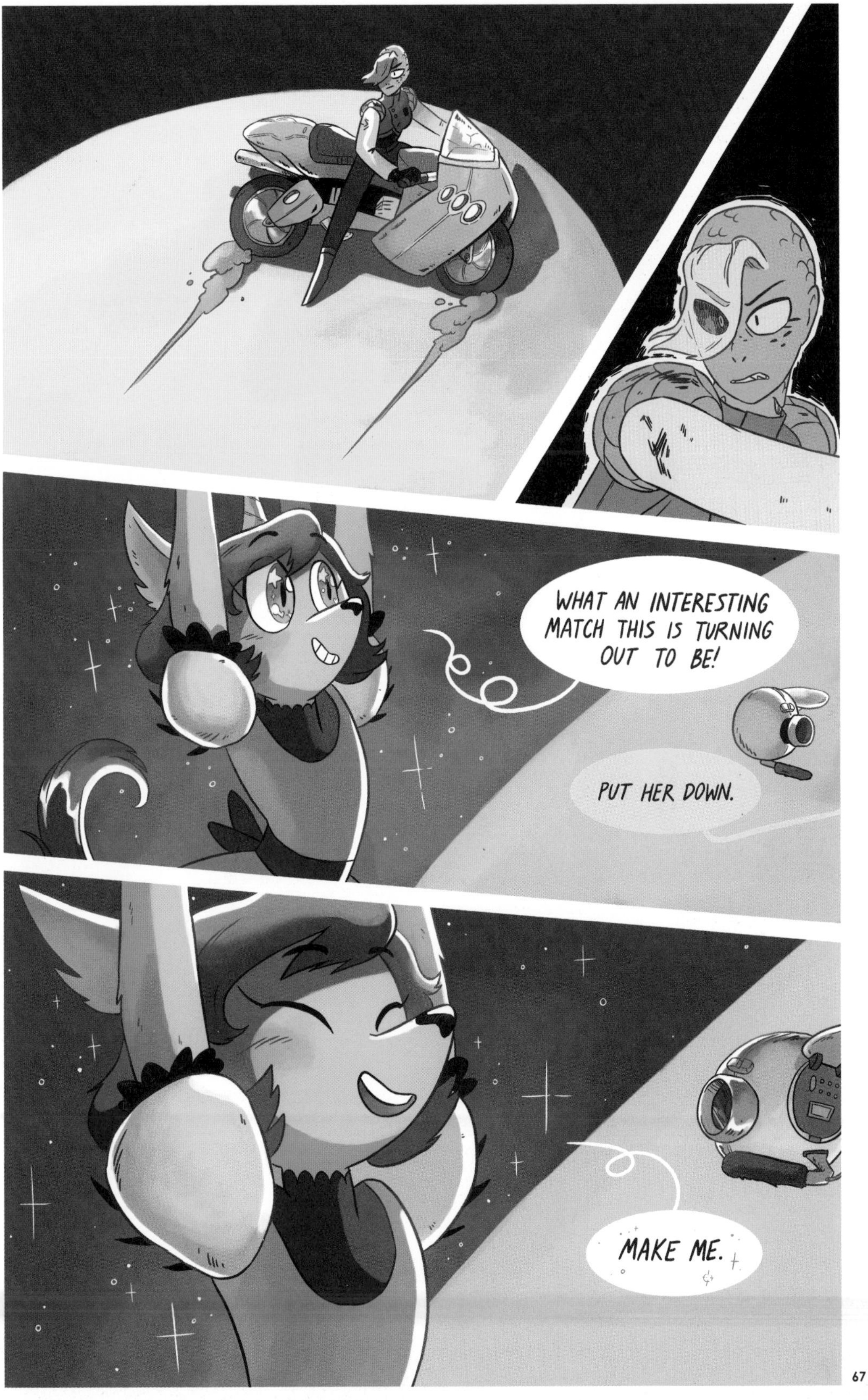
WHAT AN INTERESTING MATCH THIS IS TURNING OUT TO BE!
PUT HER DOWN.
MAKE ME.

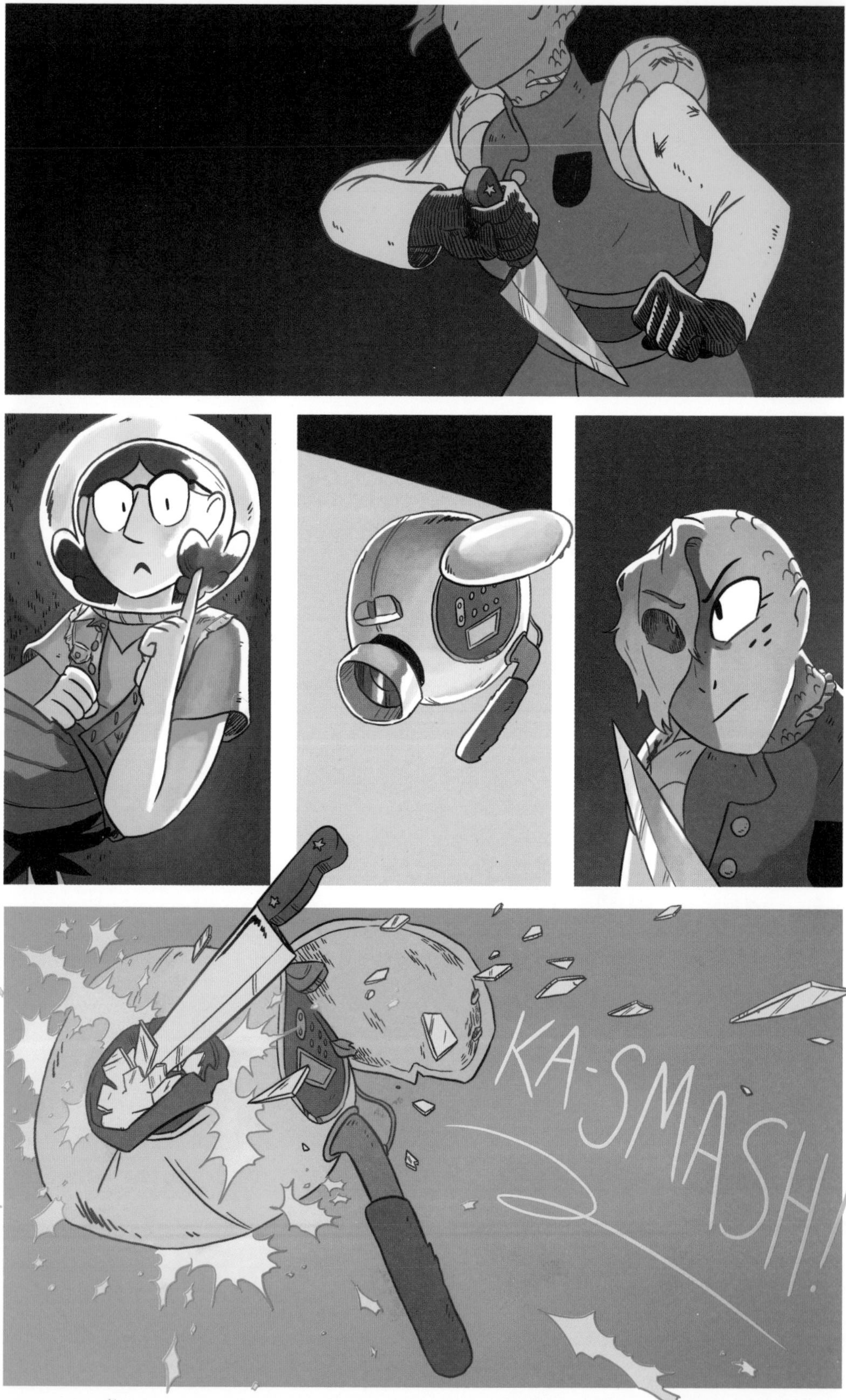
KA-SMASH!

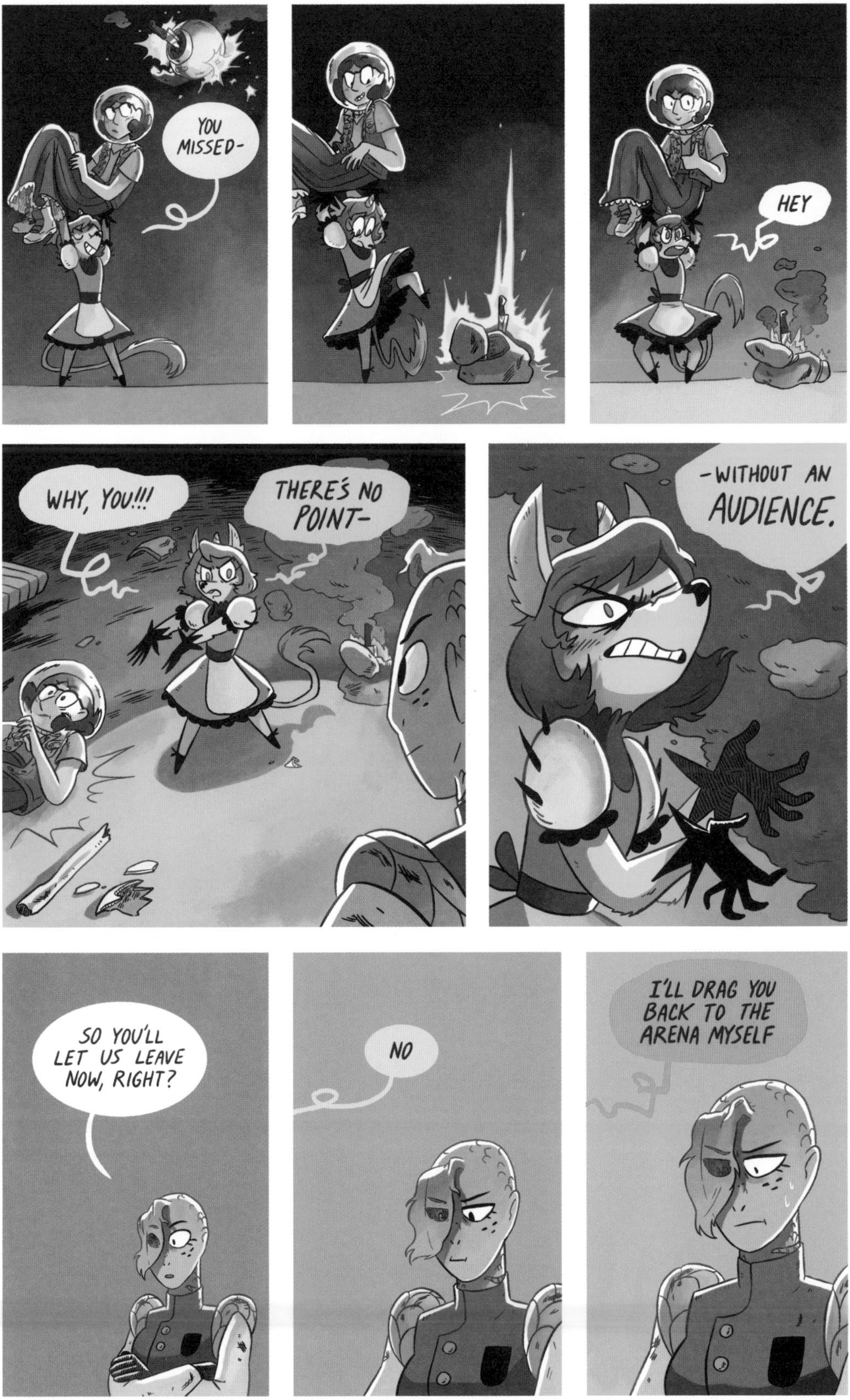
YOU MISSED-
HEY
WHY, YOU!!!
THERE'S NO POINT-
-WITHOUT AN AUDIENCE.
SO YOU'LL LET US LEAVE NOW, RIGHT?
NO
I'LL DRAG YOU BACK TO THE ARENA MYSELF

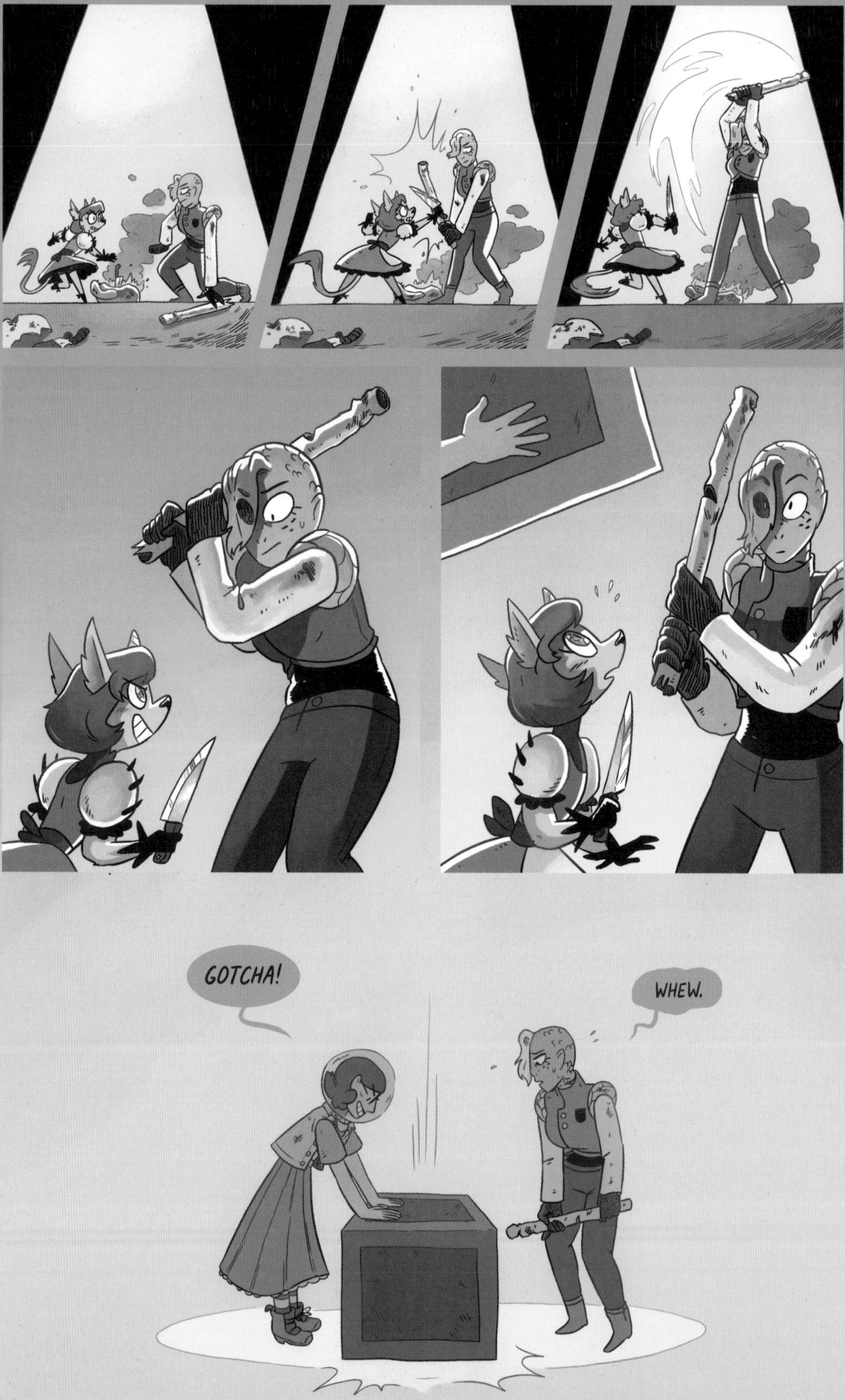
GOTCHA!
WHEW.

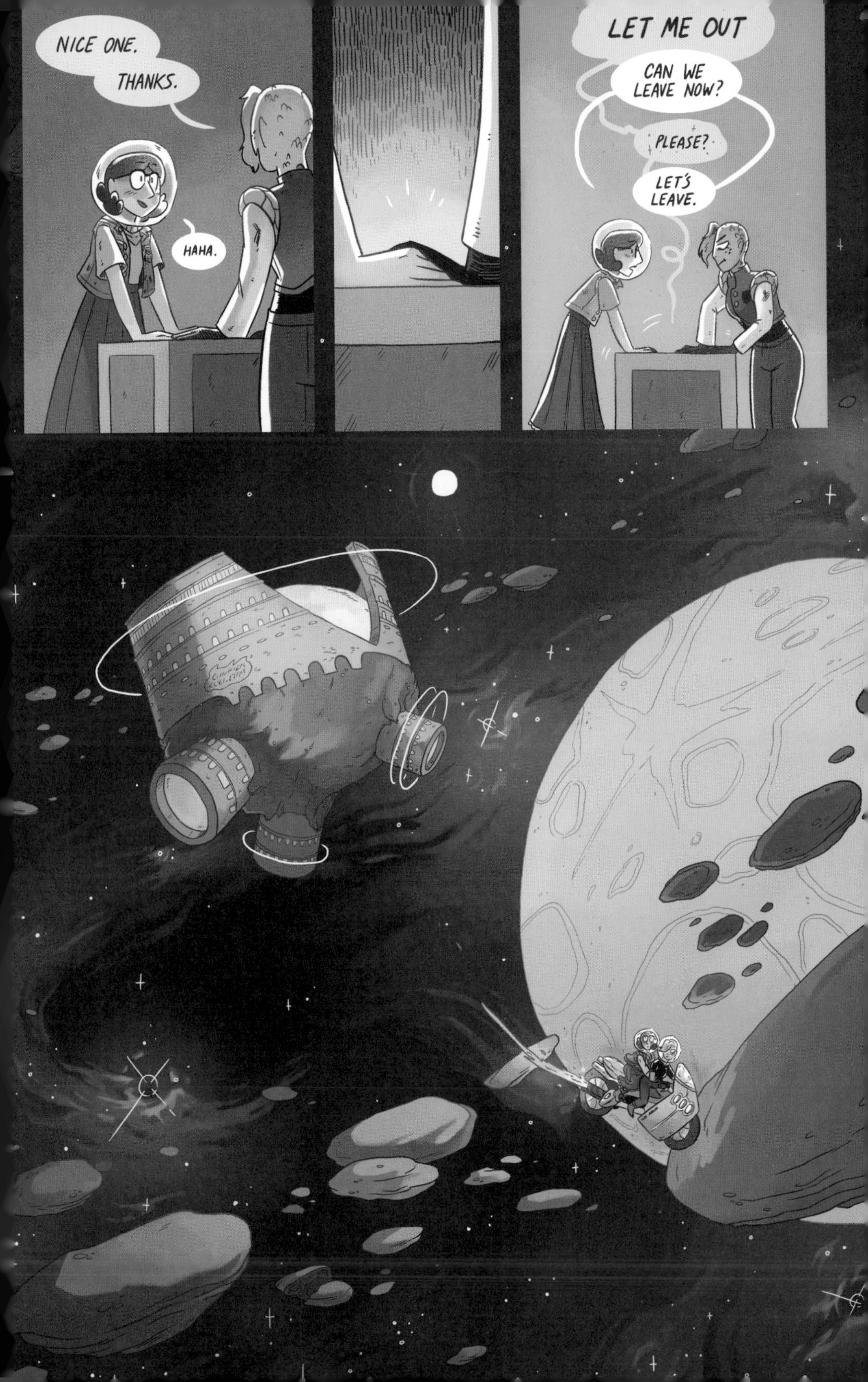
NICE ONE.
THANKS.
HAHA.
LET ME OUT
CAN WE LEAVE NOW?
PLEASE?
LET'S LEAVE.

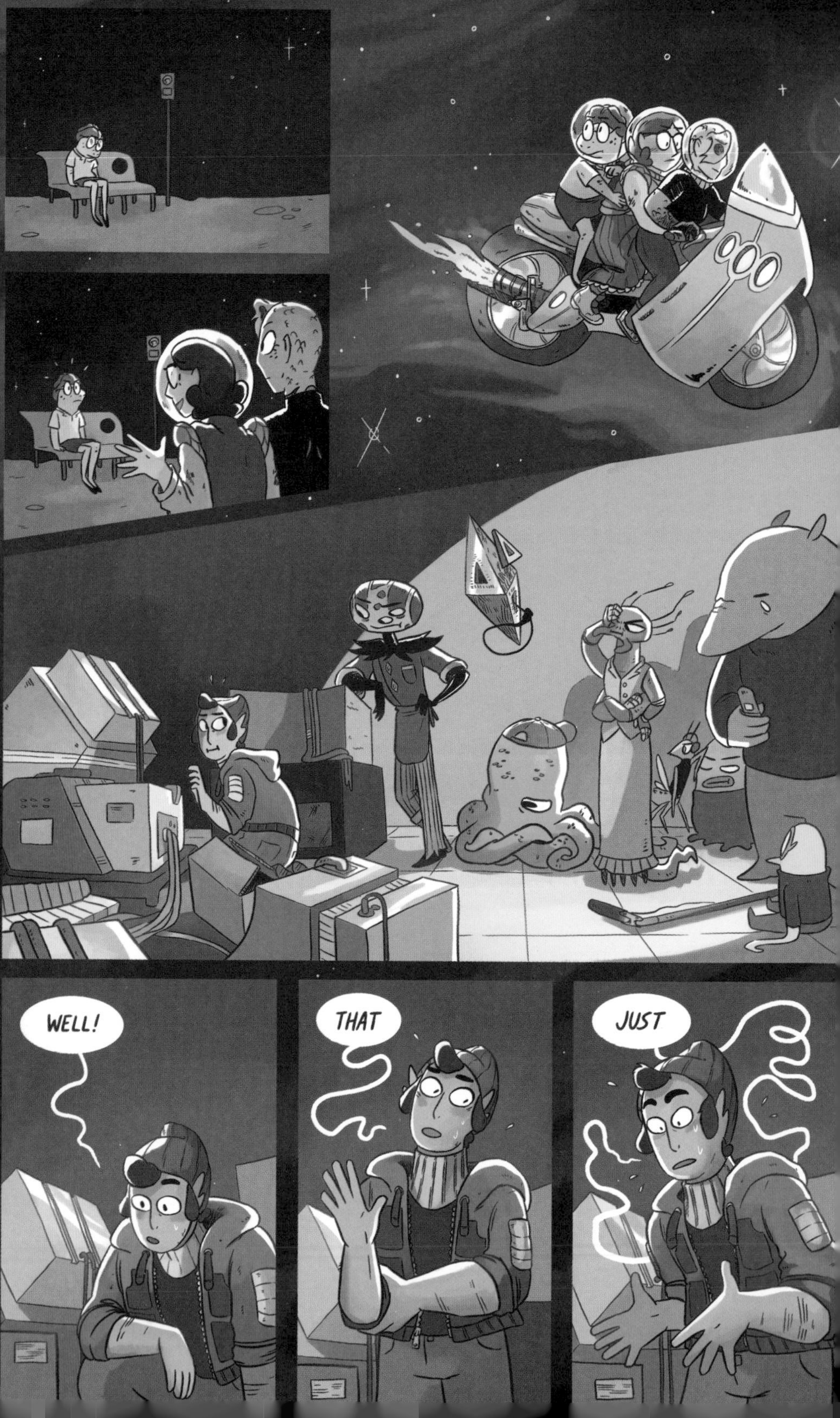
WELL!
THAT
JUST

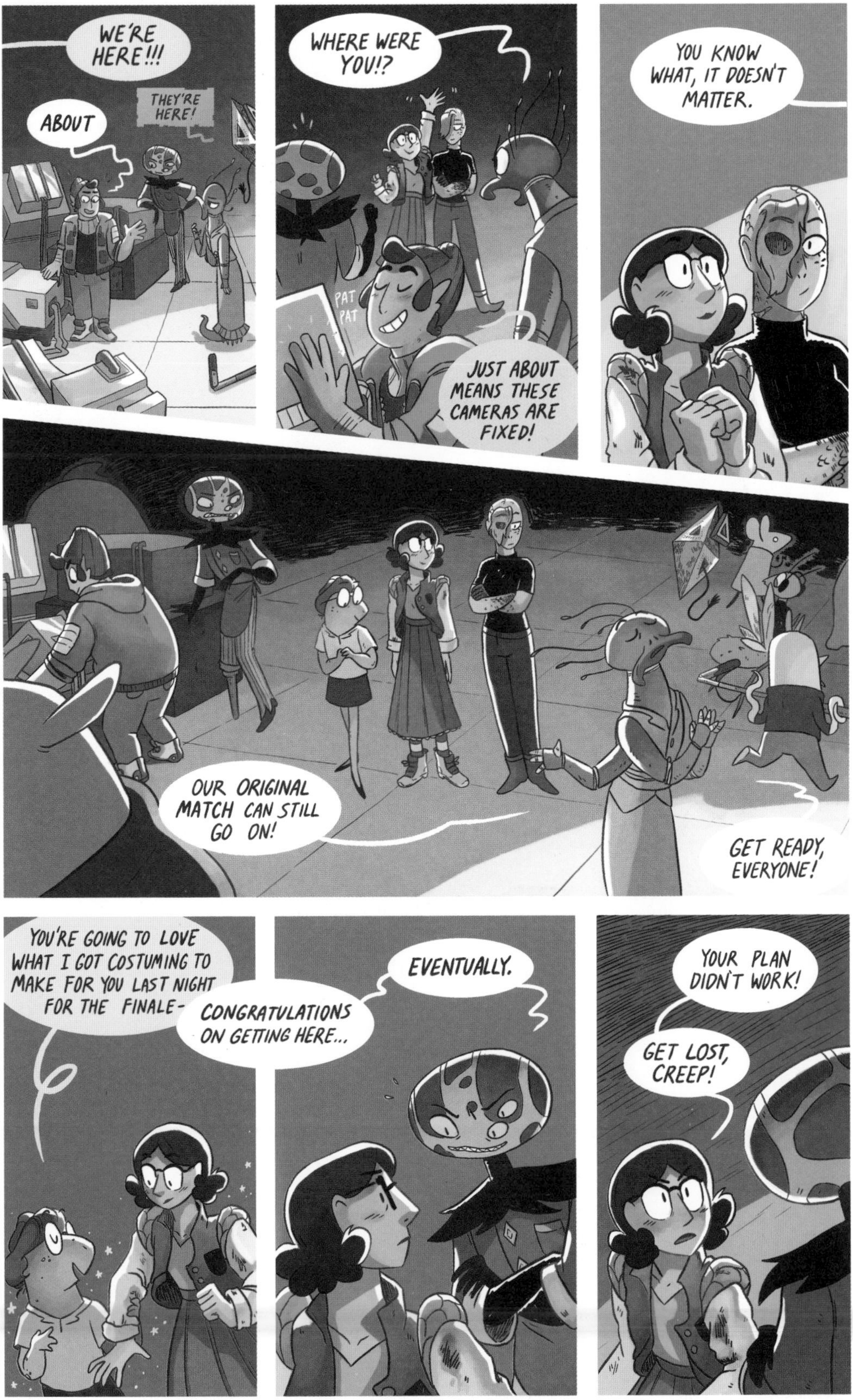
WE'RE HERE!!!
ABOUT
THEY'RE HERE!
WHERE WERE YOU!?
PAT PAT
JUST ABOUT MEANS THESE CAMERAS ARE FIXED!
YOU KNOW WHAT, IT DOESN'T MATTER.
OUR ORIGINAL MATCH CAN STILL GO ON!
GET READY, EVERYONE!
YOU'RE GOING TO LOVE WHAT I GOT COSTUMING TO MAKE FOR YOU LAST NIGHT FOR THE FINALE-
CONGRATULATIONS ON GETTING HERE...
EVENTUALLY.
YOUR PLAN DIDN'T WORK!
GET LOST, CREEP!

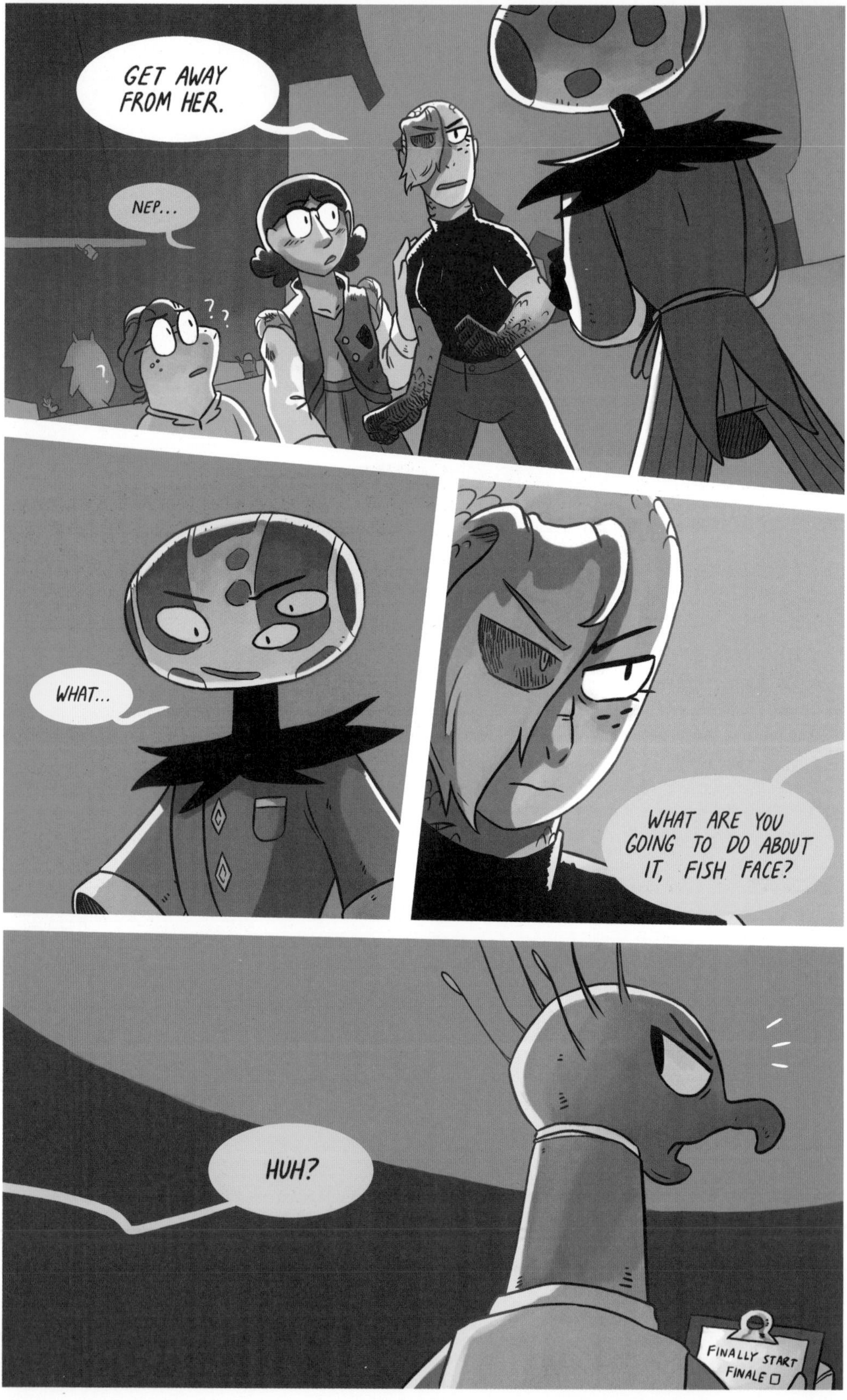
GET AWAY FROM HER.
NEP...
? ?
WHAT...
WHAT ARE YOU GOING TO DO ABOUT IT, FISH FACE?
HUH?
FINALLY START FINALE □

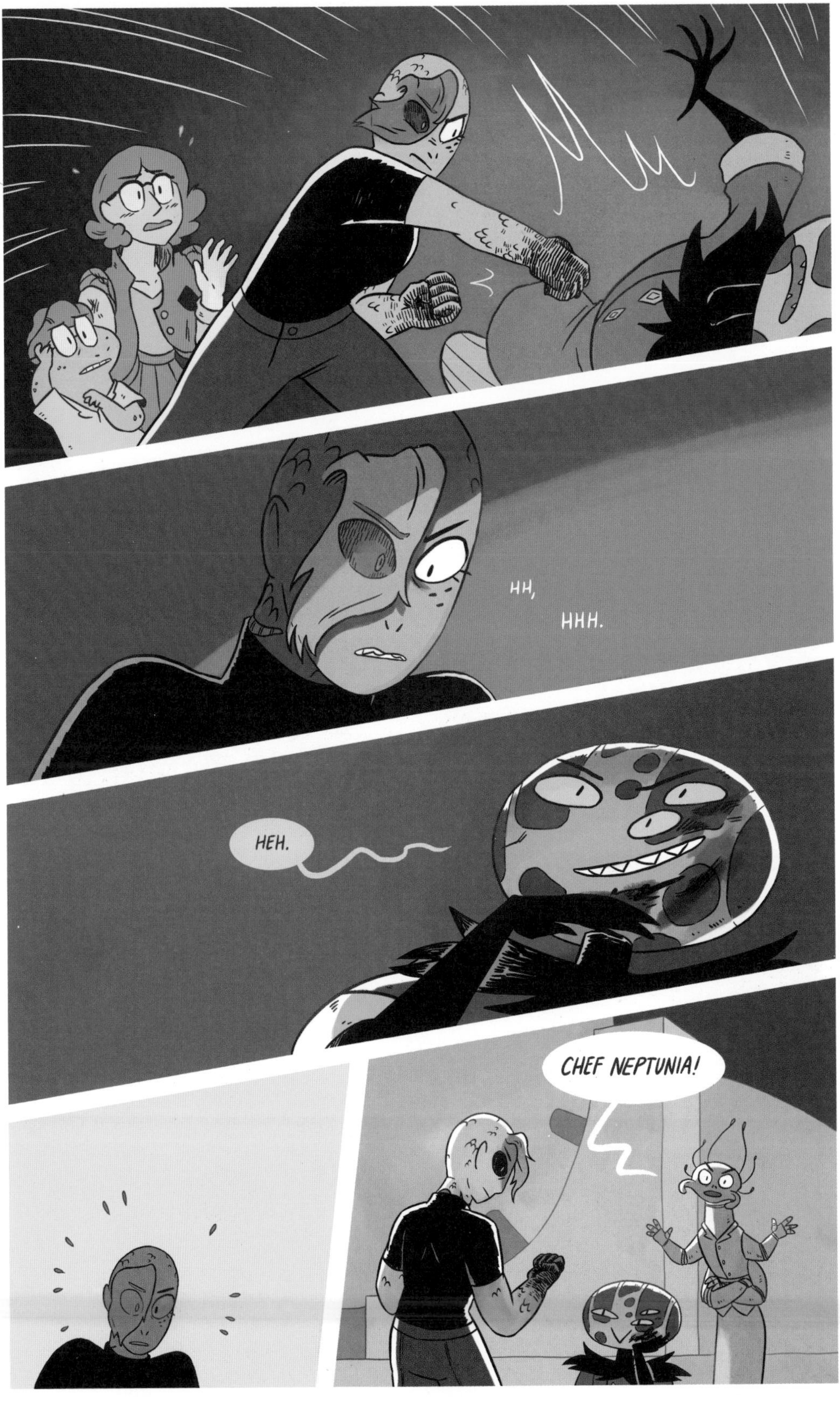

HH,
HHH.
HEH.
CHEF NEPTUNIA!

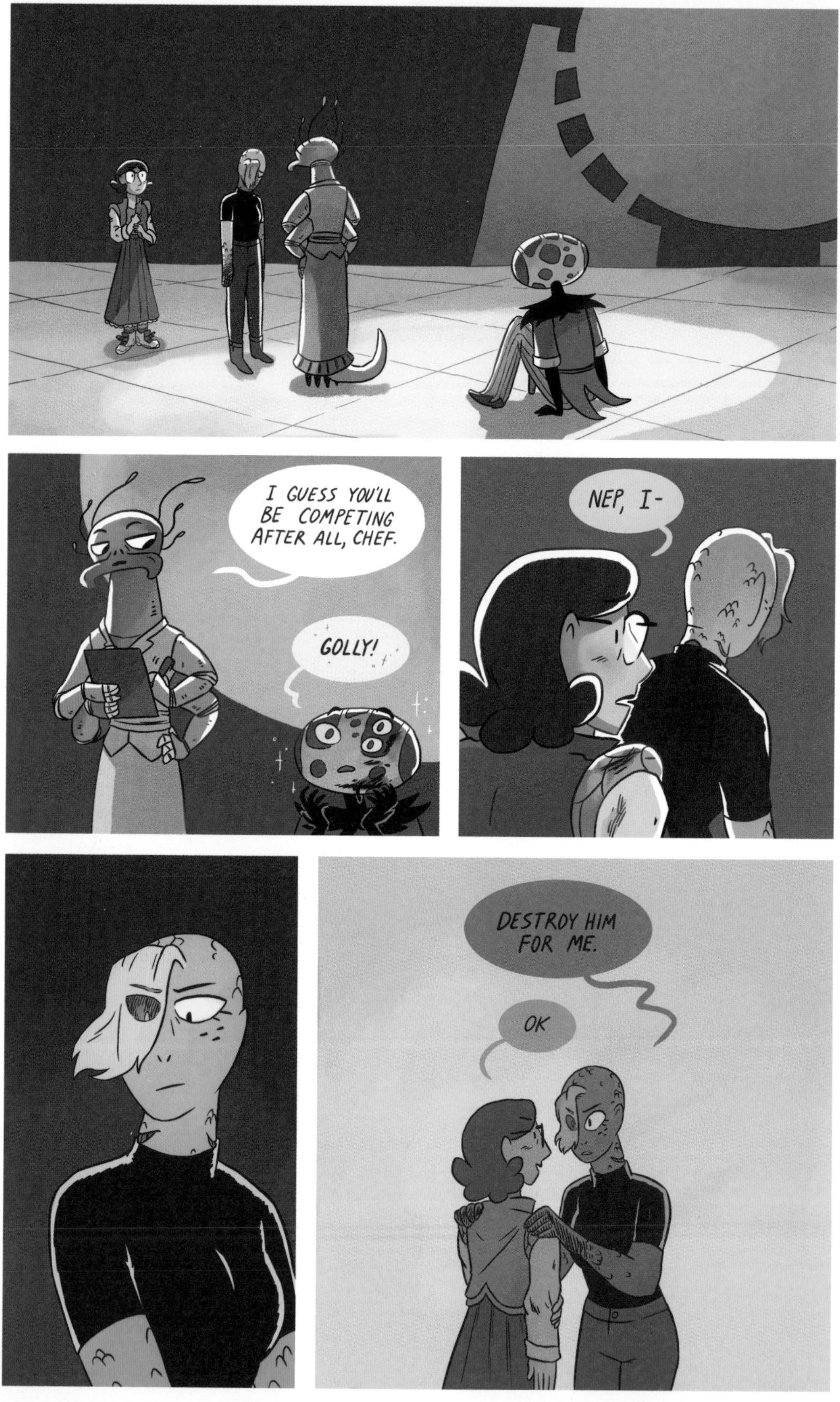
I GUESS YOU'LL BE COMPETING AFTER ALL, CHEF.
GOLLY!
NEP, I-
DESTROY HIM FOR ME.
OK

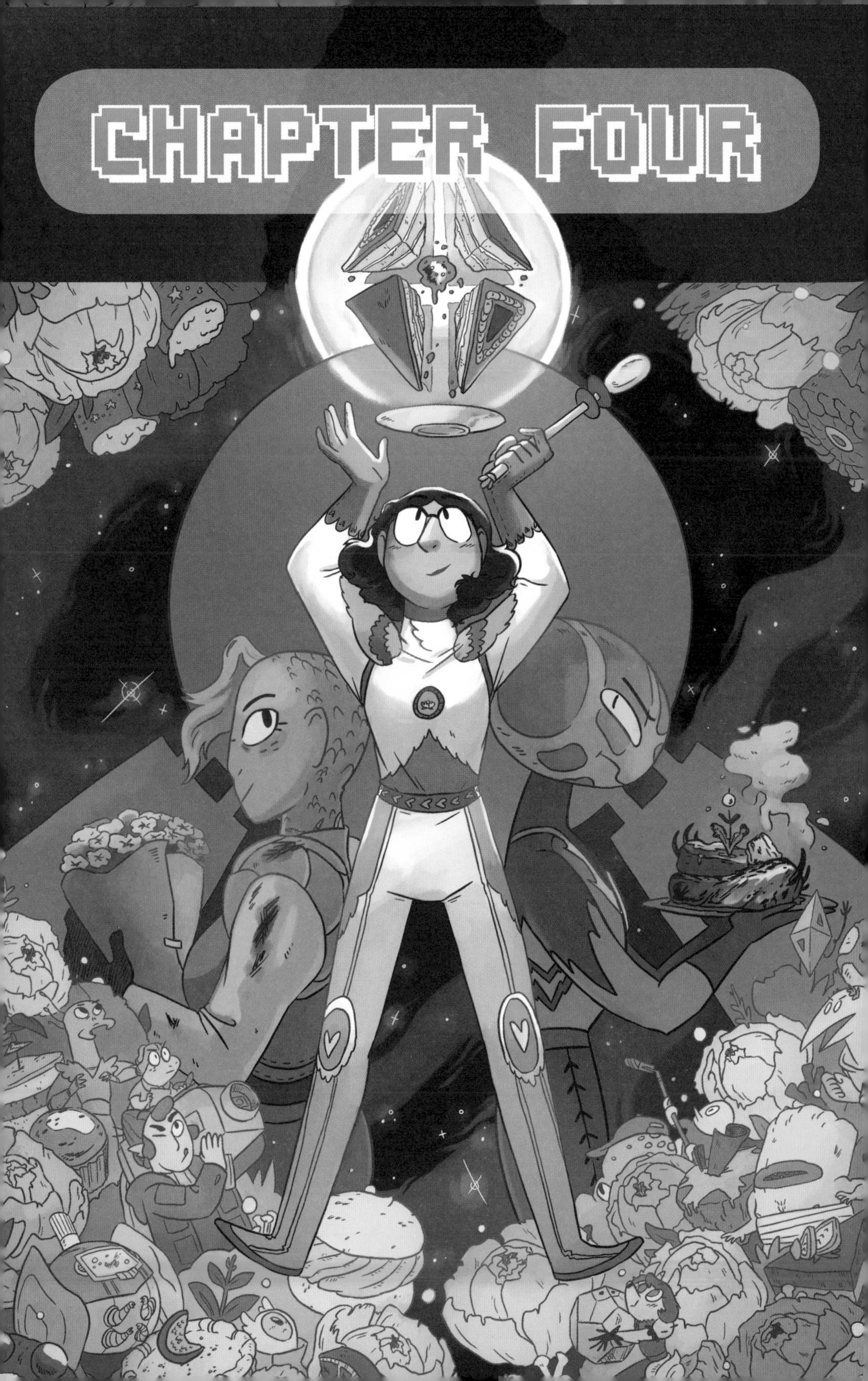
CHAPTER FOUR

PREVIOUSLY, ON SPACE BATTLE LUNCHTIME...

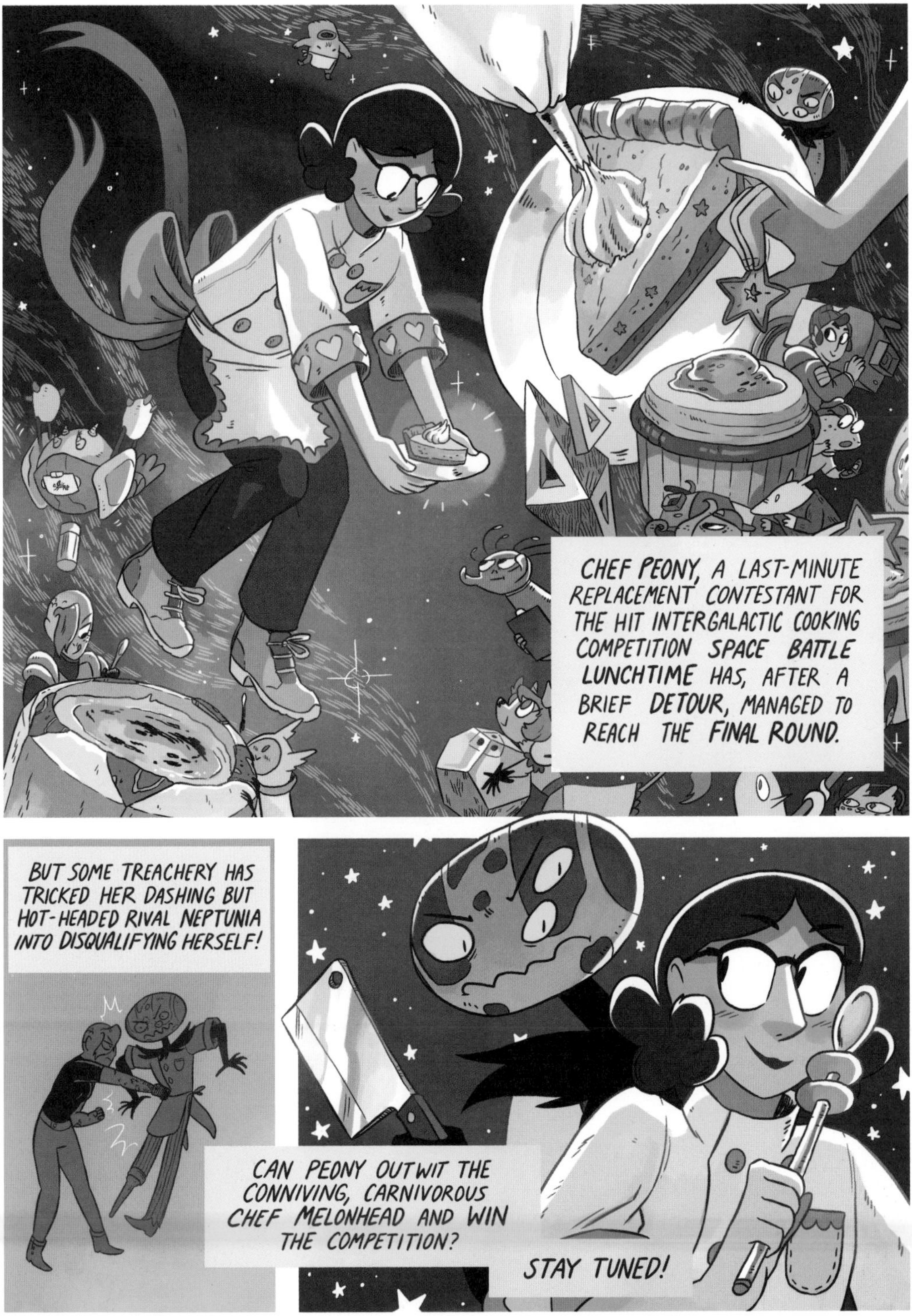
CHEF PEONY, A LAST-MINUTE REPLACEMENT CONTESTANT FOR THE HIT INTERGALACTIC COOKING COMPETITION SPACE BATTLE LUNCHTIME HAS, AFTER A BRIEF DETOUR, MANAGED TO REACH THE FINAL ROUND.
BUT SOME TREACHERY HAS TRICKED HER DASHING BUT HOT-HEADED RIVAL NEPTUNIA INTO DISQUALIFYING HERSELF!
CAN PEONY OUTWIT THE CONNIVING, CARNIVOROUS CHEF MELONHEAD AND WIN THE COMPETITION?
STAY TUNED!

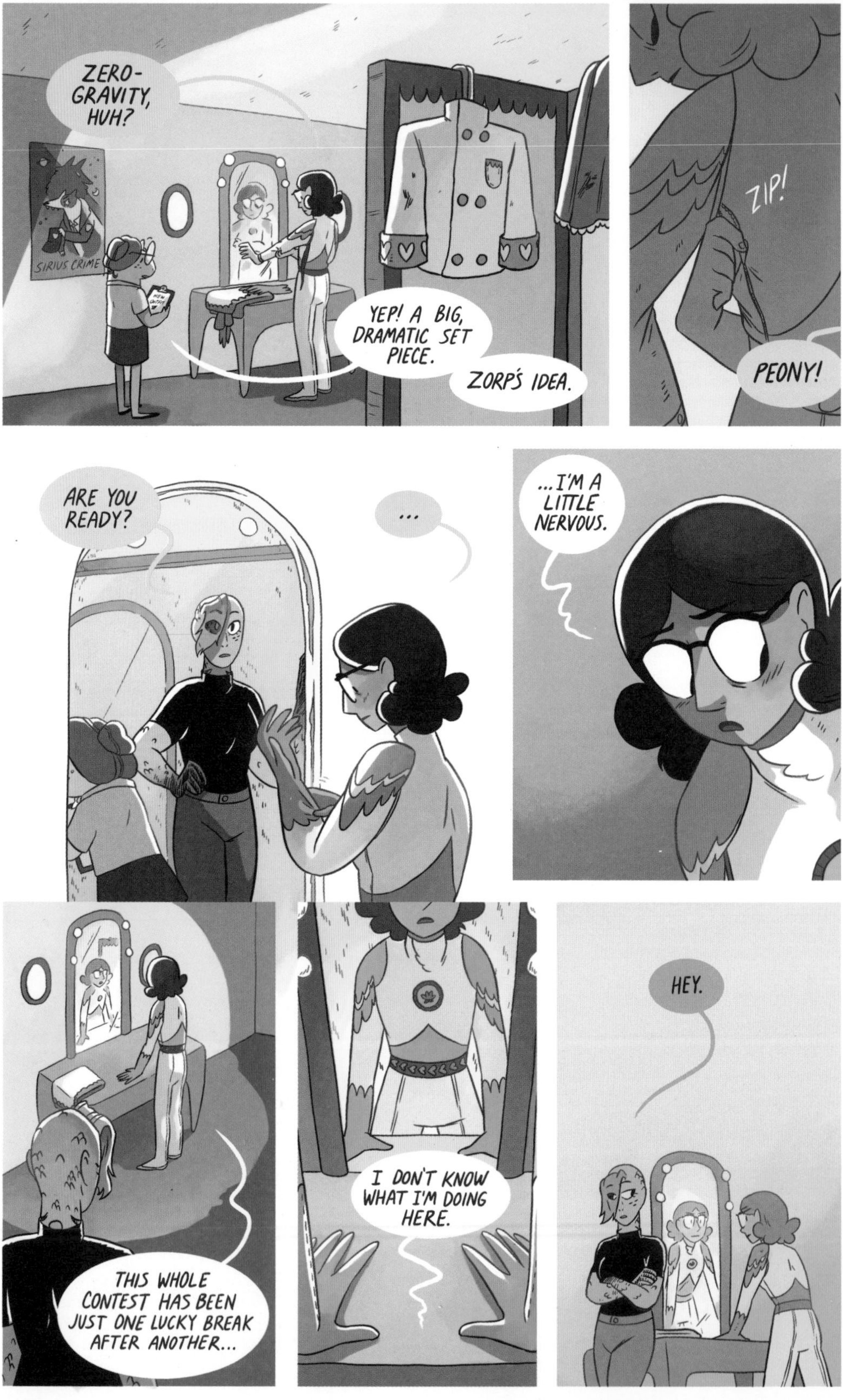
ZERO-GRAVITY, HUH?
SIRIUS CRIME
YEP! A BIG, DRAMATIC SET PIECE.
ZORP'S IDEA.
ZIP!
PEONY!
ARE YOU READY?
...
...I'M A LITTLE NERVOUS.
THIS WHOLE CONTEST HAS BEEN JUST ONE LUCKY BREAK AFTER ANOTHER...
I DON'T KNOW WHAT I'M DOING HERE.
HEY.

THERE'S A SWEET-NESS AND SINCERITY IN EVERYTHING I'VE SEEN YOU COOK.

IT'S...

...DELICIOUS.

I THOUGHT I COULD GET A FRESH START ON THIS SHOW.

BUT I DON'T KNOW IF I'LL EVER COOK LIKE THAT...

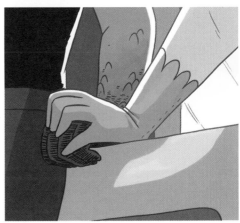

ALTHOUGH I WOULD HAVE HAD THE ADVAN-TAGE TECHNIQUE-WISE.

MY CHANCES AGAINST YOU WOULDN'T HAVE BEEN BAD.

IF I JUST HADN'T PUNCHED THAT MELON.

MHM.

ANYWAY.

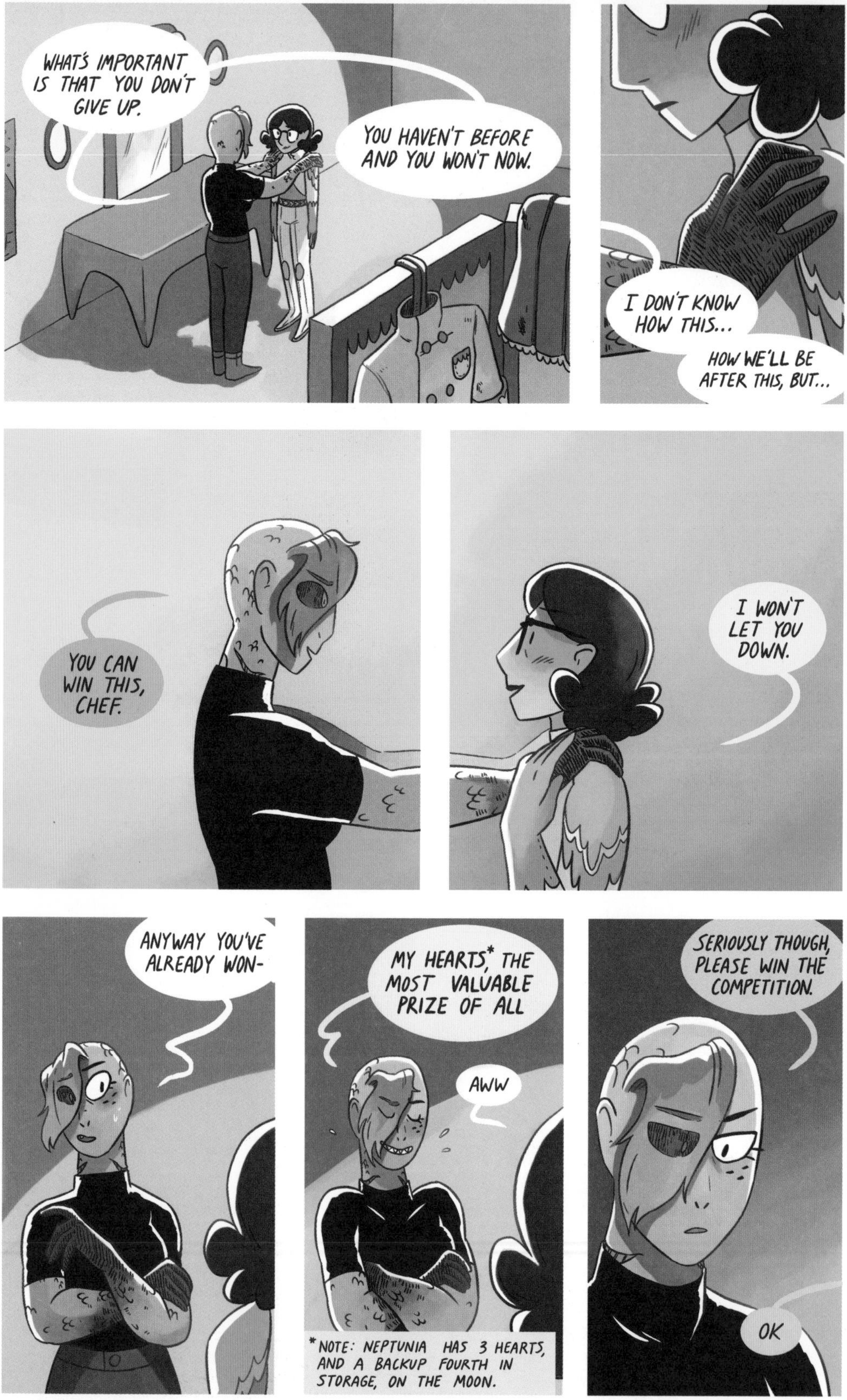
WHAT'S IMPORTANT IS THAT YOU DON'T GIVE UP.
YOU HAVEN'T BEFORE AND YOU WON'T NOW.
I DON'T KNOW HOW THIS...
HOW WE'LL BE AFTER THIS, BUT...
YOU CAN WIN THIS, CHEF.
I WON'T LET YOU DOWN.
ANYWAY YOU'VE ALREADY WON-
MY HEARTS,* THE MOST VALUABLE PRIZE OF ALL
AWW
*NOTE: NEPTUNIA HAS 3 HEARTS, AND A BACKUP FOURTH IN STORAGE, ON THE MOON.
SERIOUSLY THOUGH, PLEASE WIN THE COMPETITION.
OK

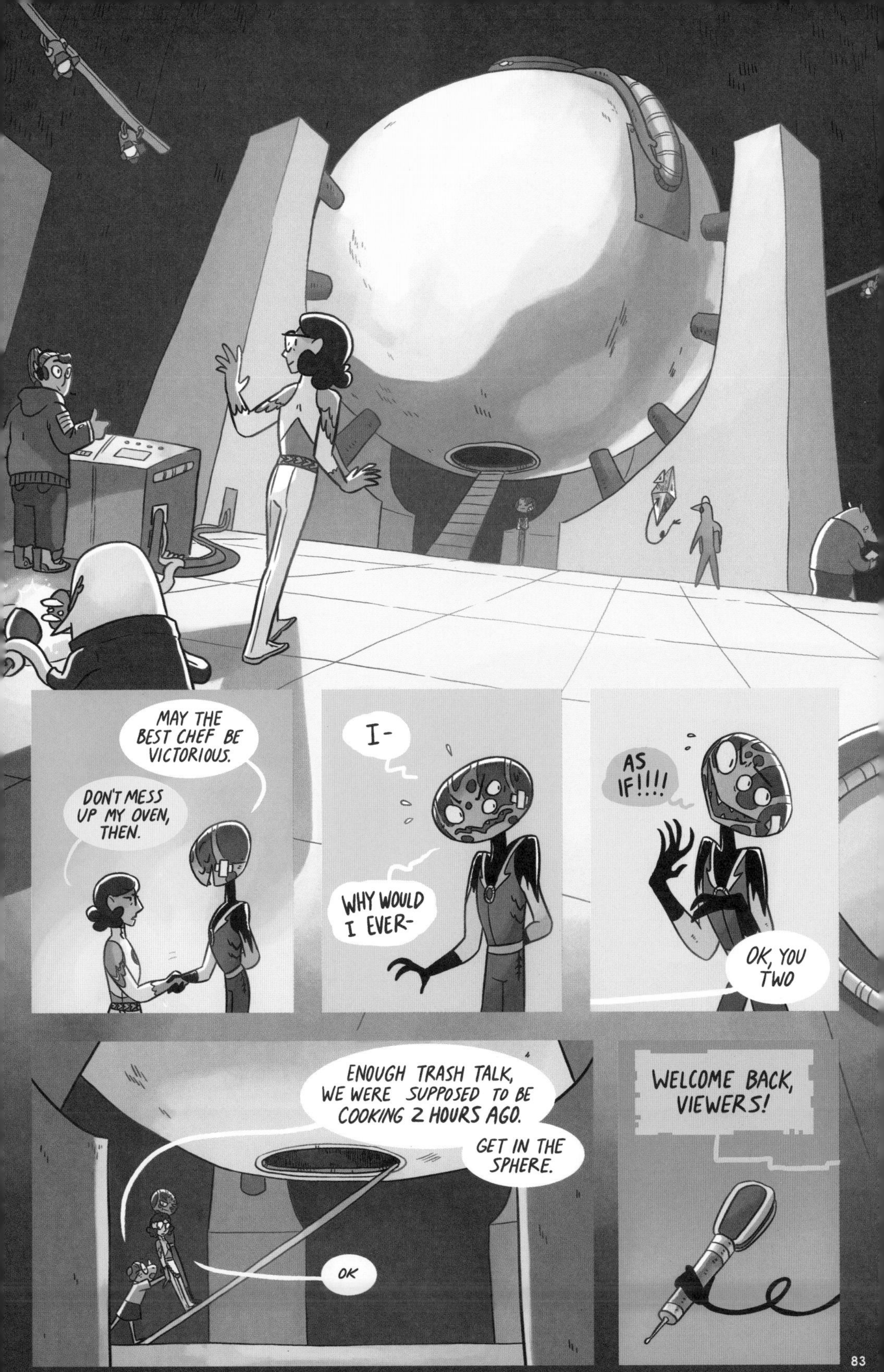
MAY THE BEST CHEF BE VICTORIOUS.
DON'T MESS UP MY OVEN, THEN.
I-
WHY WOULD I EVER-
AS IF!!!!
OK, YOU TWO
ENOUGH TRASH TALK, WE WERE SUPPOSED TO BE COOKING 2 HOURS AGO.
GET IN THE SPHERE.
OK
WELCOME BACK, VIEWERS!

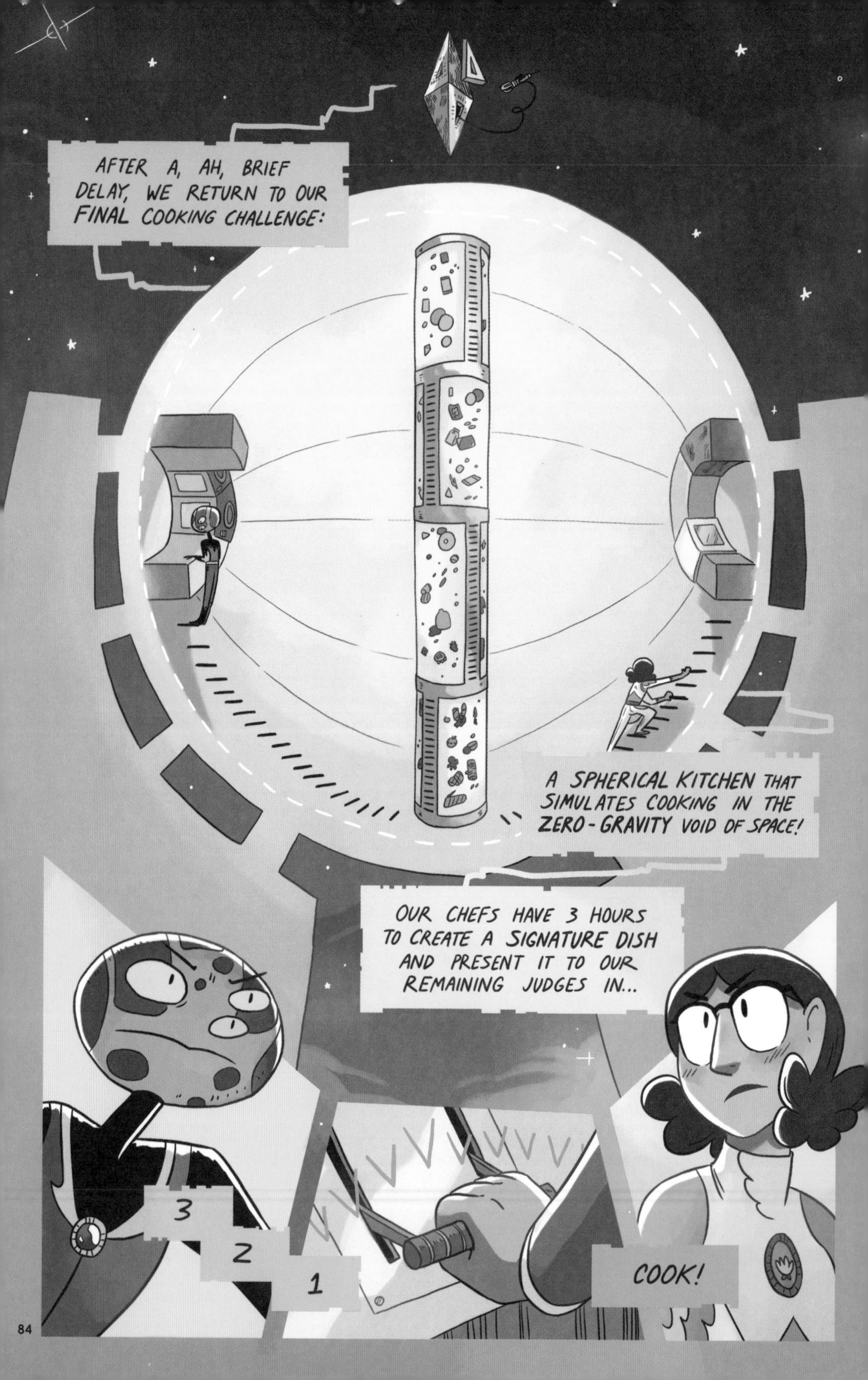
AFTER A, AH, BRIEF DELAY, WE RETURN TO OUR FINAL COOKING CHALLENGE:
A SPHERICAL KITCHEN THAT SIMULATES COOKING IN THE ZERO-GRAVITY VOID OF SPACE!
OUR CHEFS HAVE 3 HOURS TO CREATE A SIGNATURE DISH AND PRESENT IT TO OUR REMAINING JUDGES IN...
3
2
1
COOK!

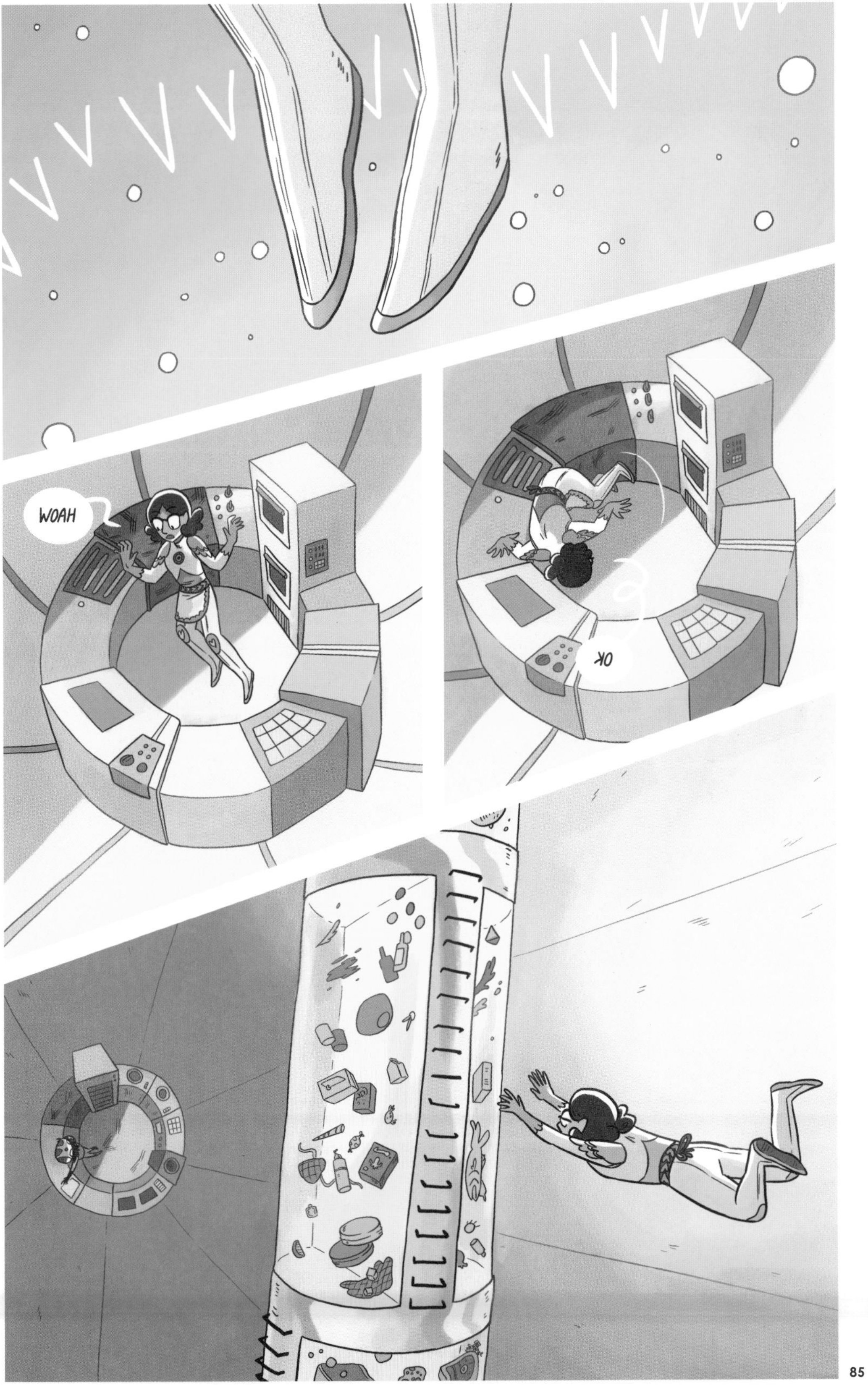
WOAH
OK

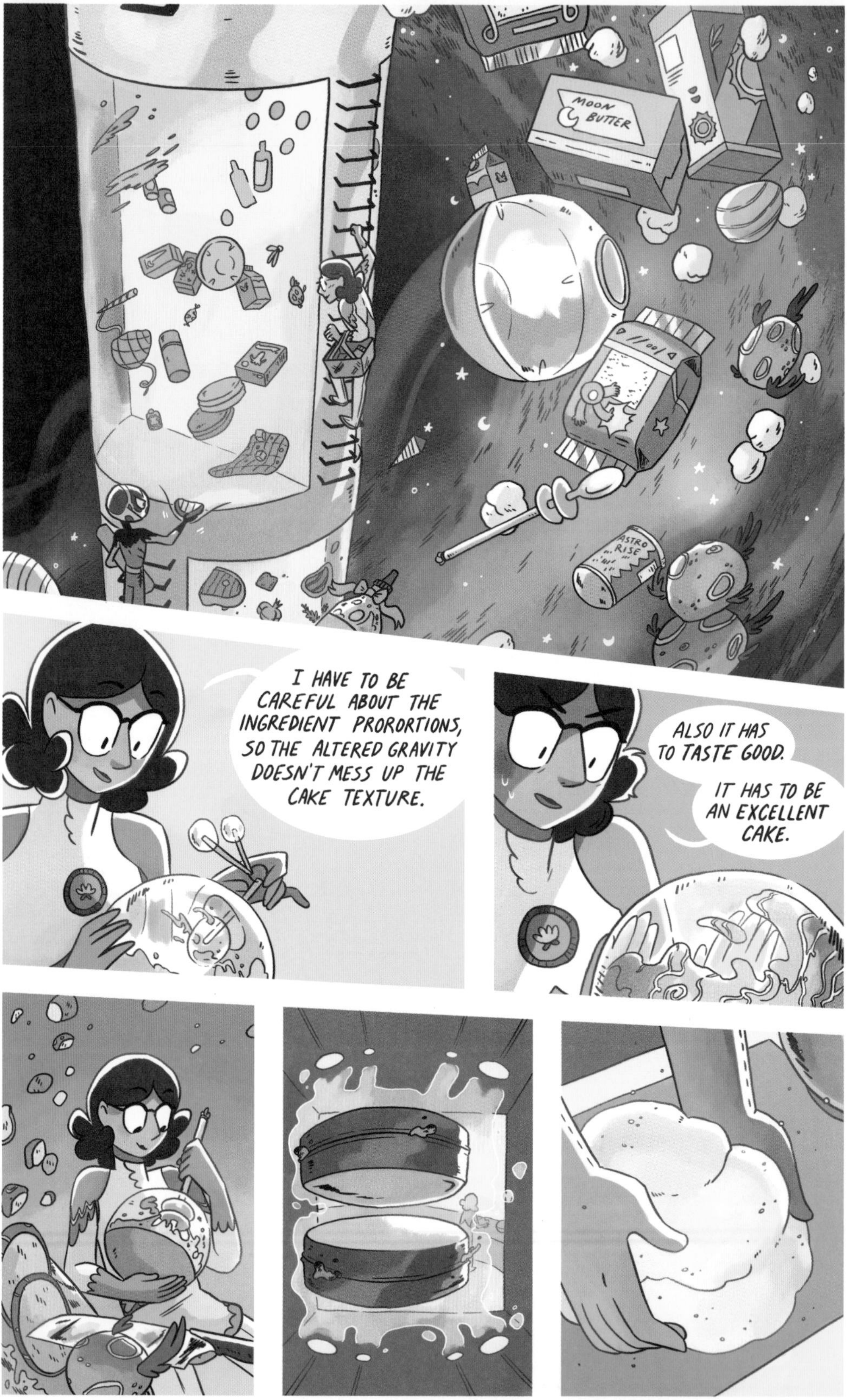
MOON BUTTER
ASTRO RISE
I HAVE TO BE CAREFUL ABOUT THE INGREDIENT PRORORTIONS, SO THE ALTERED GRAVITY DOESN'T MESS UP THE CAKE TEXTURE.
ALSO IT HAS TO TASTE GOOD.
IT HAS TO BE AN EXCELLENT CAKE.

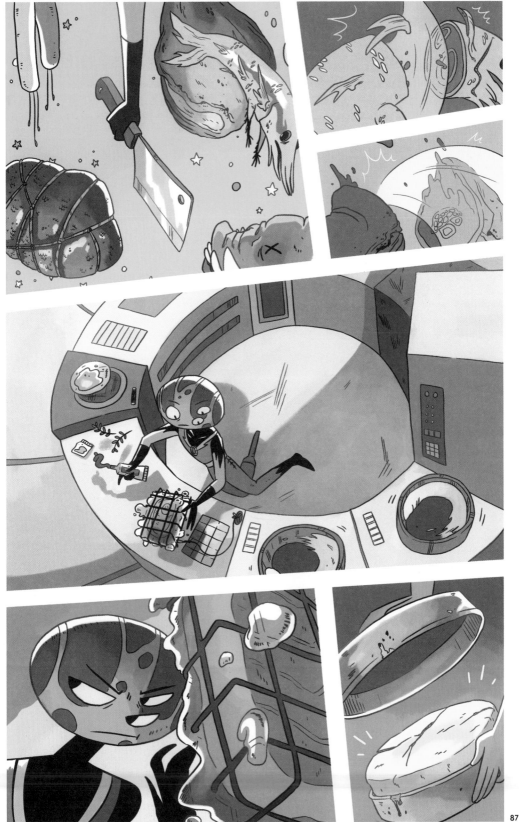

HMM...
NOT BAD!
I LIKE WHERE THIS IS GOING!
JOSTLE

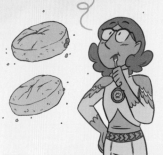

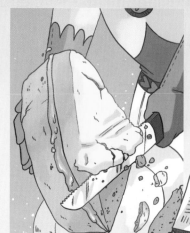

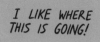

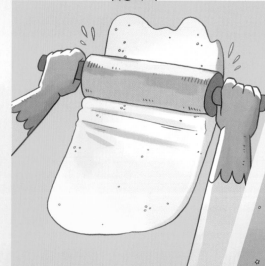

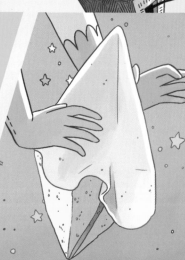

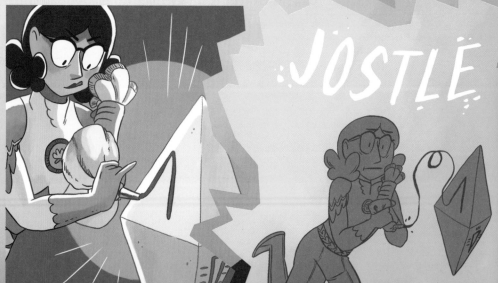

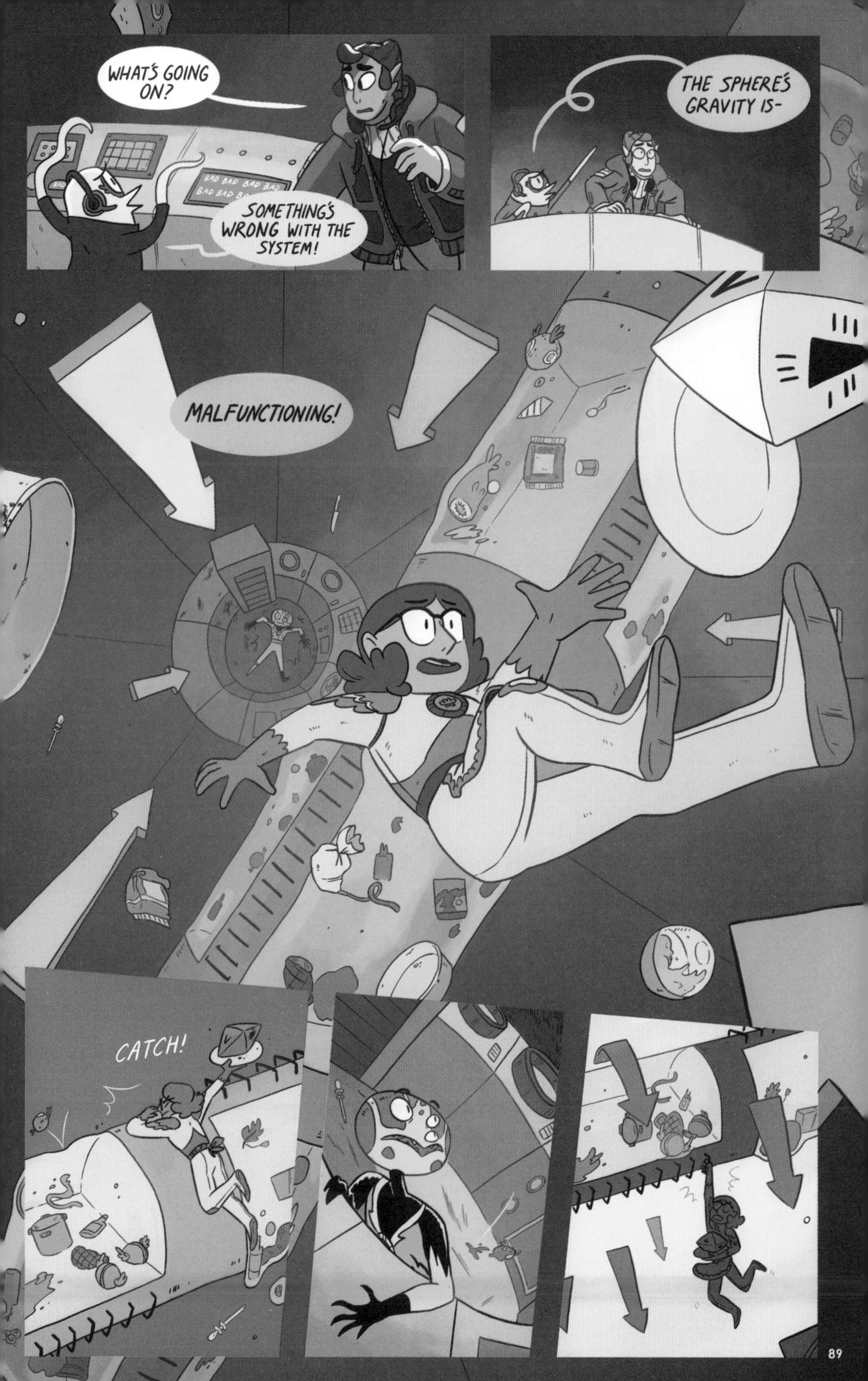
WHAT'S GOING ON?
BAD BAD BAD BAD BAD BAD BAD BAD
SOMETHING'S WRONG WITH THE SYSTEM!
THE SPHERE'S GRAVITY IS-
MALFUNCTIONING!
CATCH!

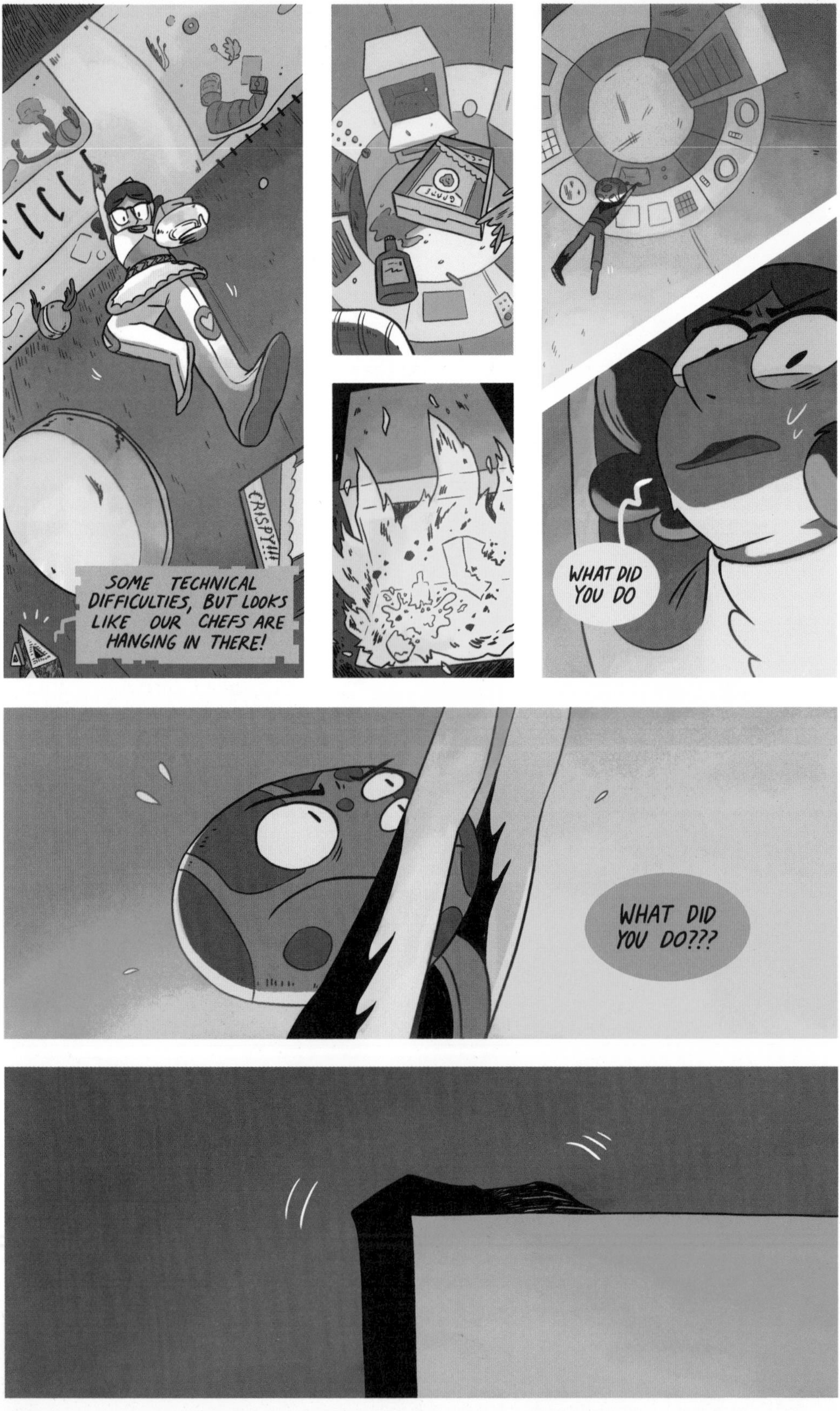
CRISPY!!!
SOME TECHNICAL DIFFICULTIES, BUT LOOKS LIKE OUR CHEFS ARE HANGING IN THERE!
WHAT DID YOU DO
WHAT DID YOU DO???

NOOOOOO

AAAAAAAAAAAAAAAAAAAAAAAAAA

WHAM!

AAAAAAAAA

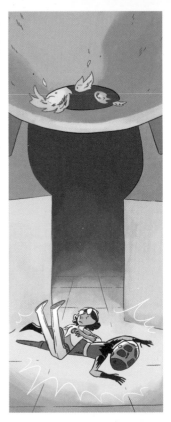

GASP

WEH

HOW ABOUT THAT HARROWING KITCHEN DISASTER, EH?

MY CAKE...

SORRY ABOUT YOUR CAKE, CHEF- IT WAS VERY HANDSOME.

PAT

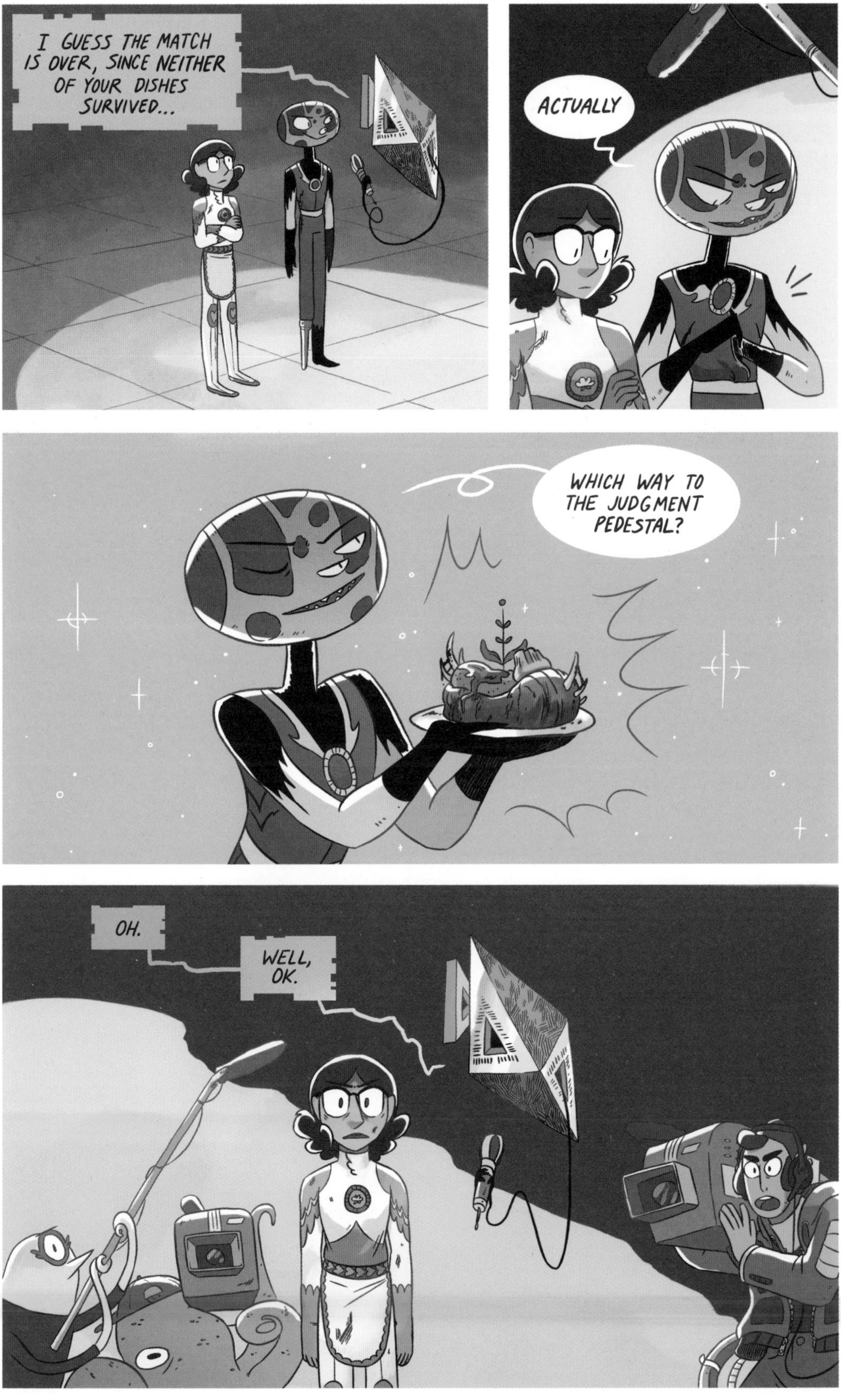
I GUESS THE MATCH IS OVER, SINCE NEITHER OF YOUR DISHES SURVIVED...
ACTUALLY
WHICH WAY TO THE JUDGMENT PEDESTAL?
OH.
WELL, OK.

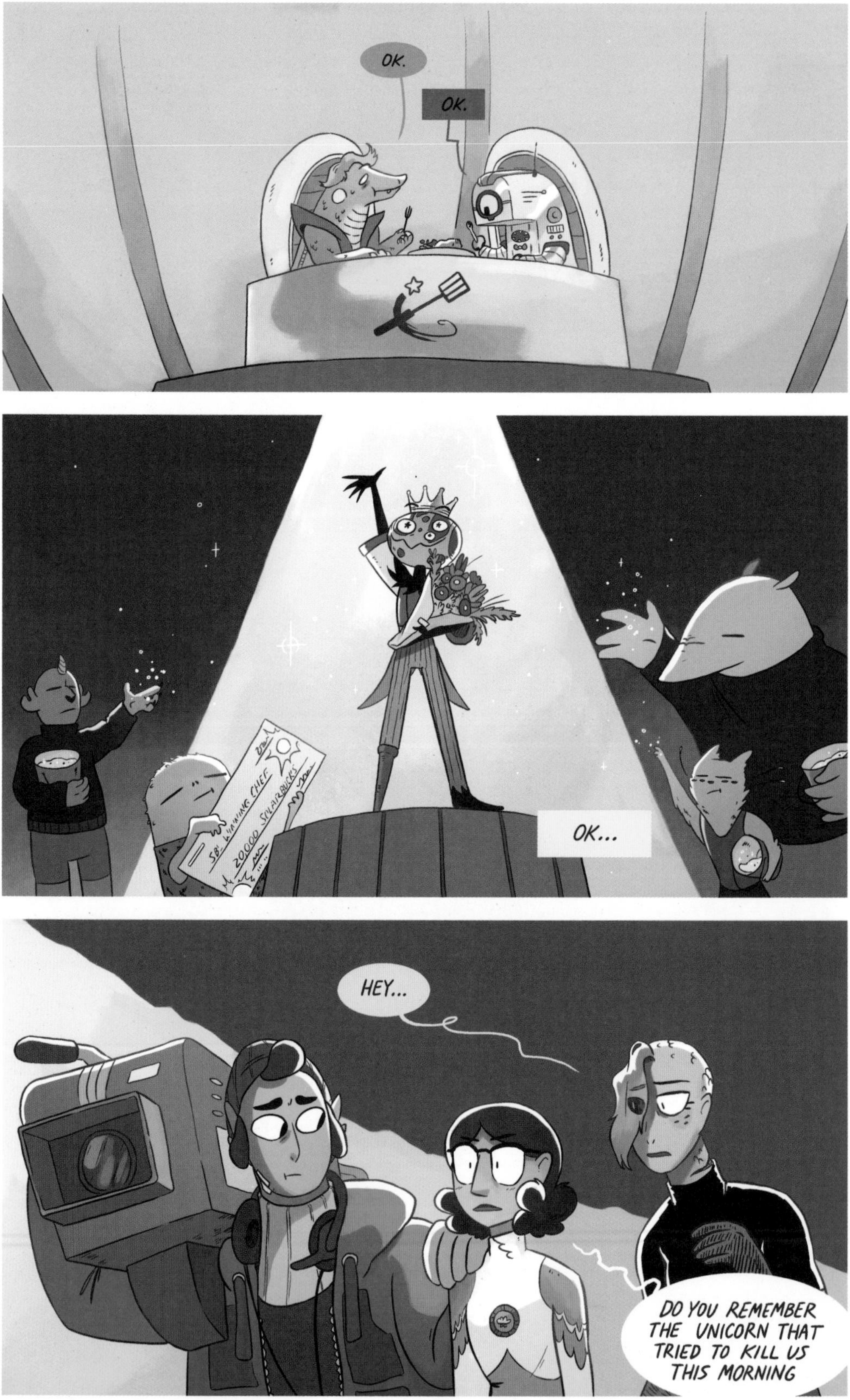

OK.
OK.
OK...
HEY...
DO YOU REMEMBER THE UNICORN THAT TRIED TO KILL US THIS MORNING

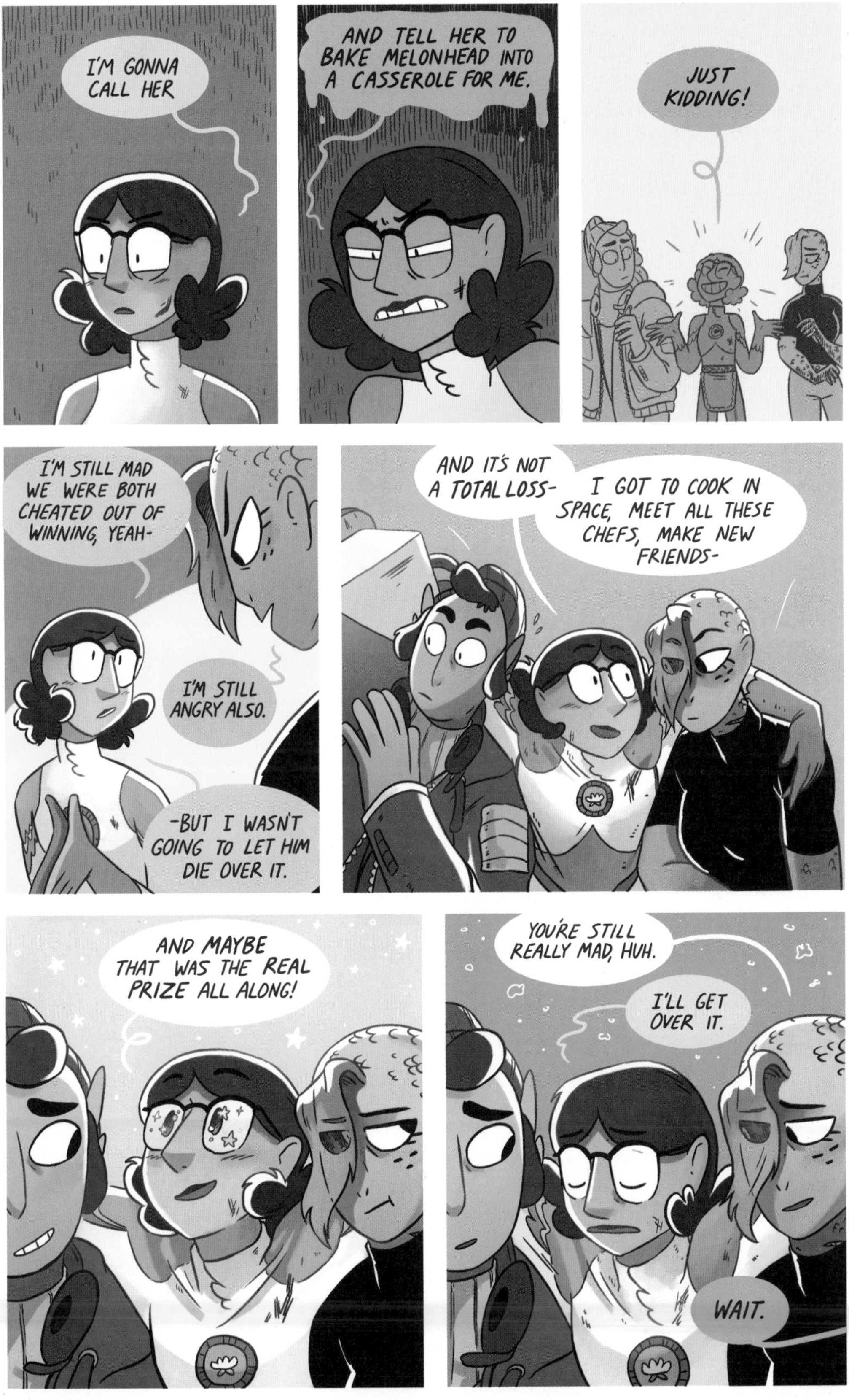
I'M GONNA CALL HER
AND TELL HER TO BAKE MELONHEAD INTO A CASSEROLE FOR ME.
JUST KIDDING!
I'M STILL MAD WE WERE BOTH CHEATED OUT OF WINNING, YEAH-
I'M STILL ANGRY ALSO.
-BUT I WASN'T GOING TO LET HIM DIE OVER IT.
AND IT'S NOT A TOTAL LOSS-
I GOT TO COOK IN SPACE, MEET ALL THESE CHEFS, MAKE NEW FRIENDS-
AND MAYBE THAT WAS THE REAL PRIZE ALL ALONG!
YOU'RE STILL REALLY MAD, HUH.
I'LL GET OVER IT.
WAIT.

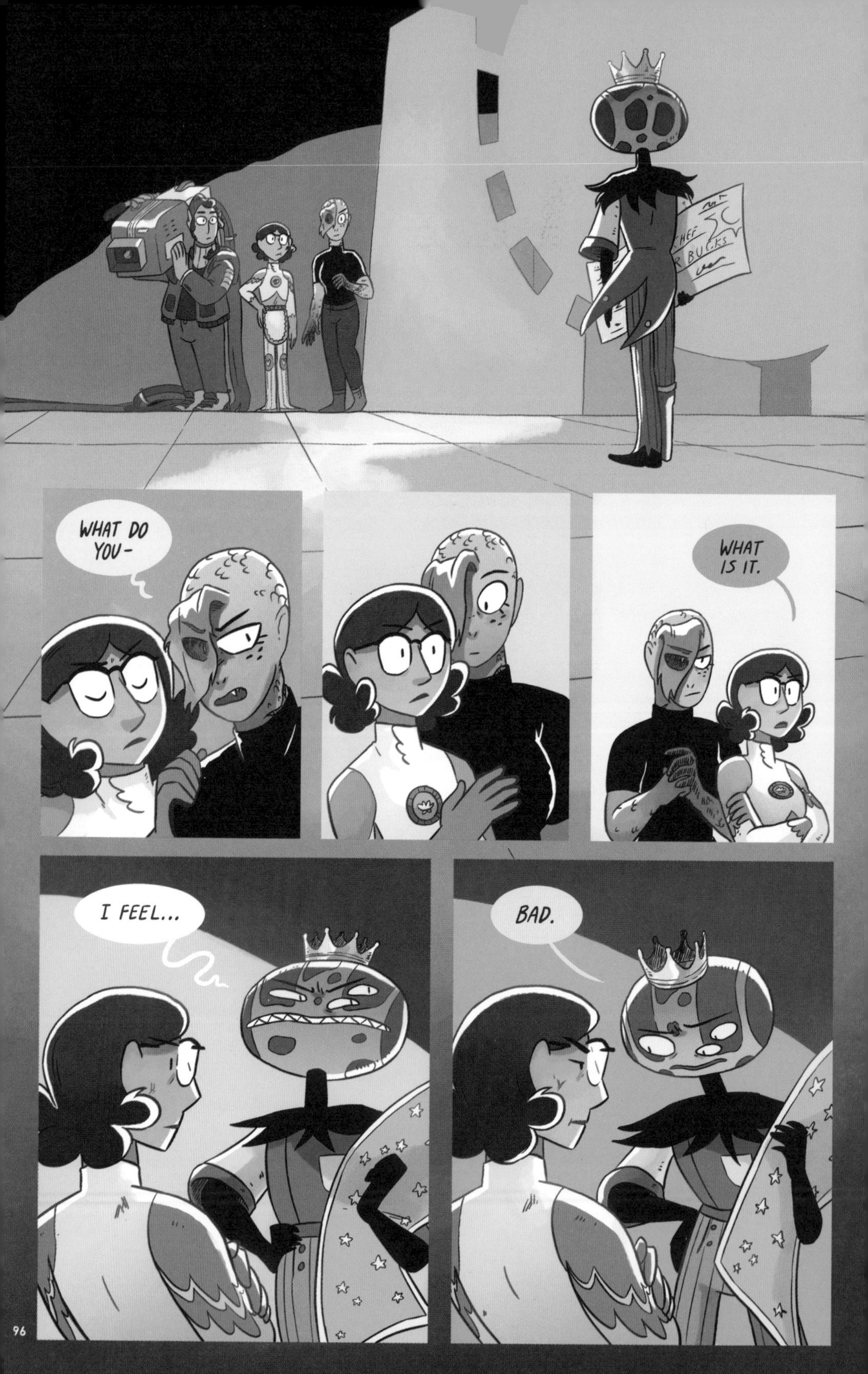
CHEF
BUCKS
WHAT DO YOU-
WHAT IS IT.
I FEEL...
BAD.

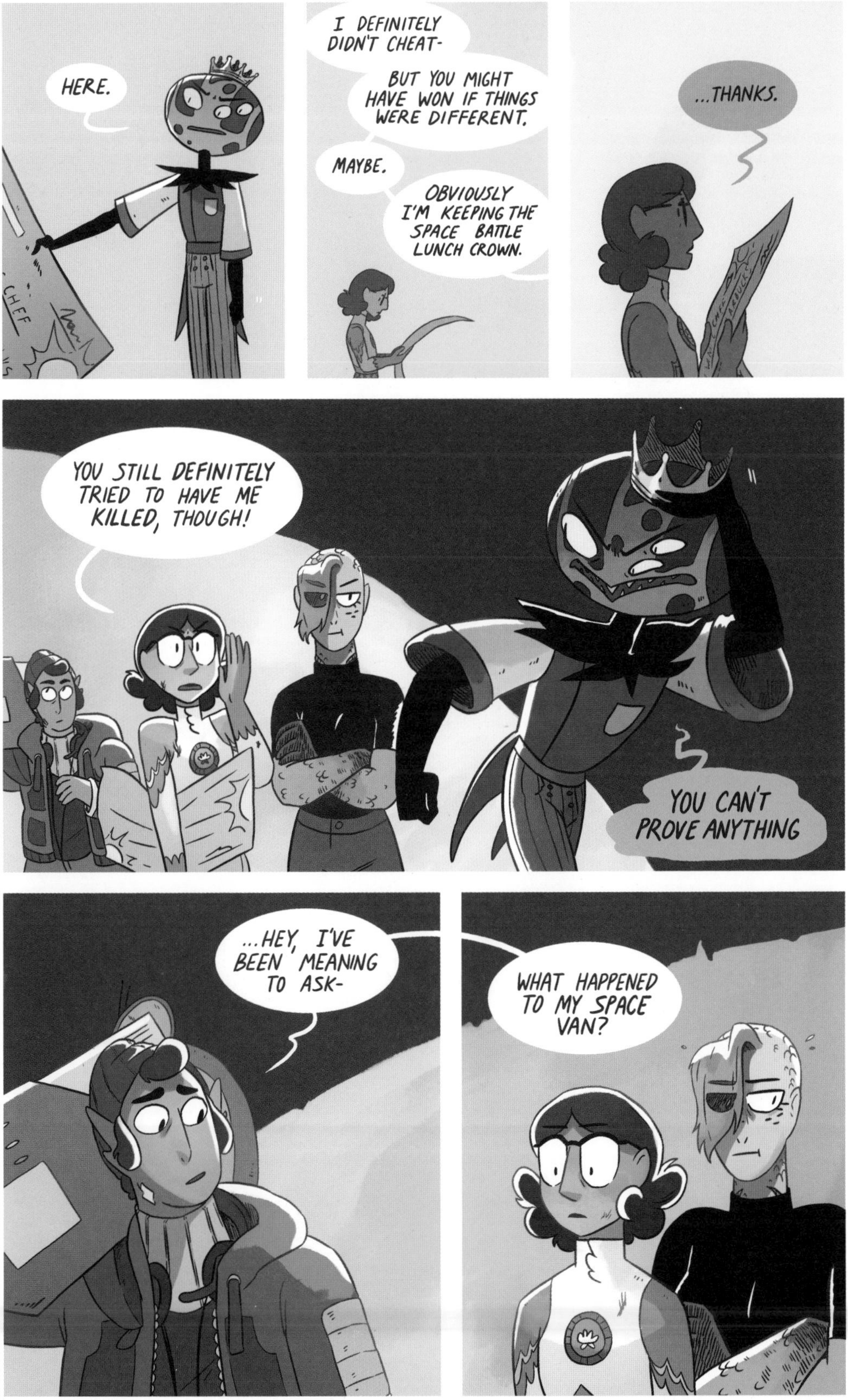
HERE.
I DEFINITELY DIDN'T CHEAT-
BUT YOU MIGHT HAVE WON IF THINGS WERE DIFFERENT.
MAYBE.
OBVIOUSLY I'M KEEPING THE SPACE BATTLE LUNCH CROWN.
...THANKS.
YOU STILL DEFINITELY TRIED TO HAVE ME KILLED, THOUGH!
YOU CAN'T PROVE ANYTHING
...HEY, I'VE BEEN MEANING TO ASK-
WHAT HAPPENED TO MY SPACE VAN?

EPILOGUE:

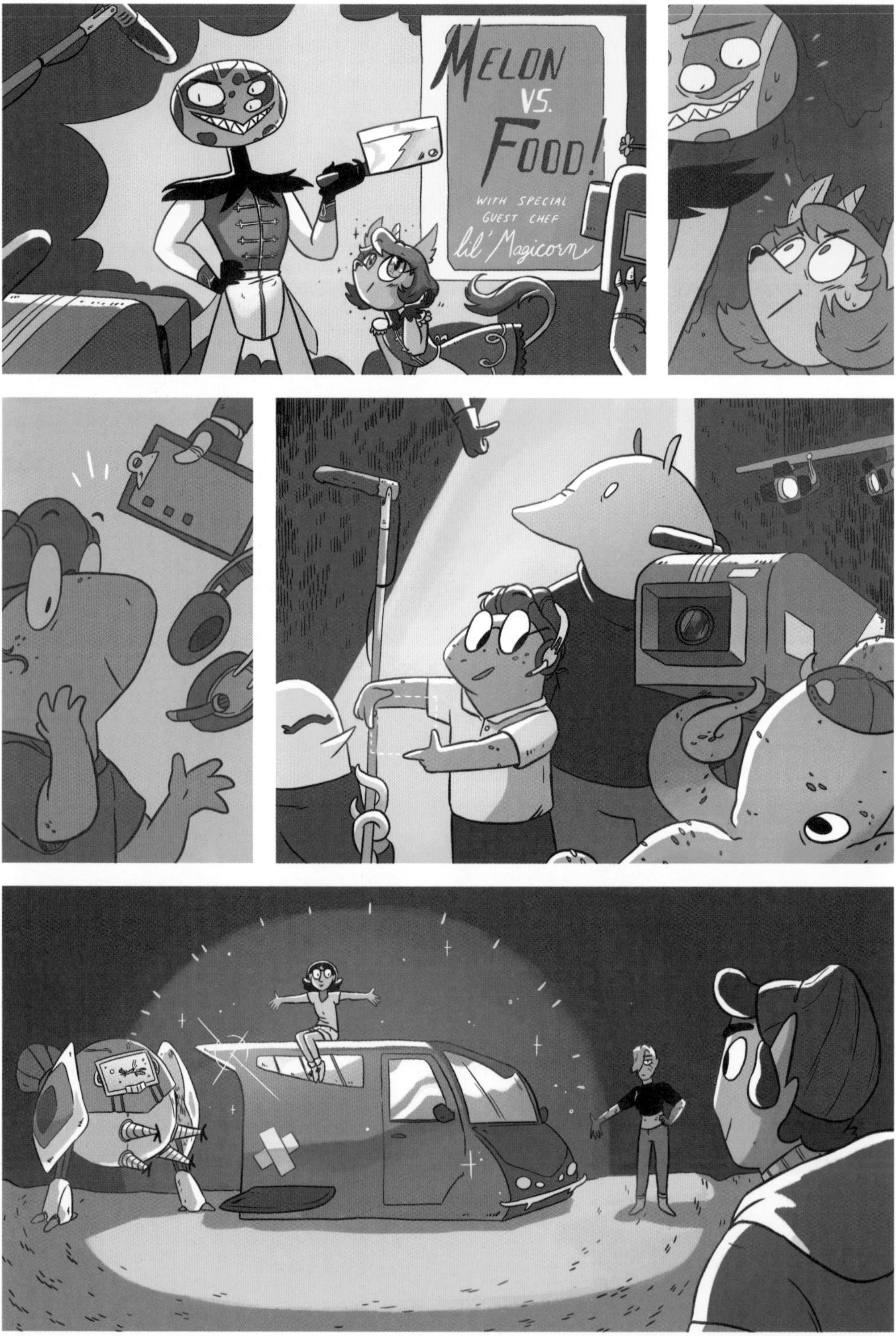

MELON VS. FOOD!
WITH SPECIAL GUEST CHEF
lil' Magicorn

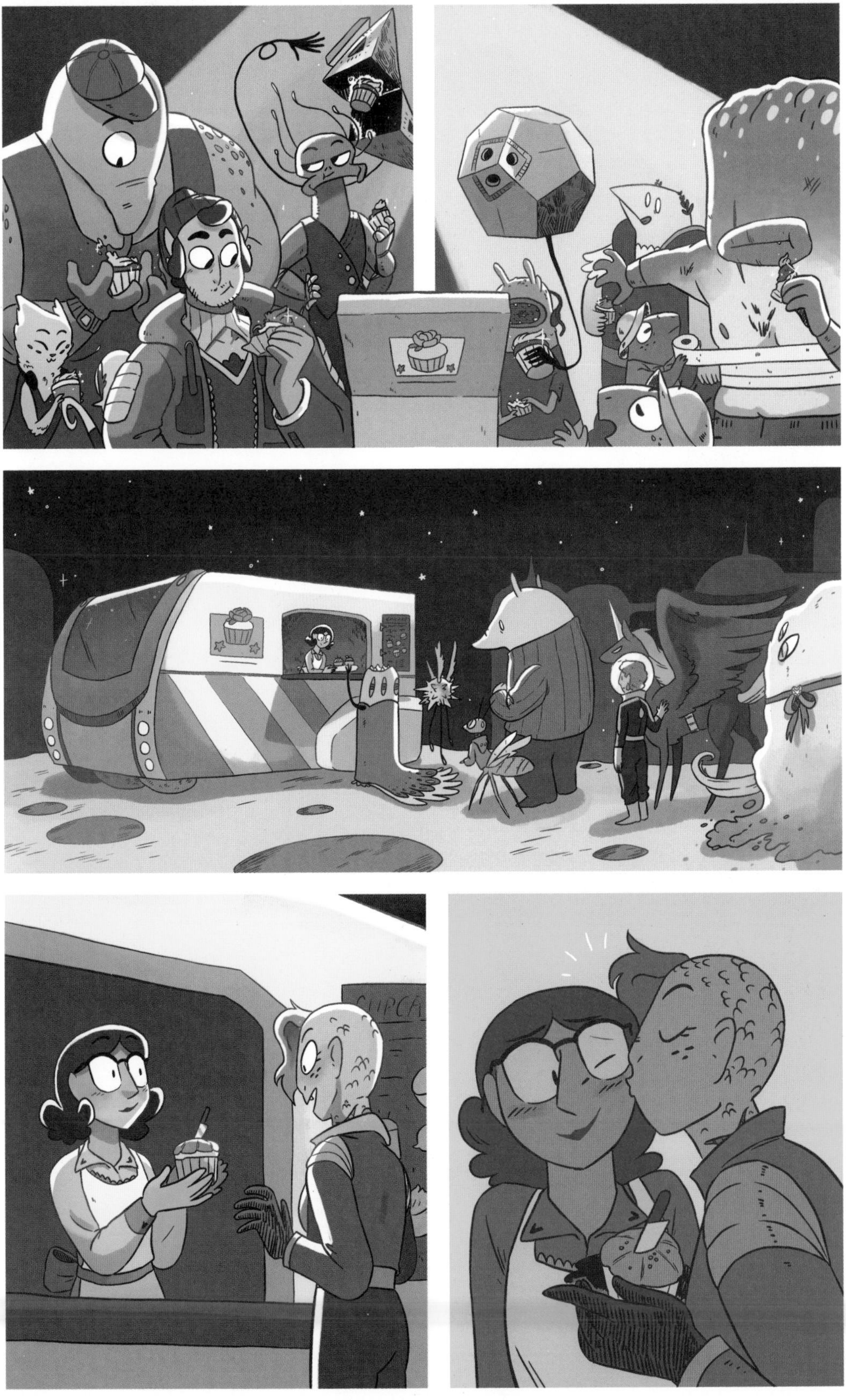

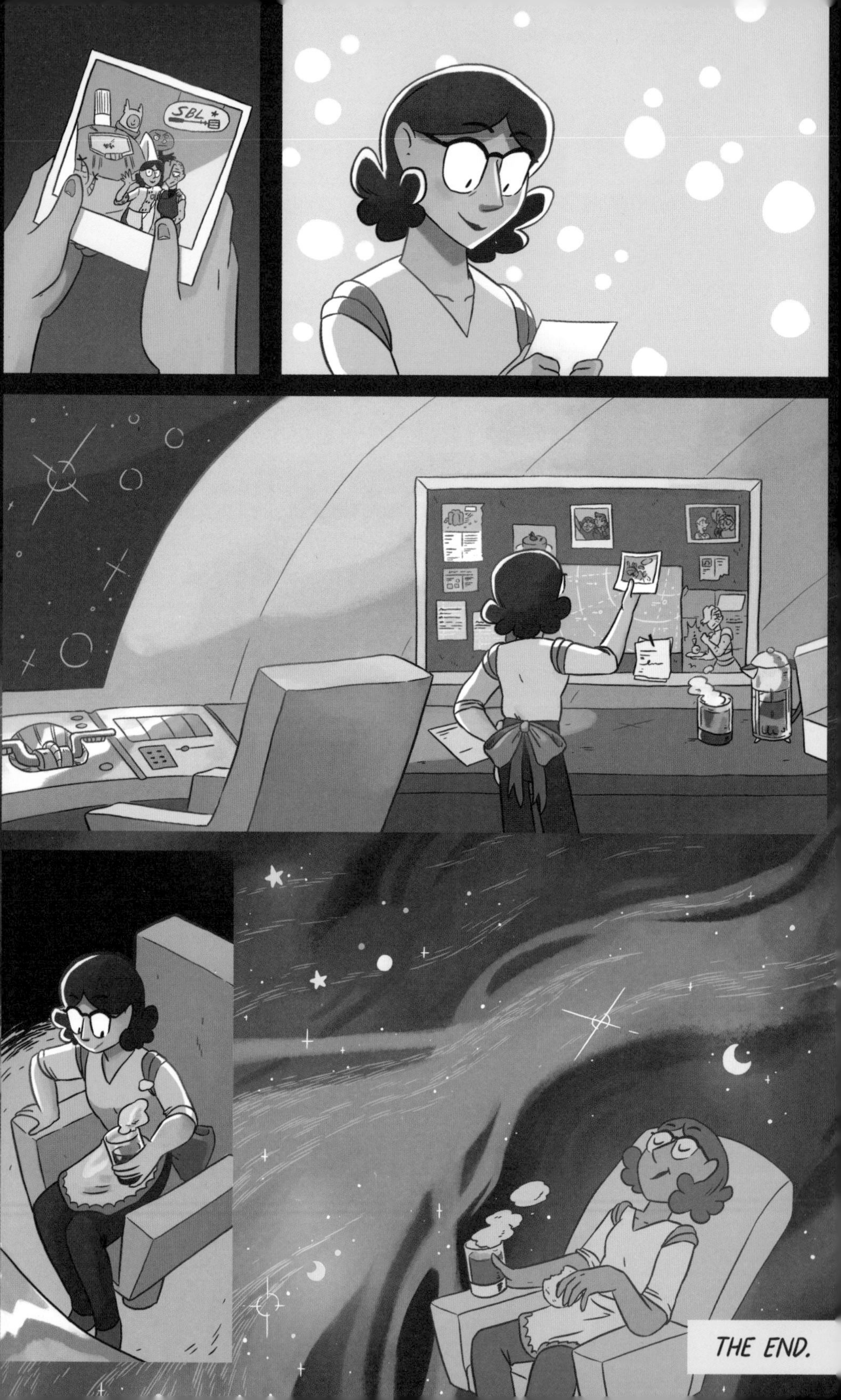
SBL
THE END.

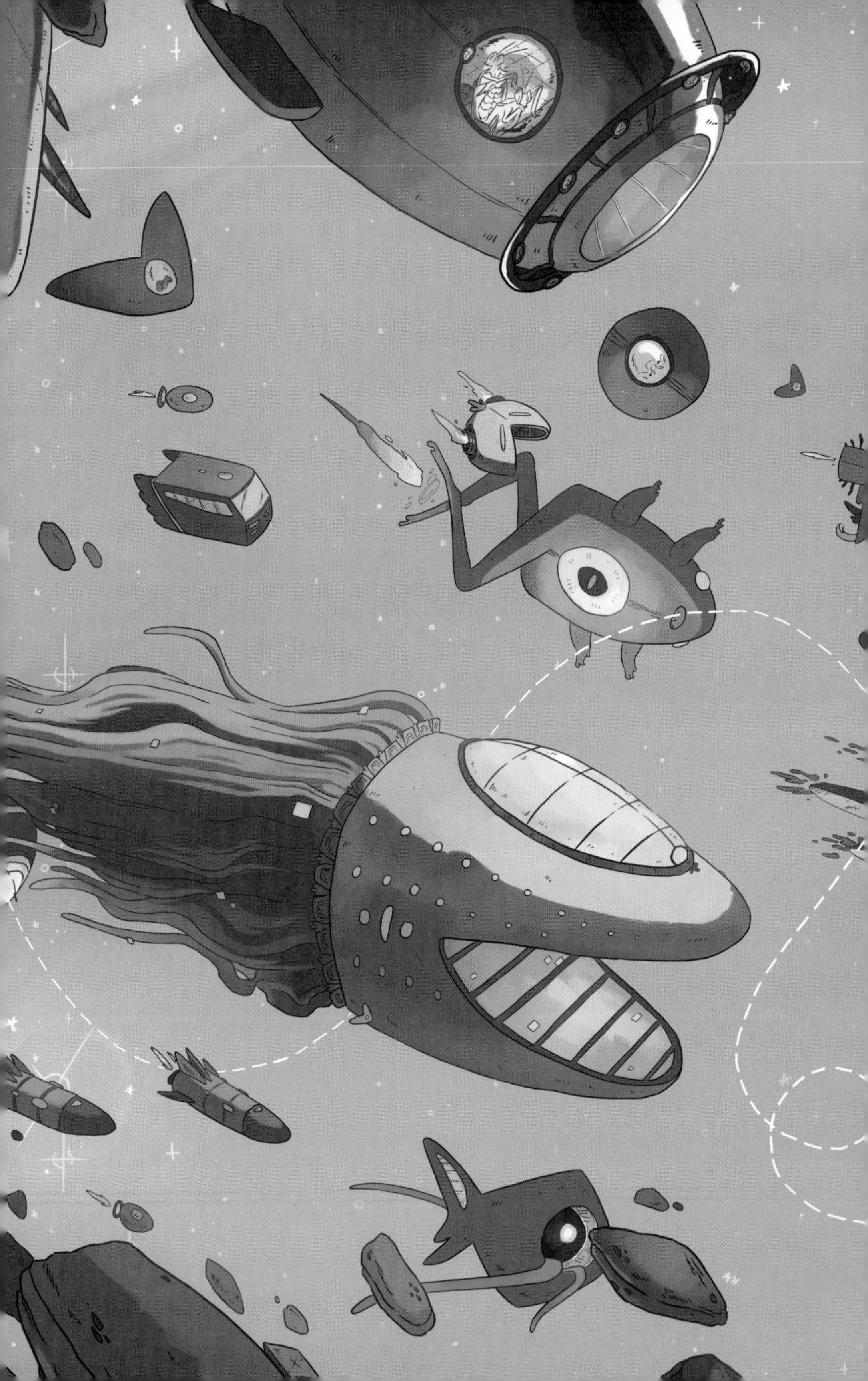

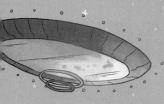

BONUS CONTENT!

Sketches, comics, and more! Turn the page.

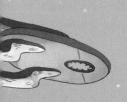

SHE'S ACTUALLY FROM EUROPA

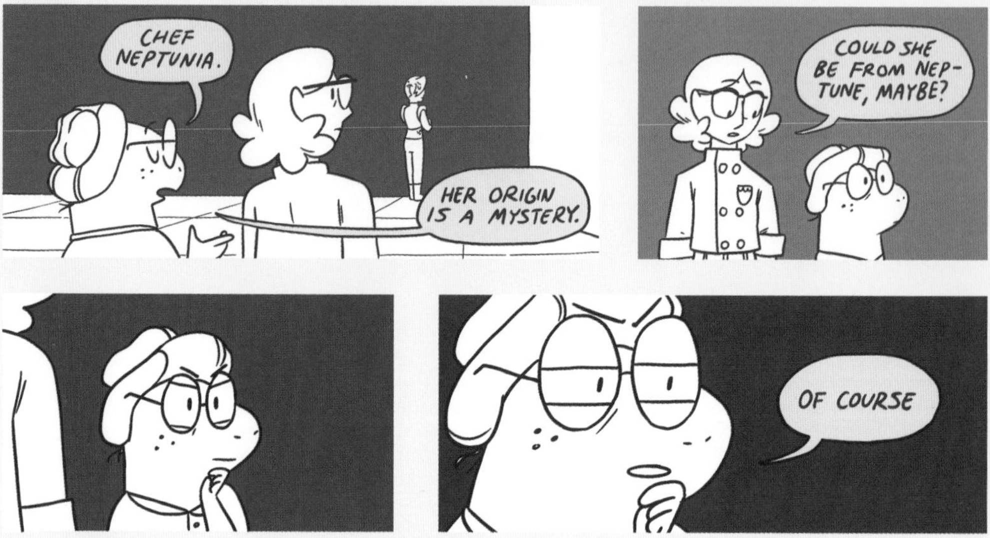
CHEF NEPTUNIA.
HER ORIGIN IS A MYSTERY.
COULD SHE BE FROM NEP-TUNE, MAYBE?
OF COURSE

KNIFE PUNS I

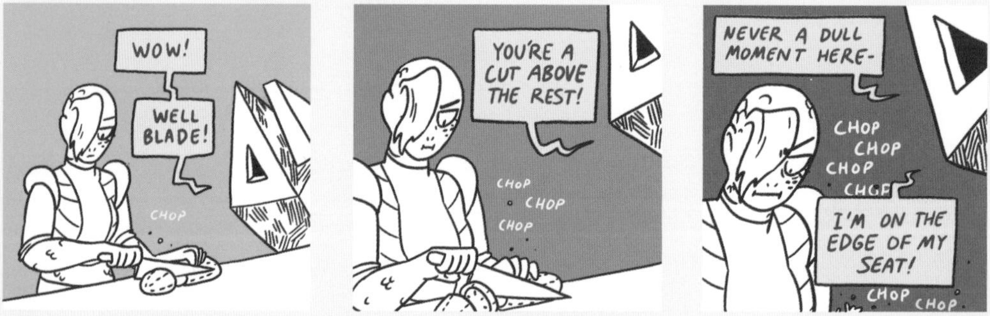
WOW!
WELL BLADE!
CHOP
YOU'RE A CUT ABOVE THE REST!
CHOP CHOP CHOP
NEVER A DULL MOMENT HERE-
CHOP CHOP CHOP
I'M ON THE EDGE OF MY SEAT!
CHOP CHOP

ABOUT THE AUTHOR

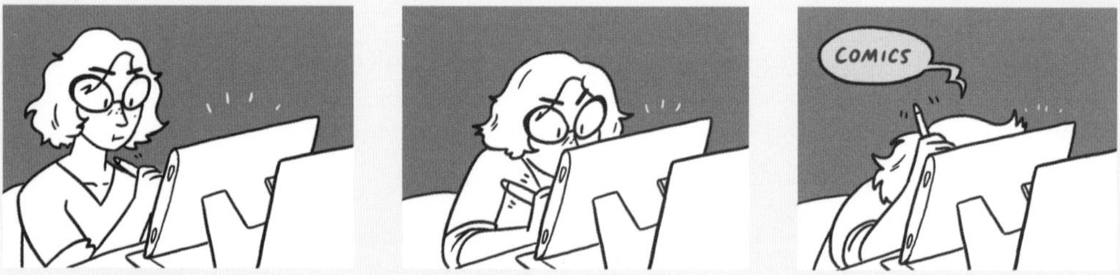
COMICS

KNIFE PUNS II

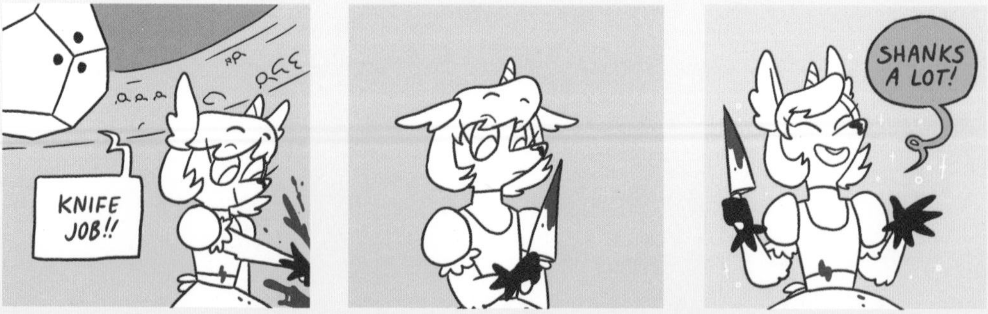
KNIFE JOB!!
SHANKS A LOT!

CONTRACT

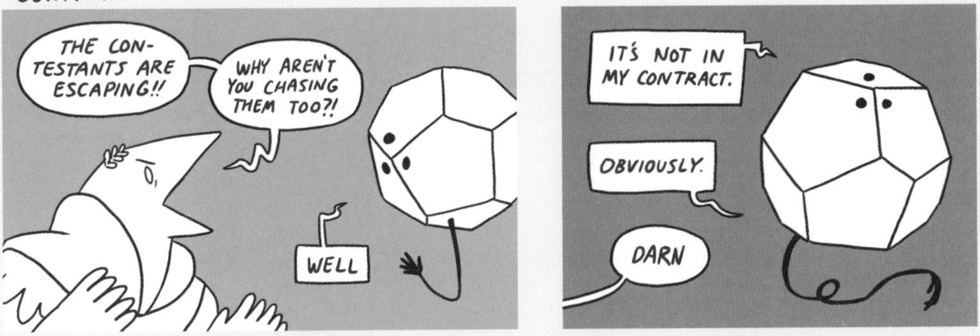

THE CON-TESTANTS ARE ESCAPING!!
WHY AREN'T YOU CHASING THEM TOO?!
WELL
IT'S NOT IN MY CONTRACT.
OBVIOUSLY.
DARN

PICK-UP LINES

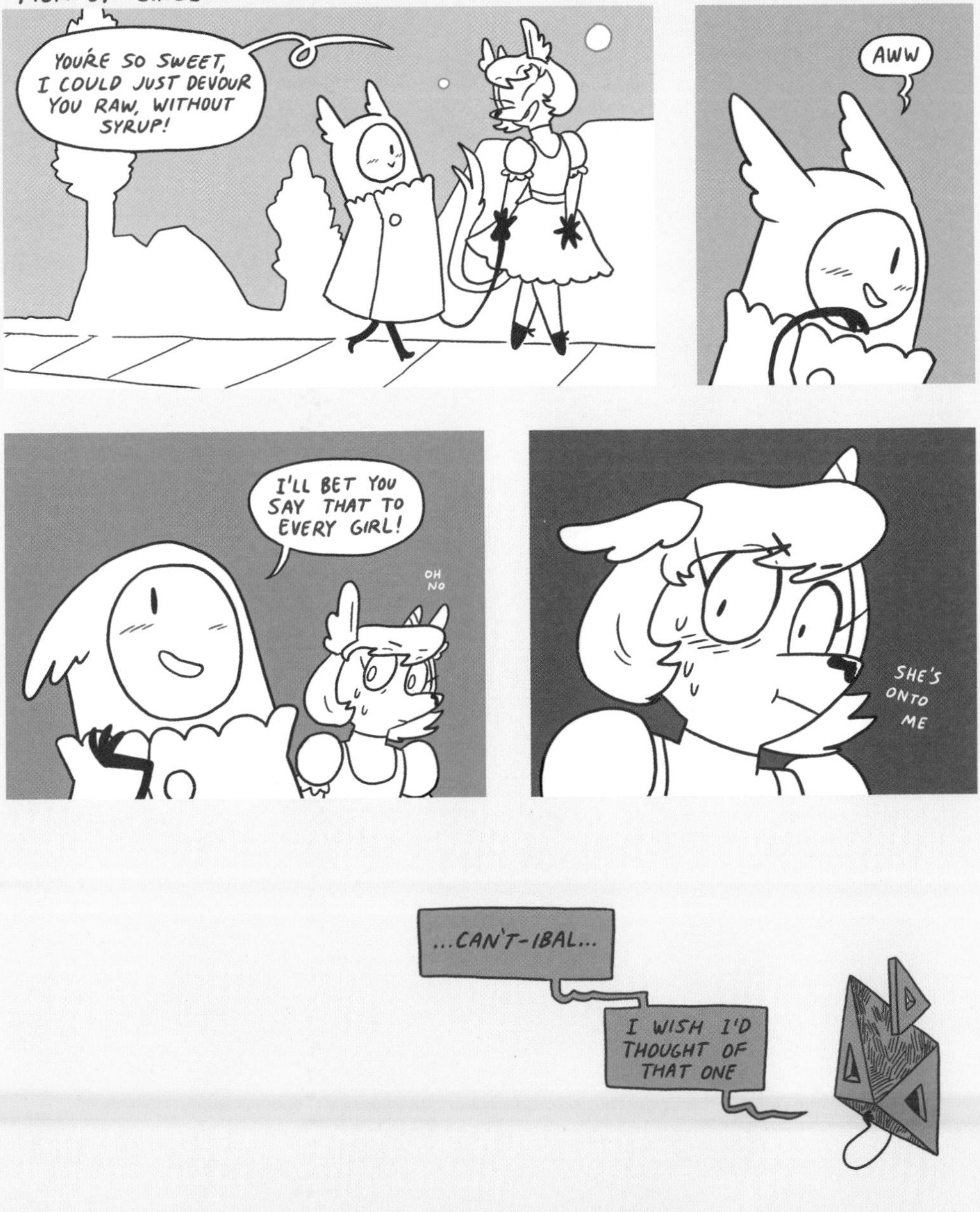

YOU'RE SO SWEET, I COULD JUST DEVOUR YOU RAW, WITHOUT SYRUP!
AWW
I'LL BET YOU SAY THAT TO EVERY GIRL!
OH NO
SHE'S ONTO ME
...CAN'T-IBAL...
I WISH I'D THOUGHT OF THAT ONE

DON'T DESSERT ME

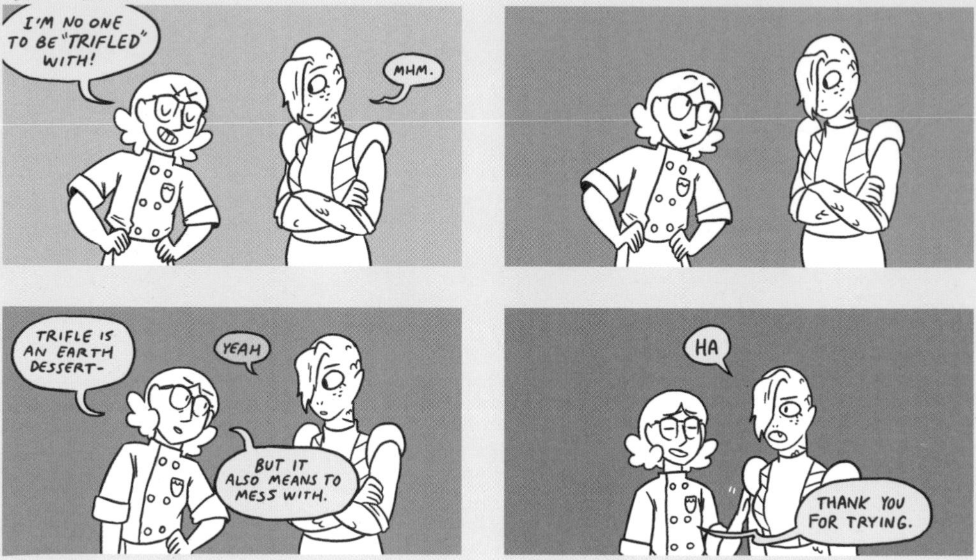
I'M NO ONE TO BE "TRIFLED" WITH!
MHM.
TRIFLE IS AN EARTH DESSERT-
YEAH
BUT IT ALSO MEANS TO MESS WITH.
HA
THANK YOU FOR TRYING.

RETURN TO EARTH

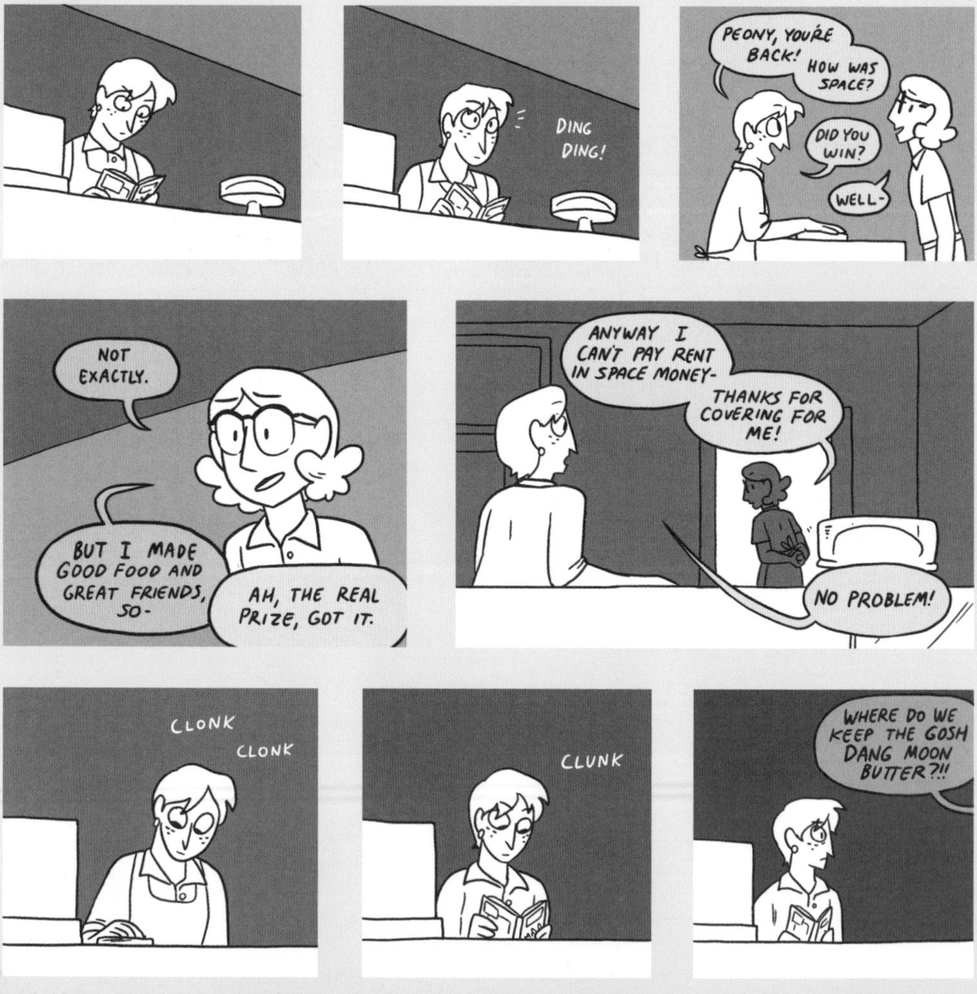
DING DING!
PEONY, YOU'RE BACK!
HOW WAS SPACE?
DID YOU WIN?
WELL-
NOT EXACTLY.
BUT I MADE GOOD FOOD AND GREAT FRIENDS, SO-
AH, THE REAL PRIZE, GOT IT.
ANYWAY I CAN'T PAY RENT IN SPACE MONEY-
THANKS FOR COVERING FOR ME!
NO PROBLEM!
CLONK
CLONK
CLUNK
WHERE DO WE KEEP THE GOSH DANG MOON BUTTER?!!

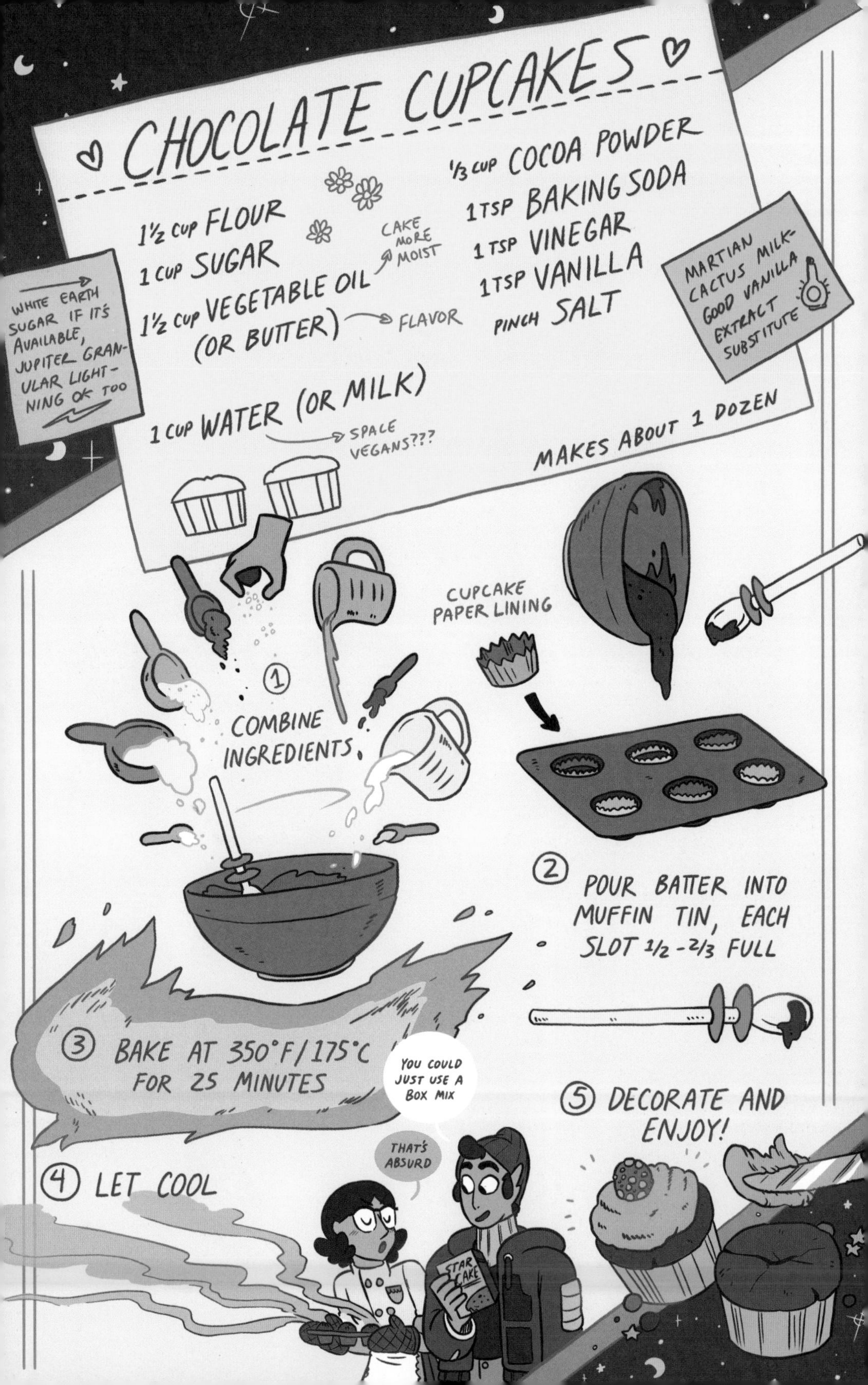

CHOCOLATE CUPCAKES
1½ CUP FLOUR
1 CUP SUGAR
1½ CUP VEGETABLE OIL (OR BUTTER)
CAKE MORE MOIST
FLAVOR
1 CUP WATER (OR MILK)
SPACE VEGANS???
⅓ CUP COCOA POWDER
1 TSP BAKING SODA
1 TSP VINEGAR
1 TSP VANILLA
PINCH SALT
WHITE EARTH SUGAR IF IT'S AVAILABLE, JUPITER GRANULAR LIGHTNING OK TOO
MARTIAN CACTUS MILK-GOOD VANILLA EXTRACT SUBSTITUTE
MAKES ABOUT 1 DOZEN
CUPCAKE PAPER LINING
1 COMBINE INGREDIENTS.
2 POUR BATTER INTO MUFFIN TIN, EACH SLOT 1/2 - 2/3 FULL
3 BAKE AT 350°F/175°C FOR 25 MINUTES
4 LET COOL
5 DECORATE AND ENJOY!
YOU COULD JUST USE A BOX MIX
THAT'S ABSURD
STAR CAKE

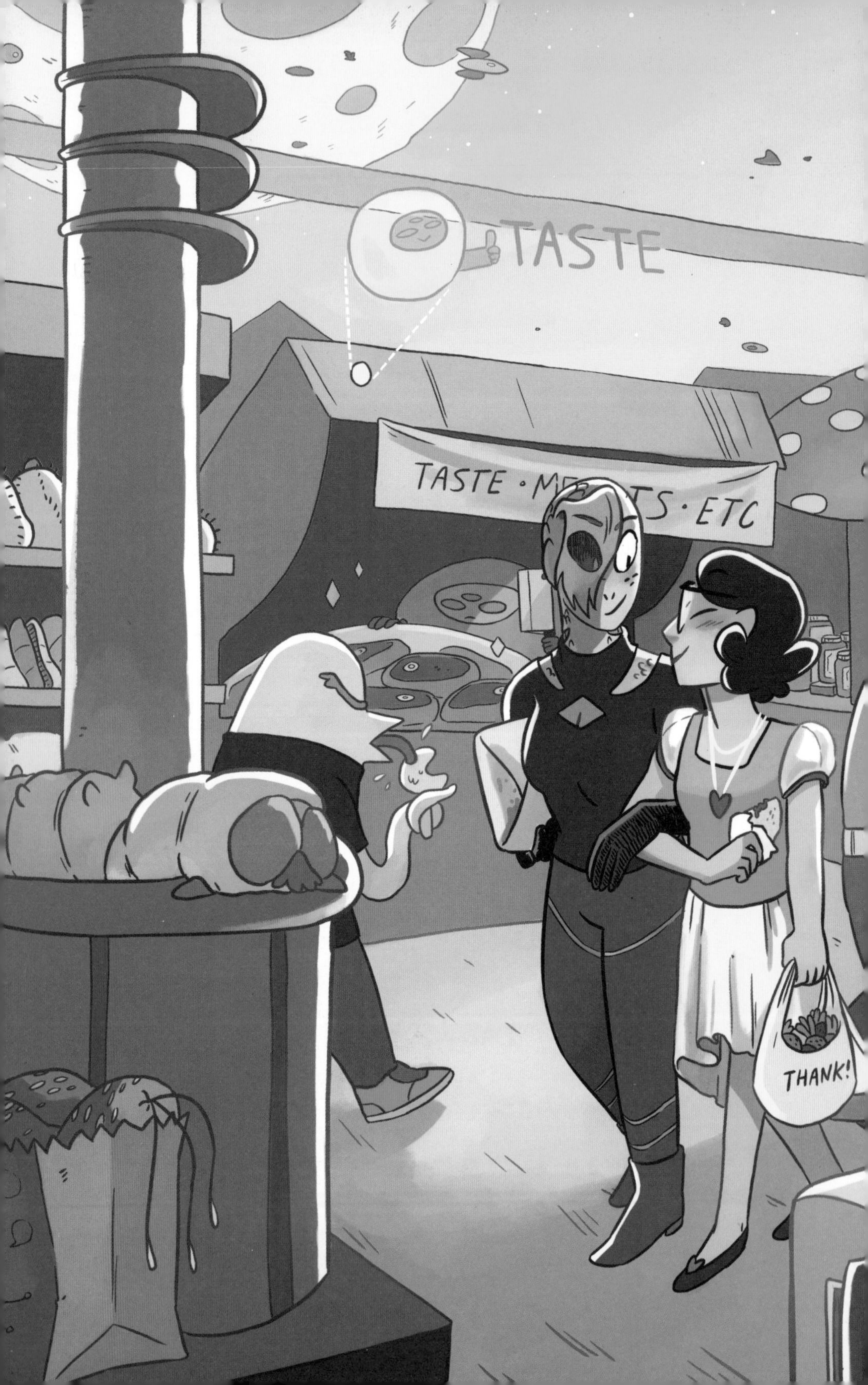
TASTE
TASTE · ME
TS · ETC
THANK!

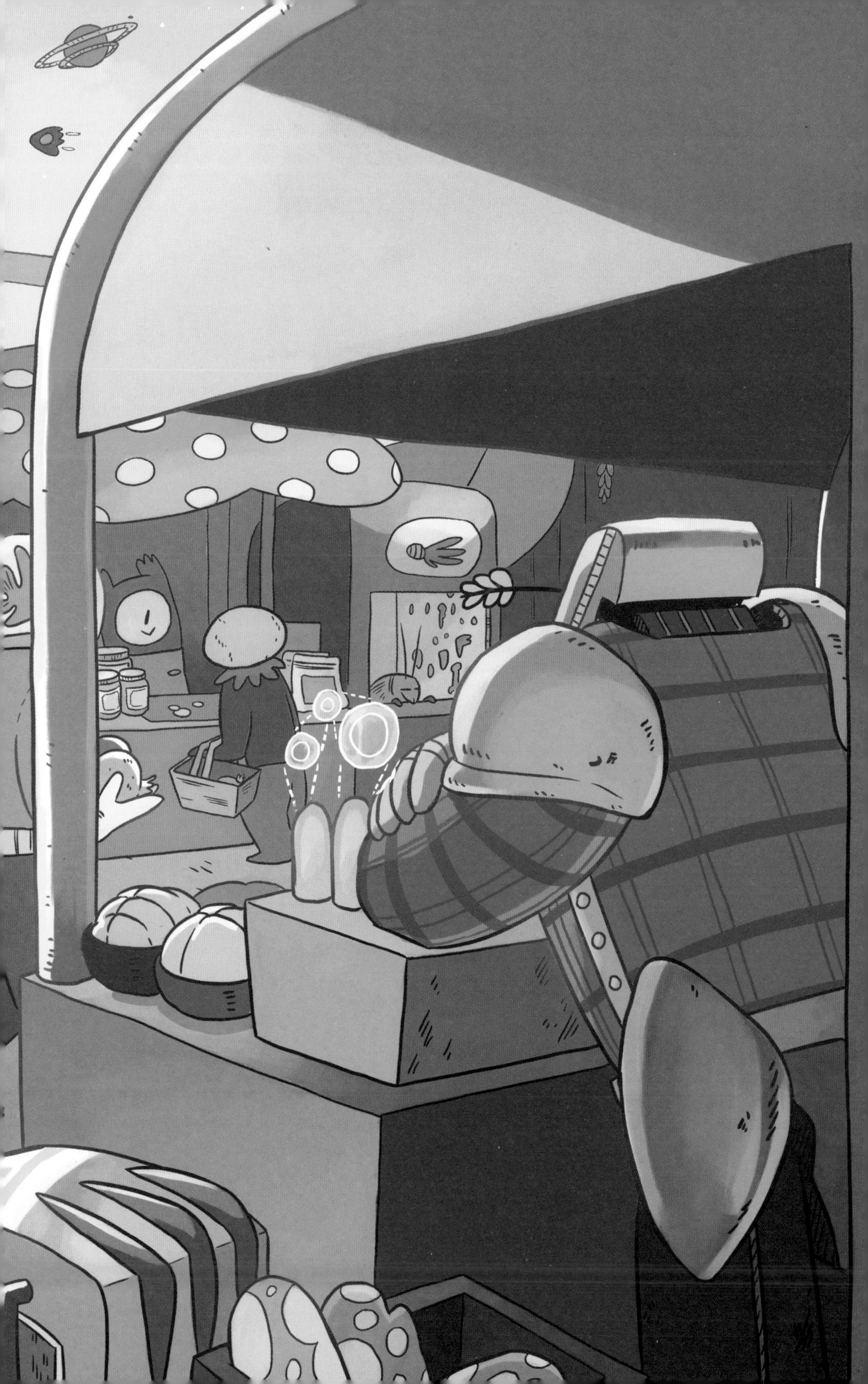

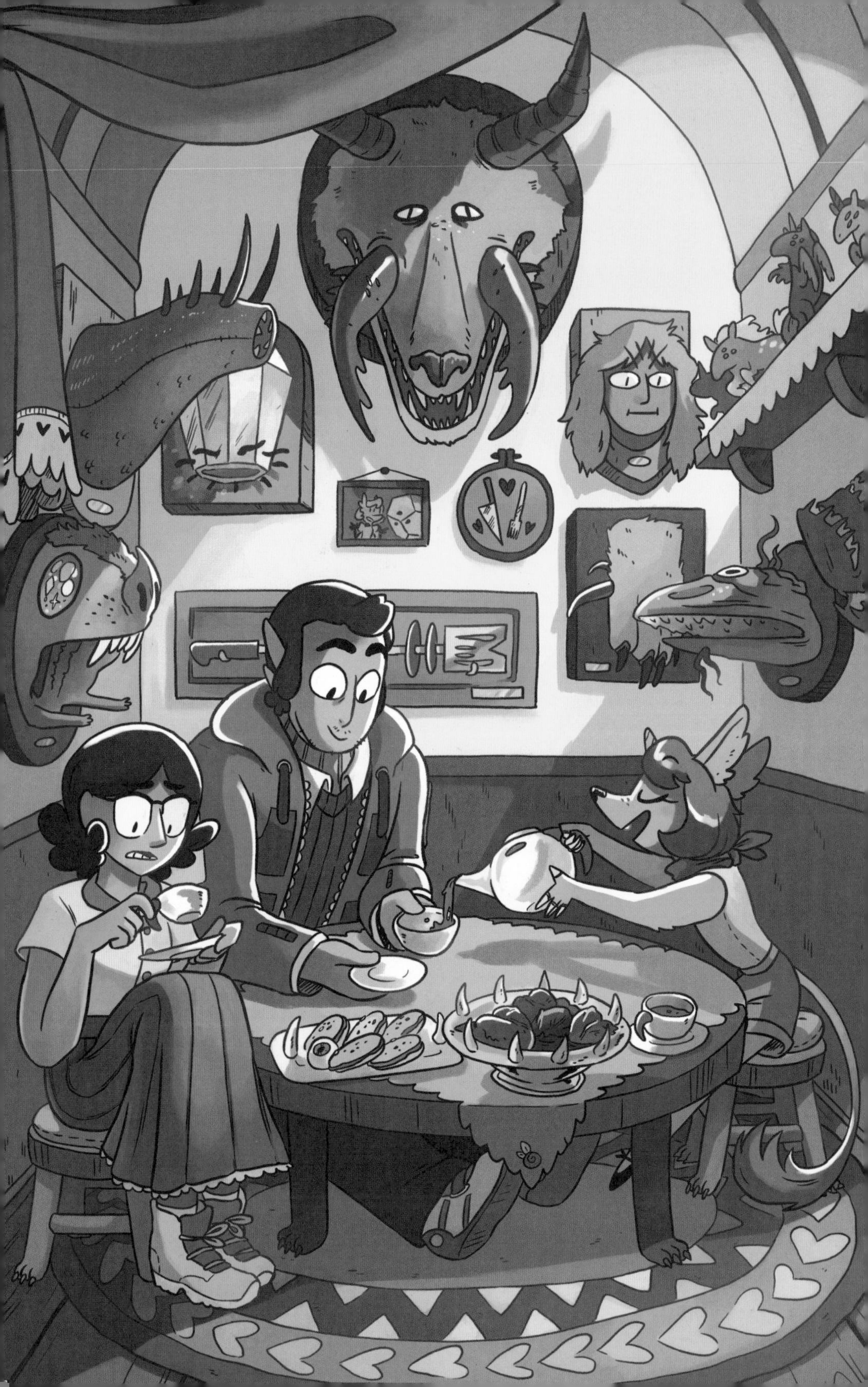

WHAT IF: *Space Battle Lunchtime*, BUT CATS!

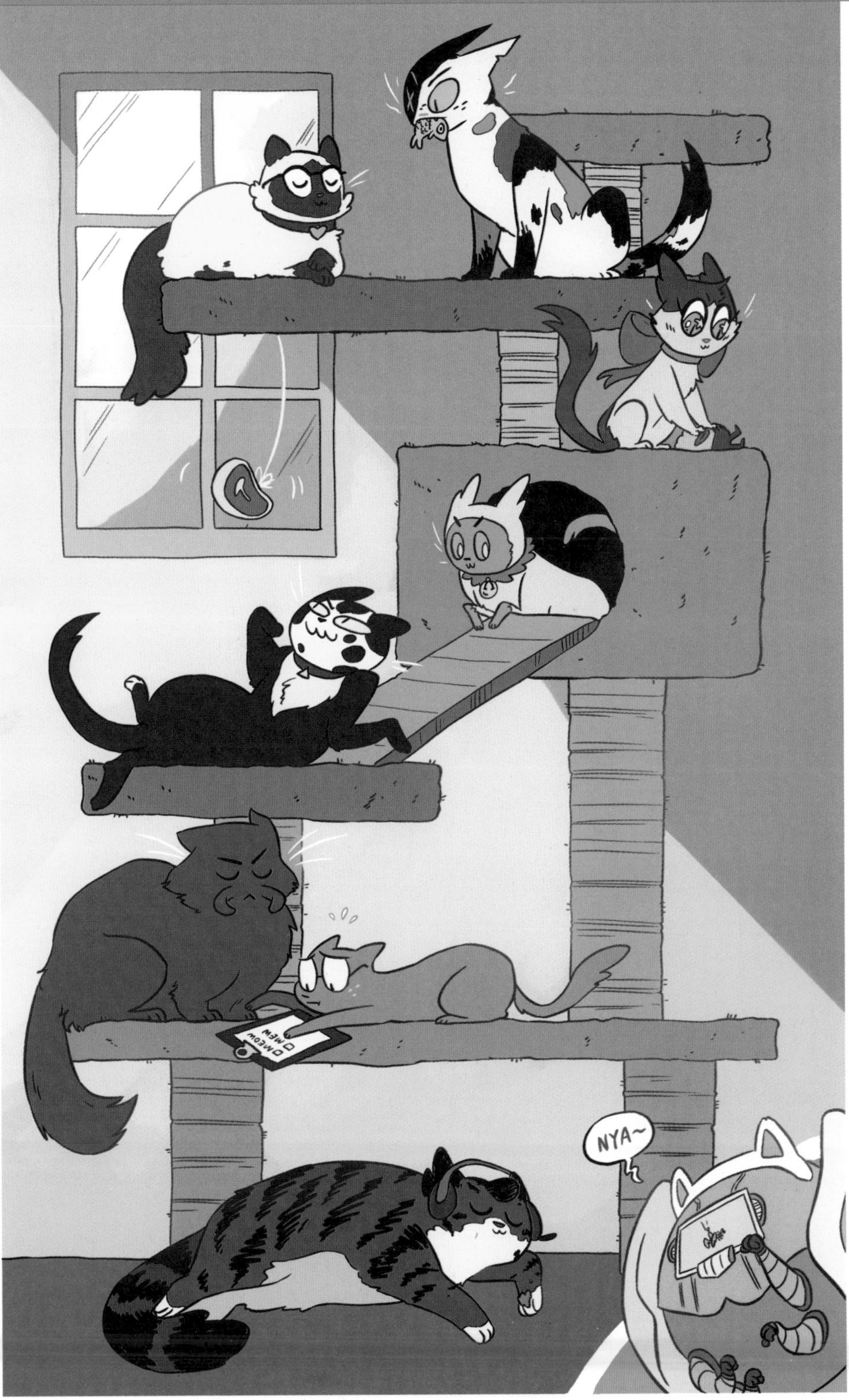
☐ MEOW
☐ MEW
NYA~

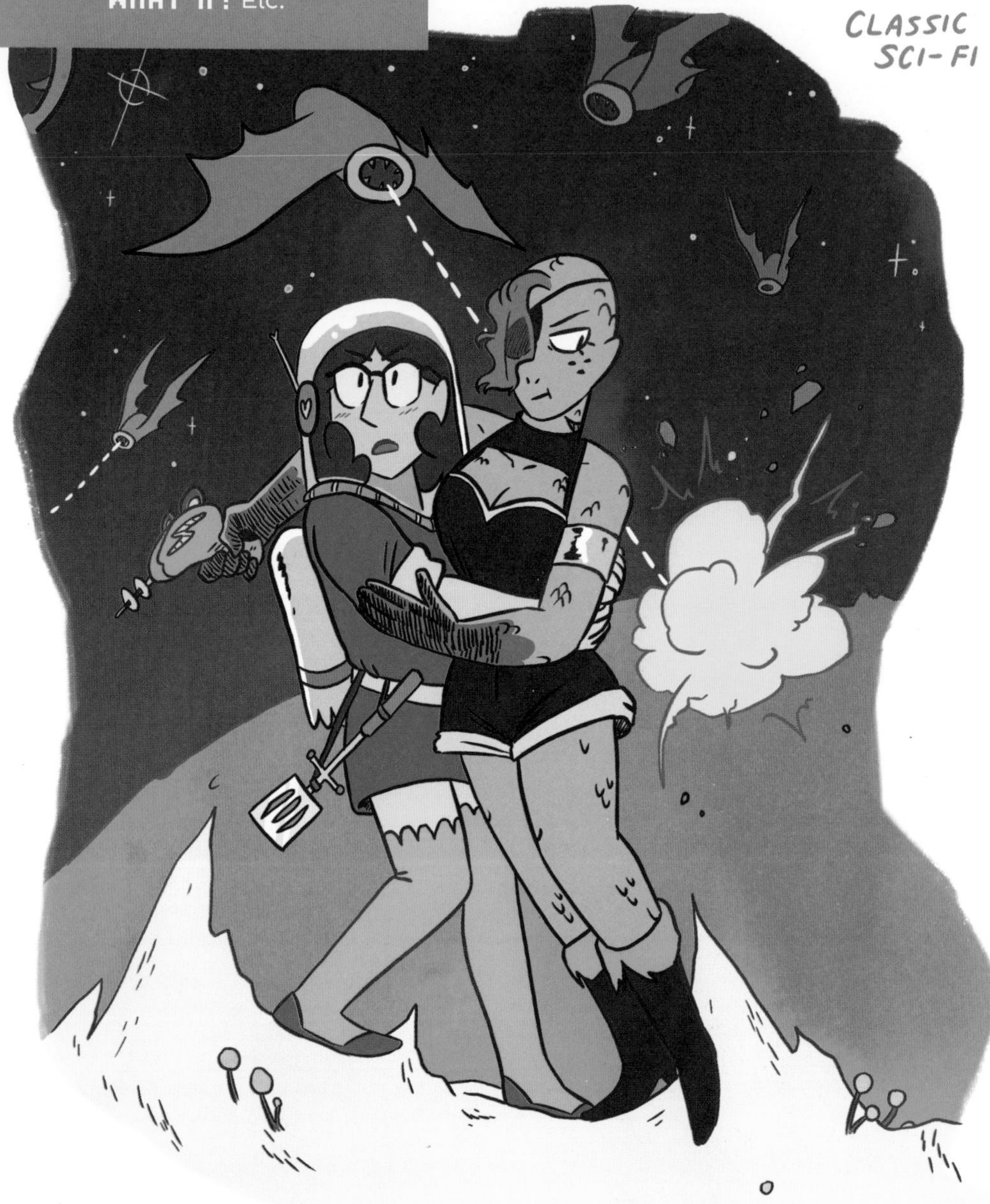
CLASSIC
SCI-FI

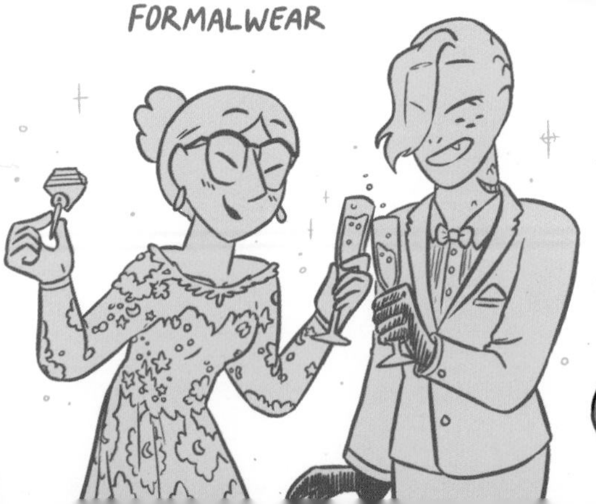
FORMALWEAR

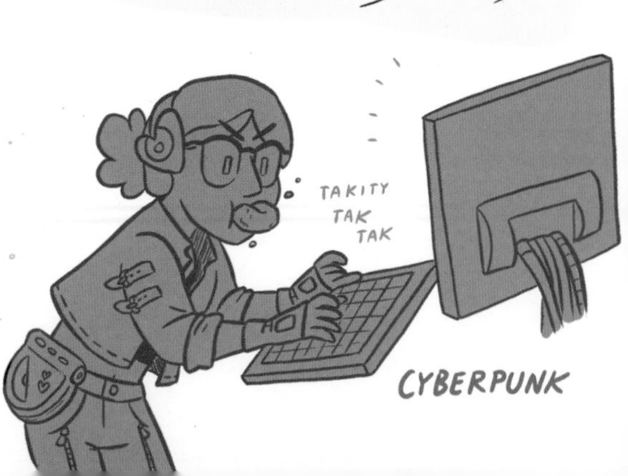
TAKITY
TAK
TAK
CYBERPUNK

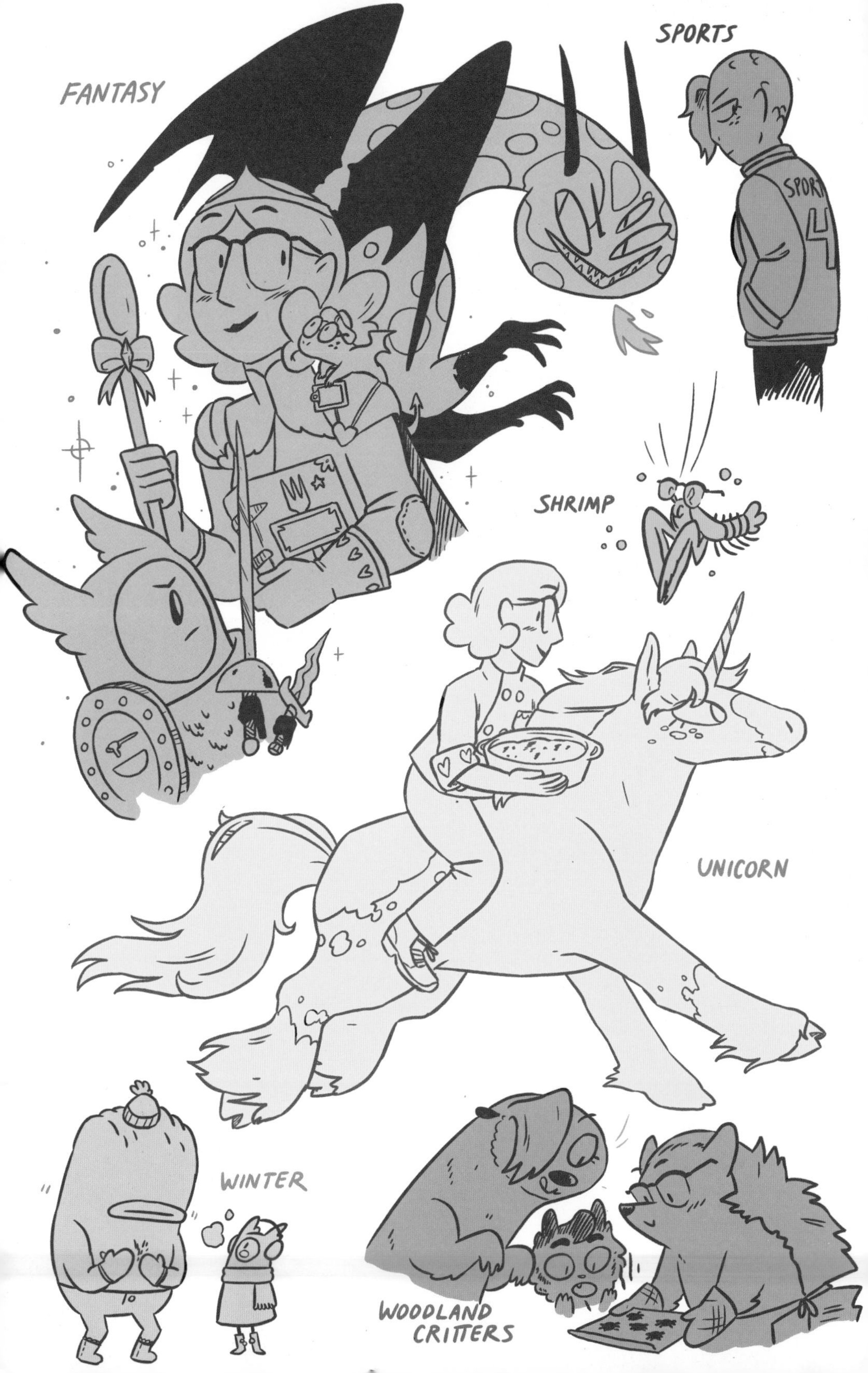
FANTASY
SPORTS
SPORT 4
SHRIMP
UNICORN
WINTER
WOODLAND CRITTERS

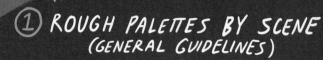

COLORING!

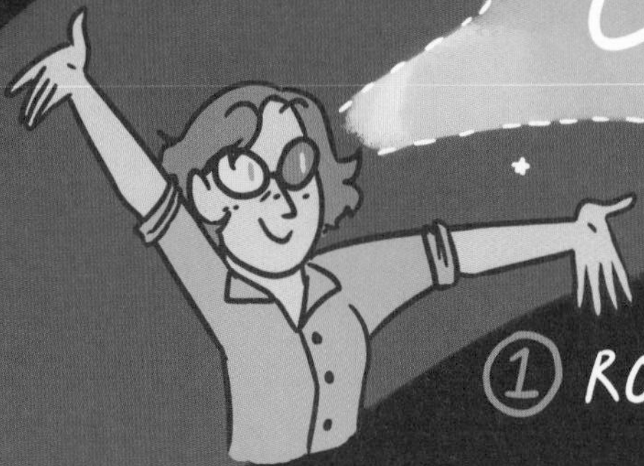

① ROUGH PALETTES BY SCENE
(GENERAL GUIDELINES)

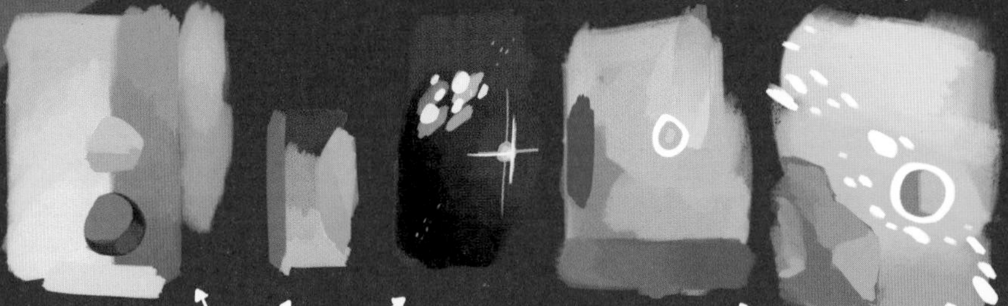
CANNIBAL COLISEUM
SPACE TRAFFIC
C.C. (MOOD SHIFT)
C.C. (NEPTUNIA ARRIVES)

CONSIDER: MOOD, COLOR TEMP, CONTRAST, THEMES/ COLORS ALREADY ESTABLISHED

② PLAN MAJOR COLOR BEATS

6 IS A MORE MUTED ISSUE, BUT I STILL USED SOME BRIGHT COLORS TO MAKE IT INTENSE!

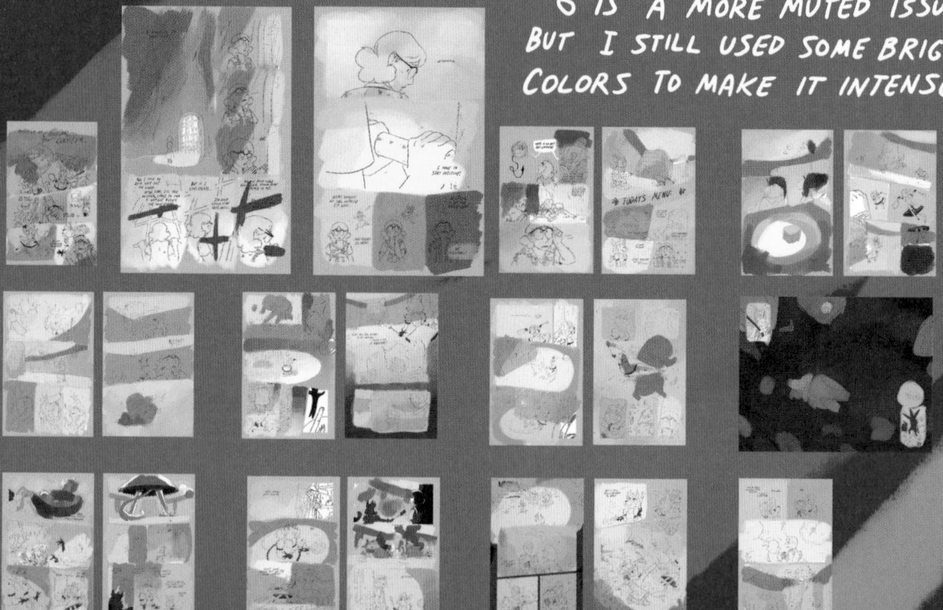

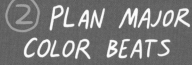

③ SEPARATE FIGURES AND BG TO MAKE PAINTING FASTER/ CLEANER

④ ROUGH PASS
PICK COLORS FROM PLAN, PREVIOUS PAGES, OR JUST WHATEVER COLORS FEEL RIGHT! TRY NEW THINGS! USE LOTS OF COLORS!!

⑤ CLEAN/RENDER, ALSO TWEAK CON- TRAST (THANKS, PHOTOSHOP!)

SOME OF MY FAVORITES:

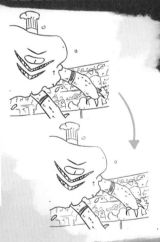

⑥ COLOR LINES
GIVES PANEL A "PAINTED" LOOK

⑦ DONE!
SEND IT TO YOUR EDITOR!

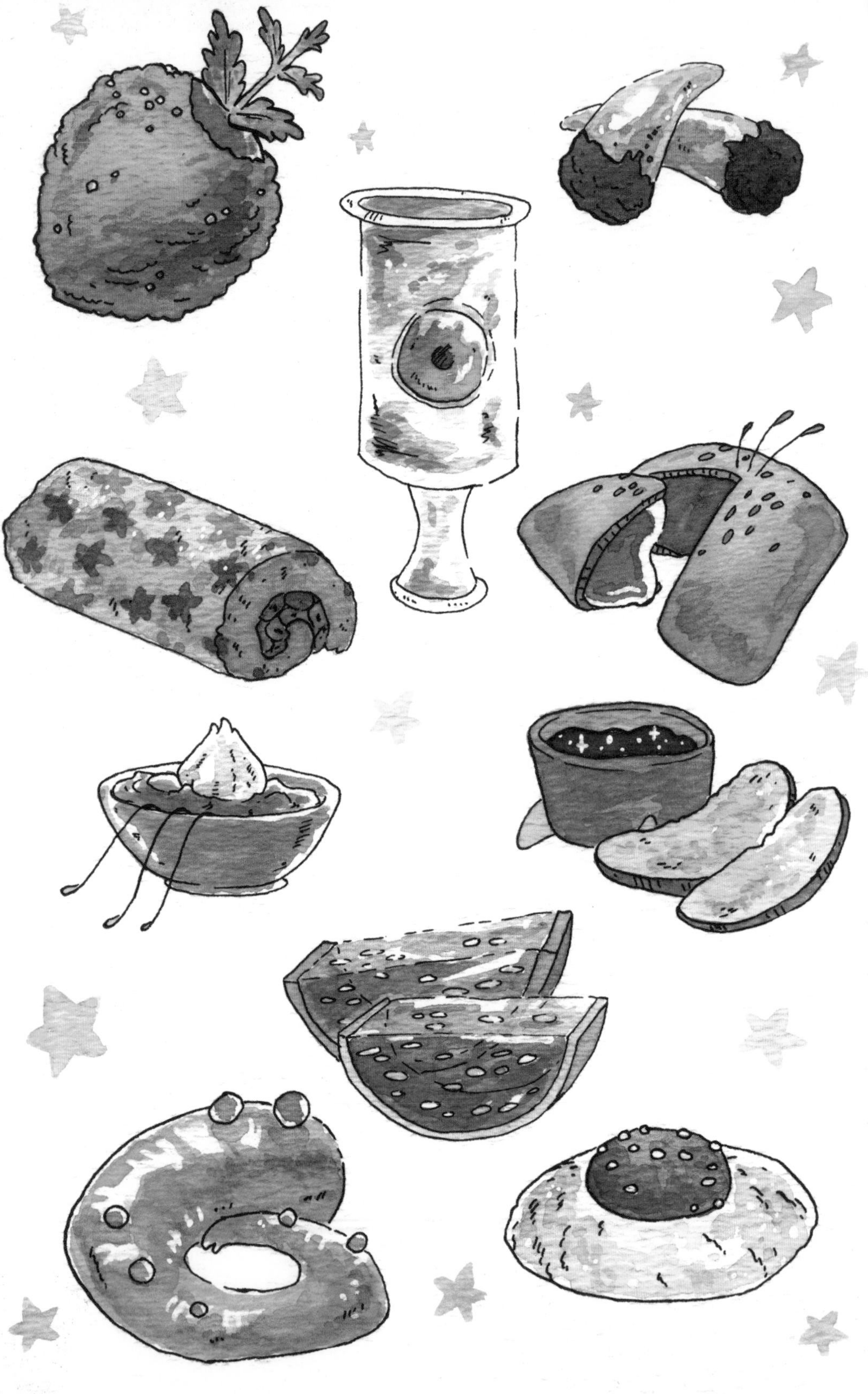

COVER SKETCHES! Many of these never made it to print, but a few did.

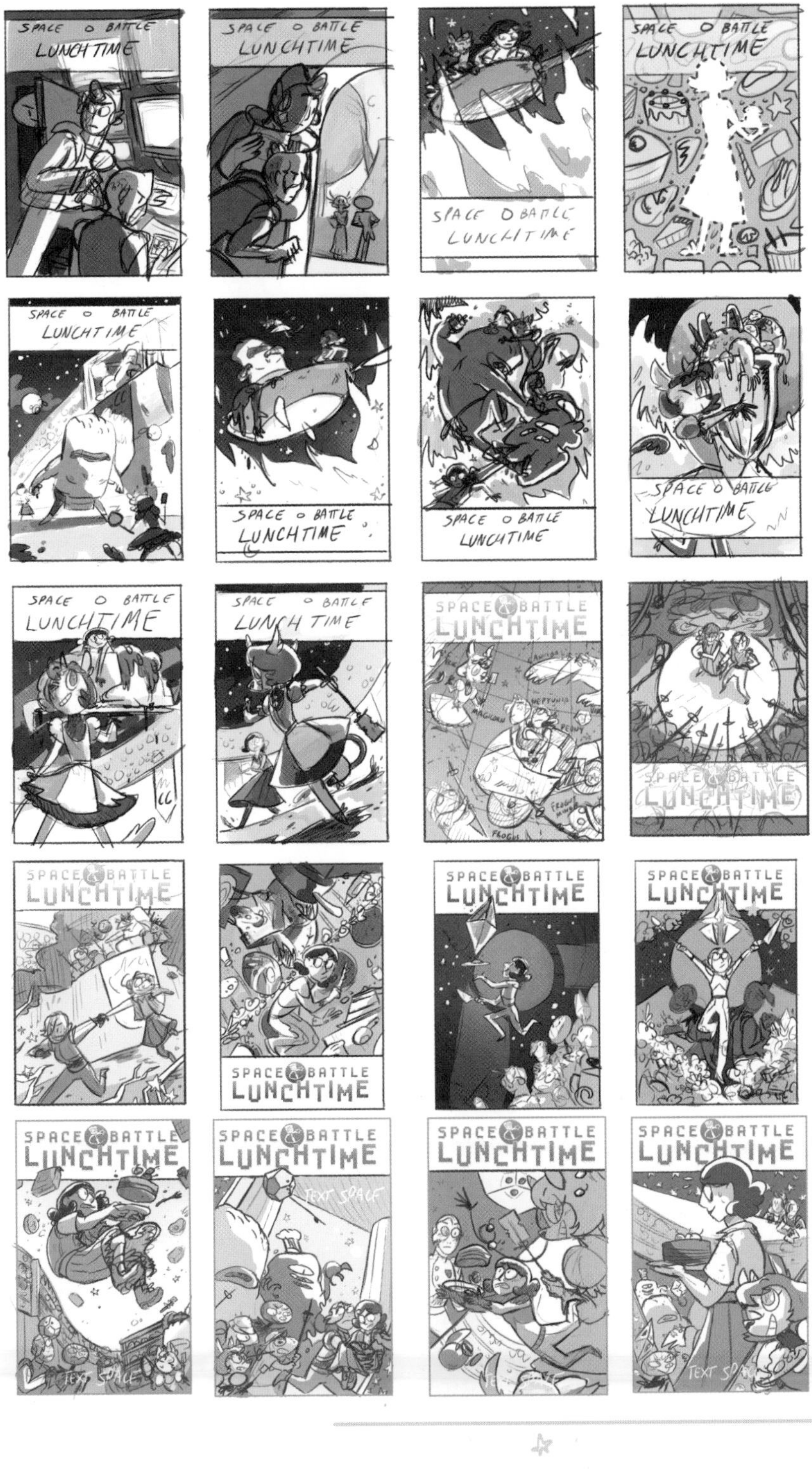
SPACE BATTLE
LUNCHTIME
SPACE BATTLE
LUNCHTIME
SPACE BATTLE
LUNCHTIME
SPACE BATTLE
LUNCHTIME
SPACE BATTLE
LUNCHTIME
SPACE BATTLE
LUNCHTIME
SPACE BATTLE
LUNCHTIME
SPACE BATTLE
LUNCHTIME
SPACE BATTLE
LUNCHTIME
SPACE BATTLE
LUNCHTIME
SPACE BATTLE
LUNCHTIME
SPACE BATTLE
LUNCHTIME
SPACE BATTLE
LUNCHTIME
SPACE BATTLE
LUNCHTIME
SPACE BATTLE
LUNCHTIME
SPACE BATTLE
LUNCHTIME
SPACE BATTLE
LUNCHTIME
TEXT SPACE
SPACE BATTLE
LUNCHTIME
TEXT SPACE
SPACE BATTLE
LUNCHTIME
SPACE BATTLE
LUNCHTIME
TEXT SPACE

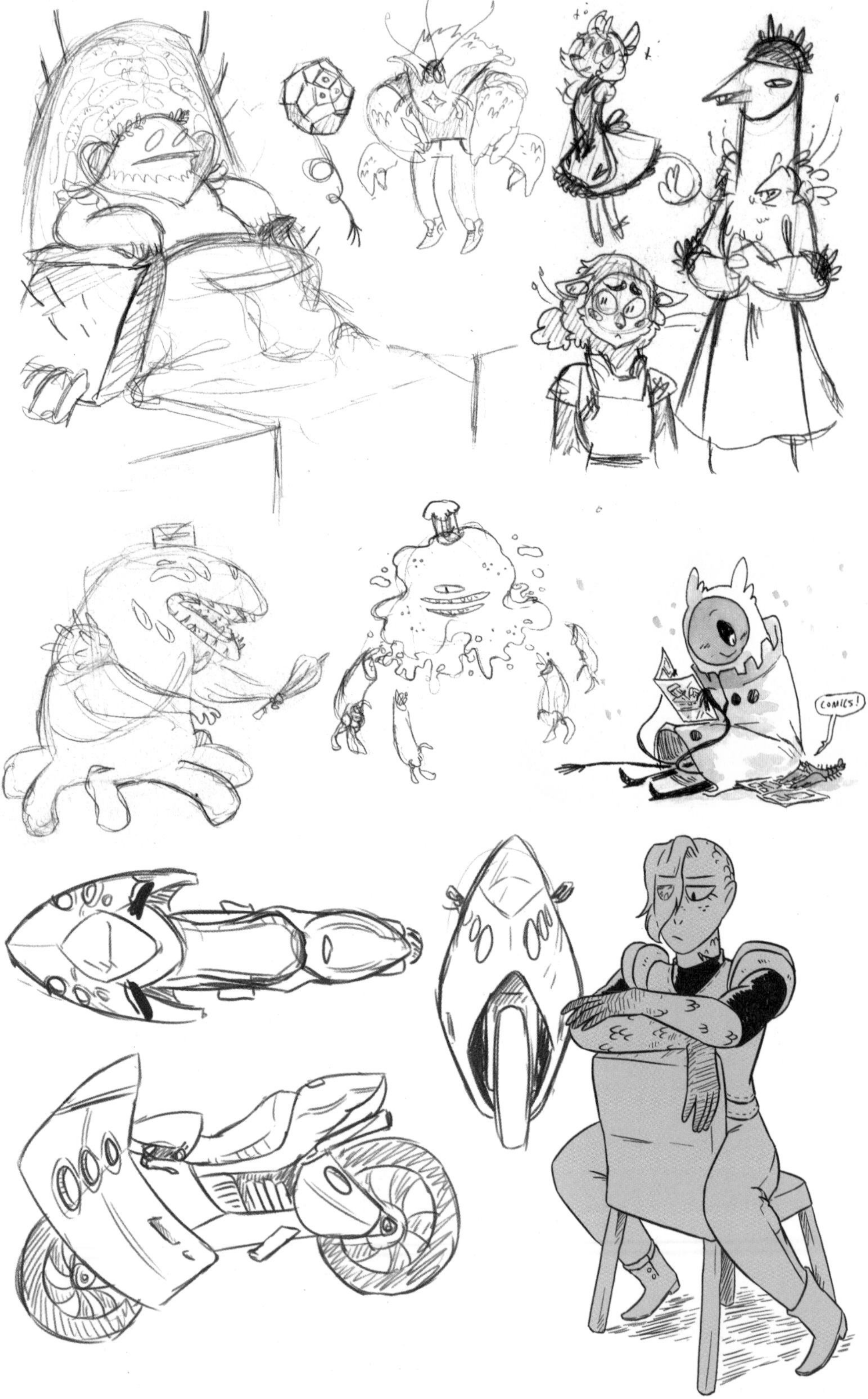
COMICS!

MORE BOOKS FROM ONI PRESS

SPACE BATTLE LUNCHTIME
VOLUME ONE:
LIGHTS, CAMERA, SNACKTION!
BY NATALIE RIESS

SPACE BATTLE LUNCHTIME, VOLUME 1: LIGHTS, CAMERA, SNACKTION!
BY NATALIE RIESS
120 PAGES, SOFTCOVER, COLOR
ISBN 978-1-62010-313-5

PRINCESS PRINCESS
Ever After
Katie O'Neill

PRINCESS PRINCESS EVER AFTER
BY KATIE O'NEILL
56 PAGES, HARDCOVER, COLOR
ISBN 978-1-62010-340-1

A YALSA Great Graphic Novels for Teens selection
BUZZ!
ANANTH HIRSH & TESSA STONE

BUZZ!
BY ANANTH HIRSH & TESSA STONE
176 PAGES, SOFTCOVER, 2-COLOR
ISBN 978-1-62010-088-2

Costume Quest:
INVASION OF THE CANDY SNATCHERS
Zac Gorman

COSTUME QUEST: INVASION OF THE CANDY SNATCHERS
BY ZAC GORMAN
56 PAGES, HARDCOVER, COLOR
ISBN 978-1-62010-190-2

Courtney Crumrin
VOLUME ONE
The Night Things
TED NAIFEH

COURTNEY CRUMRIN, VOLUME 1: THE NIGHT THINGS
BY TED NAIFEH
136 PAGES, HARDCOVER, COLOR
ISBN 978-1-934964-77-4

OYSTER WAR
BEN TOWLE

OYSTER WAR
BY BEN TOWLE
168 PAGES, HARDCOVER, COLOR
ISBN 978-1-62010-262-6

ONI PRESS
www.onipress.com

FOR MORE INFORMATION ON THESE AND OTHER FINE ONI PRESS COMIC BOOKS AND GRAPHIC NOVELS VISIT WWW.ONIPRESS.COM. TO FIND A COMIC SPECIALTY STORE IN YOUR AREA VISIT WWW.COMICSHOPS.US.

NATALIE RIESS is from a distant, unknown star. Her motives are unknown, but she seems to like drawing weird cats and comic books. She lives in Pennsylvania.